The Secrets of Solace

BOOKS BY JALEIGH JOHNSON

The Mark of the Dragonfly
The Secrets of Solace

THE SECRETS OF SOLACE

JALEIGH JOHNSON

DELACORTE PRESS

Text copyright © 2016 by Jaleigh Johnson
Jacket art copyright © 2016 by Owen Richardson
Map illustrations copyright © 2016 by Brandon Dorman

All rights reserved. Published in the United States by
Delacorte Press, an imprint of Random House Children's Books,
a division of Penguin Random House LLC, New York.

Delacorte Press is a registered trademark and the colophon
is a trademark of Penguin Random House LLC.

Visit us on the Web! randomhousekids.com

Educators and librarians, for a variety of teaching tools,
visit us at RHTeachersLibrarians.com

Library of Congress Cataloging-in-Publication Data
Johnson, Jaleigh.
The secrets of Solace / Jaleigh Johnson. — First edition.
pages   cm
Summary: "Lina is training to become an archivist in Solace,
but war threatens to upend her life. When a mysterious boy
appears, Lina must decide whether or not to trust him and reveal
a secret"—Provided by publisher.
ISBN 978-0-385-37648-8 (hc) — ISBN 978-0-385-37650-1 (el) —
ISBN 978-0-385-37649-5 (glb) [1. Fantasy.] I. Title.
PZ7.J63214Se   2016
[Fic]—dc23
2015009830

The text of this book is set in 12-point Goudy.
Jacket design by Katrina Damkoehler
Interior design by Heather Kelly

Printed in the United States of America
10 9 8 7 6 5 4 3 2 1
First Edition

For Tim, the one who holds my heart

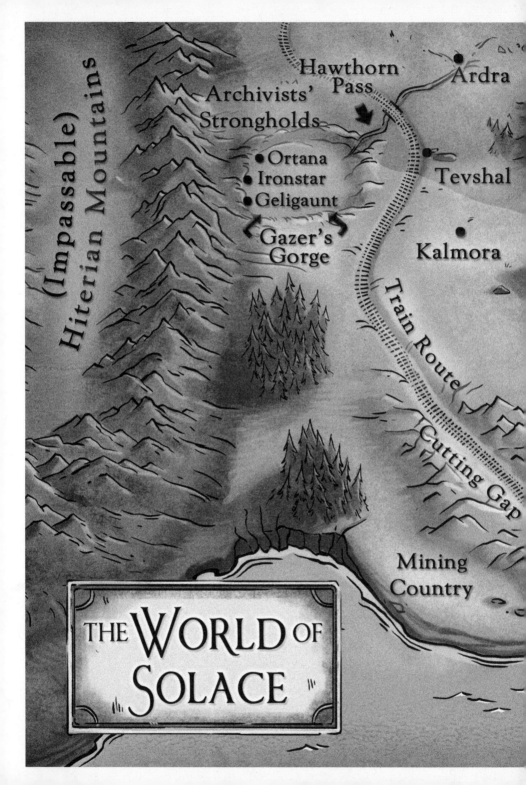

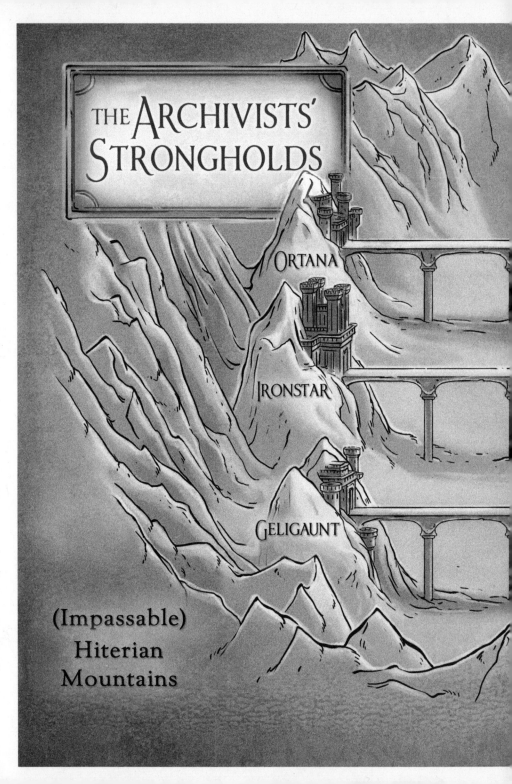

≍ ONE ≍

"Apprentices, quiet!" The excited chatter in the classroom almost drowned out Tolwin's exasperated
shout. "You'd think that none of you had ever seen a
simple box before."

From her seat near the back of the classroom, Lina
Winterbock snorted in amusement. An archivist, even a
junior apprentice like her, knew there was no such thing
as "a simple box." Not when that box had been shipped
from the meteor fields up north.

The classroom for Archival Studies was an amphitheater, the desks arranged in a semicircle on stone tiers
carved out of the cavern's natural rock formations. At
the bottom, in the teaching pit, there was a scarred
oak table and a podium beside it for the teacher. The
box that had caused the pandemonium sat in the middle of the table. Lina's teacher, the archivist Tolwin,

stood behind the podium. His apprentice and assistant, Simon, stood at Tolwin's side, scowling at all the noise. Though to be fair, the sour expression could just be Simon's version of a smile. With him, it was hard to tell.

As Tolwin swept his gaze over the fifty-odd students assembled in the classroom, Lina turned her attention away from the box and sank as low in her seat as she could manage without actually falling to the floor. It didn't matter. The teacher's sharp eyes found her anyway and narrowed as his lips pressed into a thin line of displeasure. Lina forced herself to stare back at him without flinching, but it wasn't easy. Tolwin's glare felt like a spider skittering down her spine. A large, hairy spider with fangs.

Given the *incident* last year, Tolwin's reaction to her wasn't that surprising, but Lina kept hoping maybe he would fall and hit his head and somehow forget the whole unpleasant business. Normally, she would never wish a head injury on anyone, but it might make her days in Archival Studies a bit easier.

Lina released a tense breath as Tolwin finally looked away from her, and she eagerly refocused her attention on the mysterious box. What *was* Tolwin hiding in there? Some new bit of technology? A painting? Or maybe even a manuscript? Mystery poured from the depths of the box, filling Lina's mind and quickening her heart.

Where do you come from? How far have you traveled? What secrets do you hold?

Lina had never been to the meteor fields or the scrap towns where all these strange objects were gathered. They were located far to the north of the archivists' strongholds, in the Merrow Kingdom. But she'd heard plenty of stories of the violent meteor storms that ravaged the land up there. For reasons that even the wisest of the archivists hadn't been able to discover, the boundary between their world of Solace and other lands was thin in the meteor fields, and on the night of each full moon, it dissolved completely. With no barrier, objects from other worlds tumbled from the sky in clouds of poisonous green dust. It was the poorest people in the north, the scrappers, who bravely took on the task of harvesting these meteorites. They cleaned up whatever objects were still intact and sold them at local trade markets to make money to live on.

The scrappers' best customers were the archivists, who bought up as many of these otherworldly artifacts as they could. They paid special attention to any object that might reveal hints of what life was like in unknown worlds. It was the archivists' mission to preserve the artifacts and record whatever knowledge they gleaned from them, both for its own sake and because they believed that the more people learned about these other worlds, the more they would come to understand their own. It was a unique calling, one that, even as an apprentice, made Lina's life very different from the lives of people living in other lands.

"I said *quiet!*" Tolwin barked, shaking Lina from her thoughts. Anger deepened the crisscrossing lines on her instructor's face. His bushy brown-gray hair even seemed unhappy. As he glared at the students, the noise level in the room gradually dropped to a quiet murmur. "Today I'm going to conduct a hands-on experiment, the purpose of which is to test your understanding of the archivist principles you've been taught so far." Tolwin gestured to the box on the table. "You're all wondering what I've got in here, yes? I hear you whispering about it, trying to guess which division it came from."

Naturally, Lina thought. It was the first thing any archivist would wonder. The six general divisions—Flora, Fauna, Technology, Language/Literature, Cultural Artifacts, and Medicine—formed the basis for all the archivists' work. At the end of their long years of study and apprenticeship, each of the students in this room would end up working in one of those divisions.

Tolwin rubbed his hands together as if to build suspense. "All I will tell you, to start, is that there is an object inside the box that was discovered in the meteor fields only two weeks ago."

An astonished hush fell over the classroom at this announcement, and Lina sat up straighter in her seat.

Apprentices rarely got the opportunity to *see*, let alone *study*, an object newly recovered from the meteor fields. That privilege was usually reserved for the senior archivists.

"Well, now that we've finally achieved silence," Tolwin said dryly, "we can begin the lesson. First, I will require a volunteer. Simon, would you care to select someone?"

Hands shot up all over the room as the students squirmed in their seats and shot pleading looks at Tolwin's apprentice. They all wanted to be the first to examine the object inside the box.

Only Lina sat with her hands folded tight on top of her desk. All the while, her heart banged against her ribs, begging her with each unsteady beat to raise her hand and volunteer. But, curious as she was about the secrets and wonders contained within the box, she didn't trust Tolwin. She didn't trust anyone who made her feel spider legs on her spine.

And then Simon said something that made her heart stand still. "I think . . . I think Lina Winterbock looks eager to volunteer."

Lina's stomach dropped, and she caught the malicious glint in Simon's eyes as he motioned for her to come down and join them in the teaching pit.

"Ah yes, I believe you're right." Tolwin glanced up at her, and the slightest of smiles curved his thin lips.

"Come down and stand in front of the table here, Miss Winterbock."

Lina's mind raced even as she slid her chair away from her desk with a quiet scraping sound. All eyes in the classroom fixed on her, which automatically brought a deep flush of embarrassment to her cheeks.

At times like this, Lina wished more than anything that she could look across the room and meet the eyes of a best friend, someone who would giggle and stick her tongue out at Tolwin when his back was turned, and who would mouth a few encouraging words to her while she faced down the teacher. She'd even settle for a temporary friend, one who appeared under only the direst of circumstances. She wasn't picky.

Focus, Lina.

Whatever game Tolwin and Simon were playing, the way Lina saw it, she had three possible countermoves. She could refuse to volunteer, which would thwart Tolwin but also probably get her kicked out of class. There was always the option of feigning sickness. Lina considered it as she stood up and made her way down the stairs. All she had to do was clutch her stomach and run out of the room as if she were about to vomit. If she played it up enough, Tolwin might even believe her.

But that would give him the satisfaction of knowing that he'd scared her off.

Which left option three. Lina squared her shoulders

and approached the box on the table, prepared to play along with whatever Tolwin had in store. Maybe, if she was good enough, she'd find a way to outsmart him and avoid the trap he and Simon had set.

"Now then, Miss Winterbock," Tolwin said, coming around the podium to stand beside her at the table. "We're going to play a game of make-believe." He pointed to the box. "I want you to imagine that you are a senior archivist—the very position everyone in this room aspires to—and that this object has just been delivered to your workshop. Tell me, how would you begin your examination of it?"

Easy question. Apprentices learned those steps as part of their introductory course work. Lina cleared her throat for the recitation. "Upon removal of the object from the box, I would first determine—"

He held up a hand, stopping her. "Wait a moment. You say you would remove the object from the box. Do so, please."

Lina saw the other apprentices' eyes widen. She was just as shocked herself. She'd never expected Tolwin to let her handle the object. *What* was in that box?

Cautiously, palms sweating, fearing a trick but not knowing what it was, Lina lifted the lid off the box and set it carefully on the table. She inched forward to peer inside, then let out a quiet sigh of relief.

She'd expected some ugly critter with spines or

horns to jump out at her. Reaching both hands into the box, she pulled out a small, ornate jewelry chest. Made of some kind of dark metal with bands of gold on the lid, the chest was in remarkably good shape, considering it had come crashing to the ground in a meteor storm.

And that wasn't the only thing strange about the object. Lina couldn't help wondering how the archivists had managed to acquire the item so recently, with the Iron War raging between the Merrow Kingdom, where the meteor fields were located, and the Dragonfly territories to the south. The archivists were their own separate nation and had refused to choose a side in the conflict between the two lands, but even so, trade shipments were slow in coming from the Merrow Kingdom, when they arrived at all.

But Lina didn't have time to dwell on that mystery. Tolwin wasn't finished with her.

"Now," he said when Lina put the jewelry chest on the table, "continue with your examination. How would you begin to identify this object?"

Lina scanned Tolwin's face for any clue that he was trying to trick her, but the man's expression was unreadable. She cleared her throat again and hoped her voice remained steady. "First, we need to note the material the object is made of and determine whether it's organic or inorganic," she said. "If inorganic, which this is, we then determine whether or not its composite materials are native to our world of Solace."

"Excellent," Tolwin said, though his tone was anything but warm. He turned to the class. "Would any of you care to guess what this object is made of?"

Five hands shot up in the air. Tolwin nodded to a girl who'd been sitting next to Lina. "Pewter, with gold bands," she guessed.

"Good eye," Tolwin said, smiling thinly at the girl. He turned his attention back to Lina. "So far, we have identified an inorganic object made of materials native to Solace. If we were conducting a true examination, laboratory tests would need to be done to confirm this, but for now, we'll move on with the demonstration. I assume you know the next step, Miss Winterbock?"

Lina met Tolwin's eyes and saw the look of challenge there. Of course she knew the next step, as did everyone else in the room: classify the object according to one of the six divisions of archivist studies. But that involved examining the chest more closely—at the very least, lifting the lid.

And that's where Tolwin would spring his trap. Lina could see it in his eyes. There was something in the box. Something meant just for her, and it wasn't going to be pleasant.

Lina clutched her hands in front of her to keep them from shaking. She cast about for anything that could help her and spied a ruler on a little shelf behind Tolwin's podium. Before he could protest, she walked over and grabbed it. Returning to the chest, she fitted the edge of the ruler beneath the lid and gently lifted it.

Creaking hinges echoed in the amphitheater as the chest opened, and a faint moldy smell tickled Lina's nose. Half the class leaned forward in their seats to get a better look at what was in the chest, while the other half craned away. It seemed they were all expecting something grand or dangerous to pop out.

And then Lina realized with a jolt that the chest was empty. A water-spotted lining of red velvet covered the bottom of it, but otherwise there was nothing, no waiting horror inside. Lina laid the ruler on the table and let out the breath she'd been holding. Tolwin had just been messing with her, trying to build suspense and make her afraid. She hated to admit that it had worked. Behind her, Simon chuckled, and Lina's cheeks flamed.

"Very good, Miss Winterbock. Now that you've so bravely conquered the obstacle of *opening* the chest," Tolwin said, amid titters of laughter from the class, "perhaps you could continue with your analysis?"

Lina gritted her teeth and nodded, determined not to let Tolwin get into her head. She thought the box belonged to the Cultural Artifacts division, but it didn't hurt to check to see if there were any mechanical components that might designate it as Technology. Sometimes these small jewelry chests were also music boxes. You just never knew.

She reached into the box and felt along the velvet lining with her hands, searching for any machinery, but as far as she could tell, there was none. A Cultural Artifact, then.

She opened her mouth to say so, when suddenly she noticed a slight tingling in the tips of her fingers, as if they were falling asleep. At first, she thought it was just her nervousness, but then the sensation traveled into her hands, and Lina's heart began to beat faster.

What was happening? No, it couldn't be a trap. The chest was empty. She'd checked.

"Is there a problem, Miss Winterbock?" Tolwin asked, his voice deceptively serene. "We are all awaiting the results of your analysis."

Lina tried to ignore him, focusing on her hands. She turned them palms up and saw with a growing panic that her fingers were starting to swell. A fine film of red dust coated the tips where she'd been feeling around in the chest. She hadn't noticed it at first because it was the same color as the velvet, but she could see now, looking closer, that it covered the whole inside of the chest. She reached up to try to close the lid and found that her fingers had gone completely numb. The chest teetered as she fumbled with it, and the lid shut with a snap. More faint laughter threaded through the room, ringing in Lina's ears.

How could she have been so stupid? She should have looked at the inside of the chest more closely. What was that dust Tolwin had planted? What had he done to her?

Lina tried to control her panic. She cupped her numb and swollen hands protectively against her middle and looked up at Tolwin. "What did you do?" she asked, her voice quavering.

"I did nothing, Miss Winterbock," Tolwin said, his tone smug. "I'm afraid it is you who failed to follow the proper procedure for examination of an unknown artifact. And you are, at this moment, discovering the consequences of such neglect."

Lina shook her head stubbornly. "I followed the correct procedures," she insisted. "I determined that the chest was an object made of inorganic material and—"

"You are mistaken," Tolwin interrupted her, his eyes narrowing. "You *assumed* that the object was inorganic because it appeared so to the naked eye. Based on that false assumption, you continued your examination without performing further tests, oblivious to the fact that the substance coating its interior is in fact an extraction from the lutea flower."

So that was what it was. Lina's heart sank. She knew a little bit about the lutea plant from her studies. It secreted a fine cloud of dust that acted as a paralytic on passing insects, which the plant then fed upon. In humans, the dust caused an allergic reaction when it came in contact with the skin.

But the lutea plant didn't grow naturally inside old jewelry chests.

Anger flooded Lina. "You deliberately put the dust in there," she accused.

"I don't deny it," Tolwin said, looking down at her hands and smiling. "I planted the dust to prove a point that you would all do well to remember," he said, turning to face the class. "When you are examining an object that comes from another world, you must take nothing for granted. Even the most innocuous device may contain hidden dangers."

Tolwin reached over and clasped Lina's wrist in his hand. Before she could pull away, he lifted her arm so that the entire class could see the effects of the dust. Gasps and cries of "*Eew*, gross!" filled the room.

Blood pounded an unsteady rhythm in Lina's ears as she tried to control her anger. Her fingers were now so swollen and red they looked like ugly little sausages. At least there was no pain, and so far, the sensation hadn't spread past her hands, for which Lina was grateful. But she wouldn't be able to pick anything up or even hold a pencil. No doubt that had been part of Tolwin's intention. How long would her hands stay this way?

As if he sensed her worry, Tolwin released her wrist and returned to his podium. "Take your seat, Miss Winterbock," he said, "and don't look so glum. The effects of the dust are only temporary in humans. You should be able to use your hands again in a few hours.

In the meantime, I hope you'll contemplate this lesson and perhaps take a few notes on it—when you are able to, of course." He smiled, and several of the students snickered.

Holding her head up, Lina walked back to her seat, but her face was almost as red from embarrassment and anger as her hands were from the dust. The bell that signaled the end of class began to toll just as she reached her desk. Bending over, Lina awkwardly slid her pile of books off her desk and into her arms. She tried to grab her pencil, but it skittered away from her numb fingers and fell to the floor. A group of girls giggled as they walked past her. Lina gritted her teeth and crouched down to try to pick up her pencil, but her hands were useless on the small object. Tears burned in her eyes, but Lina furiously blinked them away. She looked up to see if any of the apprentices had lingered in the classroom and might help her out, but everyone, even Simon and Tolwin, was gone.

At least they hadn't stayed around to gloat. That was something. Lina abandoned her pencil and stood up, juggling her books into a manageable pile. She walked back down the stairs and left the classroom, already dreading the journey through the passages where the other students would see her swollen hands.

As if they needed something else to point at and whisper about. They already looked sideways at her dirt-smudged face and frizzy brown hair, not to mention her rumpled and torn clothes. Today she wore a midnight-blue shirt covered with crooked black stitches where she'd tried to mend the dozens of holes. She'd grown used to people's reactions to her appearance, but lobster-claw hands were a whole different kind of strange.

Lina blew out a frustrated sigh. She was tempted to go to Councilwoman Zara and tell her what had happened. The older woman might even have something that would reduce the swelling in Lina's hands.

Like Tolwin, Zara was a teacher and a member of the archivists' ruling council, but she was also Lina's mentor and advisor. Junior apprentices—those in the first through third ranks, as Lina was—took general-knowledge classes, like science, history, reading, and mathematics, during their first several years of study. But in this time, they would also be apprenticed to a senior archivist, as Lina had been to Zara, and as Simon had been to Tolwin. Through one-on-one instruction, the archivist was responsible for mentoring and guiding his or her student toward one of the six divisions of archival work. Once the student passed into the fourth and fifth ranks of the senior apprentices, their classes would shift focus to their chosen division.

No matter what lesson he'd been trying to teach, what Tolwin had done was cruel, and Lina was sure Zara would agree with her.

But Zara was busy with her work on the council and might not be in her office if Lina went to see her. Ever since the Iron War broke out, Lina rarely had more than a few minutes alone with her teacher. Instead, she received written messages and assignments. And when they did see each other, more often than not, their conversations tended to end in arguments and shouting matches. So she didn't have what she'd call the best relationship with Zara at the moment. The thought made Lina's spirits sink even lower.

But if she wasn't going to tell Zara what had happened, that meant she would have to endure the rest of the afternoon classes with her clumsy, swollen hands. She imagined more students giggling at her as she fumbled with her books and papers, trying to work.

No, Lina decided with a fierce shake of her head. That wasn't going to happen. There were better ways and places to spend her time.

Her workshop, for instance. And the secret that was waiting there.

Excitement hummed in Lina's veins at the prospect of a whole day alone with her project. She might not accomplish much without the use of her hands, but what better way to lift her spirits than to go to the place that felt most like home?

Her decision made, she turned and followed the twisting stone corridors that led away from the classrooms to the student dormitories. She passed through several more hallways and stopped at her room so she could drop off her textbooks.

The space was small, carved out of the stone in an L shape, like all the other sleeping quarters, scarcely large enough to fit a narrow bed, a desk, and a chair. The only decoration in the room was a large map that hung on the wall above her headboard. She used the word "decoration" loosely, especially since a casual observer wouldn't be able to tell that the drawing was a map at all. It was a mess, fingerprinted and folded about ten thousand times, but Lina didn't care. It was her masterpiece: a complete map of her home in the archivists' mountain stronghold of Ortana. It depicted every secret tunnel, hidden doorway, and navigable ventilation shaft she'd ever explored—two years' painstaking work, of which Lina was extremely proud.

She'd been born for the role of explorer archivist. True, she'd created the title herself, but it made sense. The archivists' work was to uncover mysterious and wondrous things, and the archivists themselves were all about discovery and preservation of lost artifacts, history, and culture from other worlds. The problem was, they rarely stopped working long enough to realize that their own strongholds held hidden secrets and wonders lost to all but the most determined—and smallest— explorers. Also, the archivists thought the ventilation shafts and some of the tunnels were too dangerous for someone Lina's age to play around in. When Lina first began her explorations, one of the chamelins had caught her using a secret tunnel between the Menagerie and her dormitory. The archivists had sealed off the shortcut, even though she'd begged them not to. Since then, Lina had learned to be careful and secretive to avoid discovery. If that meant she tended to avoid people and occasionally forgot to check in with her teacher, well, that was just the way it had to be. Most people tended to forget about her anyway, Zara included.

Lina dropped her books on her desk and picked up her heavy coat from where she'd slung it over the back of her chair. She pulled it on, leaving the mismatched blue and copper buttons undone. She had a pair of fingerless gloves stowed in her pockets, which she would put on once the swelling in her hands went down.

Despite the steam radiators and fireplaces installed throughout the stronghold, it was never a truly warm place. It wasn't uncommon to see the archivists and apprentices walking the halls in cloaks and scarves. But the place Lina was going was colder than most, and she was used to wearing a heavy coat in her workshop.

Her gaze rested on a corner of her desk where a thick black wristband lay. She picked it up carefully, using only the tips of her swollen fingers, and surveyed the twelve black fireflies clinging to the band. A dull silver light glowed from their abdomens.

"You didn't think I'd leave you behind, did you?" she asked. The lumatites didn't answer, of course, but their light brightened, filling the small room with a silver radiance. If they fed well, a dozen of the insects were powerful enough to light a small room for hours. Lina only needed their light to guide her through a single dark tunnel, a passage no one in the stronghold knew about except her.

Satisfied that she had everything she needed, Lina took one last grimacing look at her swollen hands and left the room, kicking the door shut behind her. She made her way out of the apprentice quarters and back to the larger main tunnels of the stronghold.

The Independent Nation of Archivists, or INA, as outsiders sometimes called it, was made up of three strongholds inside three mountains. The names of the strongholds were also the names of the mountains: Ortana, Ironstar, and Geligaunt. Lina loved saying them. She thought they sounded so valiant, and she imagined the three mountains standing like sentinels amid the rest of the frigid Hiterian Mountains.

Generations of craftspeople had worked to dig the tunnels and carve the buildings and architectural fixtures out of miles of rock and caves. Lina's home, Ortana, was the largest of the three strongholds, and the seat of the nation's ruling council. It had taken centuries to finish, and the names of some of the earliest architects to work on Ortana were carved on the walls of the passage Lina walked through now. Patches of feathery green moss nested with white flowers surrounded the names. The sunlight the flowers needed to grow filtered through holes in the rock ceiling, bouncing off prisms arranged by the archivists to bring the light from the surface.

Though the archivists could be irritating at times, their extraordinary talents, like the ability to coax sunlight into the heart of a mountain, were what Lina loved most about her people.

Passing beyond the Architects' Way, Lina headed for the stronghold's centerpiece, known as the Heart of the Mountain, the hub from which all the other tunnels originated. When she walked down the short flight of stone steps into the chamber, she was struck, as always, by the vastness of the place. Stone columns and curving staircases framed the council building situated on the west side of the chamber, where the archivists' ruling body governed. The ceiling, riddled with stalactites, stretched like a tapestry of daggers a hundred feet above her head. From this chamber, she could travel to any other part of the stronghold, to the six workshops where the bulk of the archivists lived and practiced their crafts, or to the public museum, where they displayed a selection of their wondrous artifacts for the people of Solace.

Lina quickened her pace, casting glances around constantly to make sure she wasn't being watched or followed. She couldn't let anyone discover where she was going.

Ahead of her on the opposite side of the chamber was a set of tall iron gates that separated the archivists' living and work areas from the public museum. Lina turned right before reaching them and continued down a side passage.

This hallway was used for collecting the garbage from the museum. Several bags were lined up along the walls, waiting to be taken to the lower chambers and burned. Nobody wandered down this passage for any other reason, which worked greatly in Lina's favor.

She slowed, looked around again, and listened for the sound of approaching footsteps. She heard nothing, but she waited another minute anyway, just to be safe. Then she stepped up to the right-side wall and ran her hand under a large patch of deepa ivy. The plant grew wild even in the darkest caves, where the sunlight never reached, because its roots stretched deep into cracks in the earth, fed by the same volcanic vents that had formed the mountain thousands of years ago. It was an odd contrast to see them in this passage: delicate, spoon-shaped black leaves sprouting from the side of a tunnel filled with garbage.

Searching beneath the ivy, she found an empty space and lifted the black curtain aside to reveal a hole in the wall about three feet around. She bent down and ducked through the opening, letting the ivy fall gently behind her to conceal the secret entrance.

Next came the tricky part. The tunnel ahead of her was plenty large enough to stand up in and only about twenty feet in length, but it was so narrow in the middle that she had to turn sideways and suck in her breath to get through it. It was like walking through an hourglass turned on its side. Lina held up the wristband of luma-tites and whispered a quick request for light. When she could see, she began the slow, awkward shuffle down the tunnel.

No matter how much she loved to explore, the idea of getting trapped in one of these narrow spaces wasn't something Lina liked to contemplate, especially now, when it seemed like every day her body was changing on her, shoulders widening, feet getting bigger, hips all bony and awkward. She was small for her age, which helped, but someday, Lina knew, she would be too big to fit through this crucial passage. Then she would have to find some way to widen it, or she would lose access to her workshop for good. But she refused to dwell on that right now.

Finally, after she'd collected a few scrapes and bruises on her trek from one side of the Hourglass to the other, the short passage ended, and Lina popped out into a tunnel that was blessedly wider, though the ceiling was low and thick with stalactites. Weaving among them, she made her way through the passage, which sloped gradually downward. This was the longest part of her journey. She'd never actually measured how far the passage descended into the mountain, but Lina suspected that it emptied out a quarter of a mile below the museum. The air grew colder as she walked, and her breath formed thick clouds in front of her face.

She knew from studying old maps of Ortana that these chambers had once been used by the archivists as deep storage. Artifacts that were too broken to be salvaged or technologies that appeared to have no useful purpose had been consigned here. Things that had been on display for a time in the public museum had also been rotated out and stored down here to make room for more recent finds. Unfortunately, many of the oldest rooms and the tunnels leading to them had been buried long ago by a series of cave-ins. Hundreds, maybe thousands, of artifacts had been lost forever. The chambers and passages that remained intact were theoretically stable, except for a few tremors now and then, but the archivists hadn't wanted to take the chance of losing any more of their artifacts. They'd moved the storage areas to the workshops above and abandoned these tunnels for good.

Lina had reclaimed them the day she'd discovered the hole behind the curtain of deepa ivy. Her best guess was that it had been made sometime during the excavations for the museum expansion two years ago. The area had been a torn-up mess at the time, so it wasn't surprising that the workers had overlooked the hole, and the ivy had grown in later to cover it.

She knew she was getting close to her destination when the passage began to level out. The corridor narrowed again but not nearly as much as at the beginning of her journey. She skirted around the forest of stalactites until finally the passage emptied into a much larger cavern. The lumatites' glow couldn't reach the fifty-foot-high ceiling, and Lina estimated that the whole of the chamber was over two hundred feet in diameter.

To her left, in a tiny corner of the cavern, was her workshop. She'd fashioned a table by throwing two thin oak planks over a pair of sawhorses that she'd made herself. Eventually, she built a stool to go with it, although her first couple of attempts had collapsed under her when she tried to sit on them. Her carpentry skills had improved since then, and a good thing too. Everything she brought down here had to either fit through the passage or be in pieces that she'd later assemble. On the table, she had a pair of small lanterns and her tools spread out on a towel, along with her bigger maps of the stronghold and her secret tunnels.

Lina went to the table and draped her work apron over her head, though she had no hope of being able to tie the strings yet. Using both hands, she lifted a box of matches out of her apron pocket, all the while wondering if she could actually manage to strike one. No choice but to try, she supposed. She needed more light than her dozen lumatites could offer. And now that no one else was around to see her, she didn't mind looking a little ridiculous.

Ten excruciating minutes later, hands trembling and sweat dripping down her forehead, Lina heard a satisfying crackle as her tenth match scraped across the stone floor and brought forth flame.

She lit the lanterns and then moved carefully to the cluster of stalagmites surrounding her worktable. On their tips, Lina had stuck dozens of candle stubs, which she also lit, until the room was awash in warm golden light. She muffled the lumatites with her hand until their light dimmed and went out, wanting to give them a rest. "Thanks for the help," she murmured.

Now that she had more light, the workshop felt almost cozy. Lina loved to take naps down here when she forgot about the time and needed a rest, but she'd had to dig a fire pit in order to keep from freezing in the cavern. She'd also collected a pile of thick quilts and one of her lumpy old pillows, arranging them among the stalagmites like a nest.

Lina shivered and stuffed her hands in her pockets. Her fingers weren't up to making a fire yet. For now, the coat would have to be enough.

After surveying her space to make sure everything was as she'd left it, Lina closed her eyes and turned slowly toward the center of the now-lighted chamber, half-afraid that it wouldn't be there, that even after all this time it had been some kind of fanciful dream. Her heart thudded against her rib cage, but she needn't have worried. When she opened her eyes, it was waiting for her like a sleek bird of prey.

The *Merlin*.

≈ TWO ≈

L ina walked over to inspect the airship, checking to see whether any new debris had fallen from the cave ceiling since the last time she'd been here. Thankfully, everything looked the same. The ship was fine.

When Lina first discovered the chamber, the vessel was half-buried from a cave-in. Back then, the debris pile was so large in places that she could scramble up and down it to stand on top of the ship's rigid frame. That was how she came up with its name. The bluish-gray hue of the nose cone and the black bands painted on the horizontal and vertical stabilizers at the rear strongly resembled the plumage of a type of falcon called a merlin. And the ship itself, with its landing wheels only half deployed, reminded her of an injured bird resting on the ground. She found writing on the side of the ship, strange looping symbols and slashes that probably declared its name but in a language Lina had never seen before, so she decided to name the vessel herself.

For eight months, she'd been meticulously digging the ship out of its stone prison. Dozens of healing cuts and blisters covered her hands from moving all that rock, and rough calluses made the skin of her palms smooth and shiny. For Lina, these were badges of honor. She'd done the work all on her own, finally uncovering the part of the ship she'd been the most eager to find.

Lina approached the last remaining rock pile, a cluster of boulders wedged between the underside of the ship's hull and the ground. Behind the boulders was the outline of a door, barely visible through a thick layer of dirt. Using the glow of the candles and lanterns to guide her, she reached up and ran her swollen fingers along the seam between the hull and the door. The hairs on the back of her neck prickled. So close. Tantalizingly close. If Lina's examination of the ship was correct—and she'd had ample time to speculate over the last eight months— once she cleared the boulders away, the doorway would open into a gangplank and provide access to every part of the ship.

But that was also where the problem arose. Lina stepped back and surveyed the four large boulders tightly wedged against the door. *Hello, my nemeses,* she thought, rolling her eyes. *We meet again.* She'd nicknamed the boulders Pain, Wrath, Ruin—and Lumpy. She'd run out of inspiration on the last one. Lina had tried everything she could think of to pry the boulders loose, scraping, yanking, digging, and heaving with every tool in her arsenal. She'd worked until her hands and arms bled, but she hadn't been able to dislodge any of them. They were wedged too tightly. She figured she needed at least one more pair of hands to help her lever the boulders out of place.

Only help was the one thing Lina couldn't ask for.

Partly, the issue was size. Lina sat down on Wrath and rested her chin on her hand as she contemplated the puzzle. Very few people in Ortana were small enough to fit down that first narrow passage to the chamber. And she wasn't about to trust her secret to the ones who were. All it would take was for somebody to let it slip to the archivists that she'd found an intact airship. Lina didn't know how long the *Merlin* had been here or who had built it, but she knew that if the archivists discovered the airship's existence, they would come with shovels and excavators and dig the ship out for themselves.

Lina wasn't about to let that happen. Not after she'd worked so hard for so long.

Compiling accounts from numerous other worlds, the archivists had conducted extensive studies of the technology of flying vessels, and Lina had spent many late nights in the library studying their findings. The *Merlin* most closely resembled the design for a rigid airship, or dirigible, with its twenty-five-foot-long cylindrical body and two steam propeller engines situated near the rear of the craft. If this were the case, the internal framework would contain a set of lifting bags that, when filled with a gas lighter than air, provided the means of flight. But as far as Lina knew, dirigible technology was purely theoretical, at least in her world. No one had ever built, let alone successfully flown, such a craft. The only type of airships in regular use in Solace were small, short-range gliders, which were almost exclusively flown by sky raiders, because they were unstable and prone to crashing.

Not long ago, King Aron of the Dragonfly territories announced his intention to develop a new kind of airship—one that was equipped to handle a long journey and could travel safely over the impassable Hiterian Mountains to the uncharted lands of Solace. But the war stalled his efforts, and the ship was never built.

The *Merlin* was exactly the type of ship King Aron must have envisioned: sleek yet powerful, roomy enough, even with the gasbags, to carry a crew. The engines were a problem, though. They were far too small to handle the *Merlin's* bulk, which would make maneuvering the vessel extremely difficult. So why had such small engines been used? The answer to that mystery, if it existed, lay inside the ship.

Lina stood up and walked over to her worktable. She'd arranged her books on airship technology in a small alcove in the wall behind the table. She selected one on engines and managed to get it open to a book-marked page. Since she hadn't been able to get inside the ship, her secondary goal was to attempt to start one of the steam engines, but Lina hadn't tried it yet. She wanted to make sure she studied all the manuals thoroughly, but she had to admit that part of her hesitation was the unsettling length of the list of things that could go wrong if she mishandled the pressure.

"Although all my research indicates that the engines should work perfectly," she said, glancing at the luma-tites. Again, they didn't answer her, but it was so quiet and lonely in the cavern, Lina liked to make some noise every once in a while, even if it was only the sound of her own voice. "I mean, it's not like I can compare exact models," she continued. "This technology is still sub-stantially different from anything the archivists have re-corded in their accounts, but the evidence is there, and in the end, a steam engine is a steam engine." In theory, she could start it without getting inside the ship. She'd studied the schematics that were most similar to the *Merlin*. She could make it work. Probably.

Lina closed her book with a snap and walked over to the ship. Restlessness took hold of her. Maybe it was be-cause of her encounter with Tolwin and Simon. They'd taken her hands away, made her weak and helpless. She couldn't stand feeling that way. But it was more than that. Lina was tired of studying. She wanted action, to put her theory about the ship into practice.

"And you don't want to lie there dormant forever, do you?" she asked, this time addressing the ship. Lina approached the starboard engine and laid her red, swollen hand against its smooth metal surface. As soon as she did, she noticed that some of the feeling had returned to her tingling fingers. She breathed a sigh of relief. She wouldn't be helpless much longer.

As Lina stood there in the silence, considering what she was about to do, her restlessness shifted, becoming something desperate, like longing. The feeling came on her so suddenly and so intensely, it made her gasp. She took a step back from the ship, shaking her head as if to clear it. After a moment, the emotion subsided, and she felt like herself again.

Lina took a breath and forced herself to calm down. She couldn't let her emotions take over. She needed all her concentration for this. But she knew what she had to do. If starting up the ship's engines was the only way to make progress on her own, well, then she would take the leap of faith that she could keep the steam pressure stable.

She had to wait another hour for the swelling to go down enough for her to use her screwdriver, but then Lina removed the large, curved metal plate that covered the engine components. Truly, the engine was in fine condition, which was surprising, considering the size of the craft. Lina would have expected it to be damaged beyond repair when it was scavenged from the scrap fields up north. Typically, something this large would have fallen in hundreds of pieces. But maybe one of the archivists had worked to repair the ship long ago, using bits of their own technology. It would explain the odd mix of familiar and strange mechanics, Lina thought as she ran her hands over the engine. It might also account for the engine's small size.

You're stalling, she scolded herself. *It's time to do this.*

She'd already loaded the airship's small firebox with coal as part of her advance preparations. Her water had come from an underground stream that flowed through the back of the chamber. Once she checked that her quantities were right, she needed to start the fire and increase the heat gradually, monitoring the pressure as steam production began. All together, the process would likely take several hours, so she was in for a long day and night.

Lina took a deep breath and, before she could change her mind, reached into her apron for her matches.

A little before midnight, about the same time Lina's hands finally returned to normal, the airship's propeller started to turn. Lina quickly backed away from the engine as the buzz and whir picked up, stumbling and sliding over rocks in her haste to get a good view. When she was steady again, she stood, openmouthed, and stared at the ship.

It worked. Lina's heart pounded. *It worked.* Pressure was stable, and the engine itself showed no sign of damage or deterioration. The *Merlin*, so long forgotten by the world, was coming back to life. She just needed someone at the controls to bring her the rest of the way.

Lina was no pilot, of course, but she longed to be inside the ship, sitting at those controls. She dreamed about flying over the mountains to the uncharted lands. Goddess, it wasn't fair! Frustration burned in her chest, and she picked up a rock and hurled it against the wall of the cavern. She was so close! If it weren't for those stupid boulders! There had to be a way to move them.

Careful to avoid the propeller, Lina ran to the front of the ship and crouched down beside Lumpy, the smallest of the boulders. She took out her pry bar and fixed one end in a spot between the boulder and another, smaller rock. Grunting, she gathered the pent-up anger and frustration that raged inside her and pushed down with all her strength. Blood rushed to her face, and she clenched her jaw as she threw her weight against the pry bar. Sweat rolled down her face, stinging her eyes, and the sound of the whirring propeller filled her ears.

And for a brief instant, she thought that this time the boulder would give way.

But suddenly, Lina's strength gave out, and she collapsed beside the boulder, her pry bar clattering to the ground. Tears burned in her eyes, and she raised her fist, wanting to punch the boulder. Instead, she let her hand drop. She'd lashed out once before in a fit of anger—that was how Wrath had gotten its name—and ended up with bruised and bloody knuckles to show for it.

Dragging herself to her feet, Lina trudged over to the engine to start bringing the pressure down. She didn't want to leave it running long on its first test. As she worked to shut the engine off, the noise of the propeller gradually died away, and the familiar hollow silence consumed the chamber, which made her misery complete. Again, Lina found herself wishing there was someone here with her. Between activating the steam engine and Tolwin humiliating her in front of the other apprentices, she'd experienced incredible success and spectacular failure all in one night—but no one had been there to share any of it with her.

It doesn't matter, Lina told herself sternly. The most important thing was that the engine had worked. She used the thought to try to pull herself out of her dark mood. All her work over the past eight months had been worth it for this moment.

She walked along the length of the ship, running her hand over its metal surface as a slow grin spread across her face. "I promise I'll find a way to open the door," she whispered, and this time the words were for herself.

I will open the door. She turned to go back to her work-table, reenergized.

And then she heard the rumbling.

A chill went through Lina's body. *No, it can't be. Please, no.* But the rumbling continued, building steadily in intensity. Instinctively, Lina stepped toward the ship, bumping against the hull as a tremor shook the cavern. The *Merlin* trembled—Lina felt the vibration through her back. She whipped her head around wildly, seeking shelter from what she knew was coming, even as thin streamers of dust and small rocks fell from the cavern ceiling. She looked up, and a scream welled in her throat.

A thick cloud of dust billowed from above as a shower of much bigger rocks began to fall, landing in a rush of noise all around her. A stone clipped her shoulder, and Lina flinched, dropping to her knees. She threw up her hands to protect her face just as another rock glanced off her arm, and she cried out in pain.

Her worktable—if she could just get there . . . crawl underneath.

Another rock smashed to the ground, inches from crushing her leg.

She'd never make it across the room. Frantic, Lina crawled toward the gap beneath the edge of the ship's hull and one of its half-deployed landing wheels. Tucking into a tight ball, she put her arms over her head, careful to cover the wristband holding the lumatites with her other hand. The stones were still falling dangerously close, bouncing off the ship's hull, but it was the best protection she had. She squeezed her eyes shut and braced for more rocks and pain. She wanted to scream for help, but fear choked her silent. There would be no one to hear her anyway. For all she knew, she was about to be buried alive with the ship, and no one would find either of them.

Suddenly, the grinding shriek of metal against metal filled her ears. The sound came from somewhere above her, drowning out even the deafening crash of falling rock. Despite her fear, Lina opened her eyes, looking for the source of the sound.

Stone dust filled the chamber, but through the brown clouds and by the faint light of the lumatites at her wrist, Lina saw something that didn't make sense. A shadowy curtain hung above her head. Was it just the ship? No, it was bigger, a sheet of metal that extended outward from the ship's upper hull. Whatever it was, it blocked the shower of debris, forming a wide shield above her. Lina didn't dare move to get a better look at it while the rocks were still falling.

She stayed tucked beneath the ship for what felt like an eternity but was probably only a few minutes. Gradually, the tremors in the cavern quieted, and the deadly rock falls ceased. For once, Lina was thankful for the ensuing silence. She lifted trembling hands and checked her head, searching for wounds. Her arm and leg hurt where the stones had hit her, but they were no worse than the other scrapes and bruises she'd collected that night.

Still, a trip to the medical wing was probably a good idea, before anything else went wrong.

Lina shook the dust out of her hair as she stood up. Her knees trembled, threatening to buckle. She took a deep breath to steady herself. *That was close. Too close.* There had been small tremors in the cavern before, but never anything like this.

She took a few more breaths, and when she'd calmed down, Lina raised her arm to shine the lumatites on the metal curtain above her. She wanted to get a closer look at what had saved her life.

The first thing she noticed was that, unlike the *Merlin*'s hull, this metal had a liquid, shimmering quality to it. Scrambling up on a pile of rocks so she could reach, Lina ran her fingers carefully over its surface and encountered a softness that reminded her of silk. But no, the surface was rigid. Wasn't it? She dropped her arm and walked from the ship, examining the surface as it tapered to a point roughly twenty feet away.

Lina gasped as the truth of it hit her like one of those falling rocks:

The metal curtain was a wing.

She ran to the front of the ship and faced the nose

cone. Sure enough, another wing sprouted from the starboard side. Somehow, when she'd started the engine, she must have inadvertently activated a mechanism that caused them to deploy.

"But that doesn't make any sense!" Lina burst out, elated but equally confused by her discovery. None of the dirigible designs she'd seen in her books had said anything about wings—the lifting gases made them unnecessary—let alone ones that extended and retracted from the ship. And why hadn't they activated when she'd had the engine at full steam? Were there other power sources at work in the ship she didn't know about, ones that had triggered when she'd started up the engine?

So many questions, and with them came the excitement; it bubbled up, banishing her earlier fear. Lina ran back to the rock pile she'd been standing on and grabbed some more stones lying nearby to build it higher. She climbed up on them again, this time raising both hands to lay them flat against the wing.

Suddenly, with a yelp, Lina snatched her hands back. That feeling—had she imagined it? No, she hadn't. She touched her fingers to her lips, and a slow smile spread over her face. Giggling nervously, she reached out again to press her palms against the wing. This time she was prepared for the warmth and subtle vibration humming under her hands.

The hairs on the back of her neck stood up as she

considered the implications of what had just happened. She had triggered something when she'd started that engine. And the tremor she'd felt just before the cave-in—could it have come from the ship? Maybe it was some sort of internal power source that was now running independently of the steam engine. Without being at the control panel, she had no way of knowing.

I have to get inside the ship! But Lina tamped down her excitement and forced herself to think about the situation logically. Maybe it was just a matter of getting bigger tools or a longer pry bar. The archivists' Technology division—or Gears and Steam, as most people called it—had to have something she could use to get those boulders loose. But would the tools fit through the narrow passage? She had the overwhelming urge to go find out, but she knew it was pointless. This late, the workshops in the Technology division would all be locked up tight.

With a sigh, Lina had to admit she'd done all she could for now. But what a day! It had started out perfectly miserable and ended in a breakthrough with the *Merlin* that was better than anything she could have dreamed.

She jumped down from the rock pile and went over to her worktable. Dust and stones littered its surface. The lanterns were out, their glass shattered, and most of her tools and books were scattered all over the floor. Lina gathered them up and put them back on the table.

Then she went around to the handful of candles still burning on the stalagmites and blew them out. Using just the lumatites for light, she made her way back to the passage, squeezing through the Hourglass and earning herself a few more cuts and scrapes on her way to the Heart of the Mountain.

When she reentered the Heart, Lina was surprised to see lights shining in the council building and about a dozen people milling around outside, as if they were waiting for something. She slowed her pace, curiosity overcoming her fatigue.

Ortana's ruling council must have called another emergency meeting, she guessed, though it was awfully late at night for it. Then again, the council had been having more and more closed sessions lately. Lina didn't have to guess what the meeting was about: the Iron War. Even the people standing around the building were talking about it.

The conflict, which had been raging for more than a year now, started when the Merrow Kingdom began stockpiling weapons, and rumors flew that they were out to conquer the Dragonfly territories. In response, Dragonfly's King Aron halted the iron trade, cutting Merrow off from its most necessary resource for making weapons. Furious, Merrow's King Easmon declared war anyway.

The archivists had refused to fight for either side, but

that didn't mean their world had gone untouched, as evidenced by the daily flood of refugees they'd taken into their care. Innocent people from both kingdoms had lost their homes, sometimes their whole town, and they had nowhere else to go. But since the archivists had opened their nation to the refugees, that meant the strongholds were now overflowing with people, and it was all the archivists could do to care for them.

It was one of many reasons Lina rarely saw her teacher Zara for her private lessons anymore. As part of Ortana's ruling council, Zara was responsible for the well-being of everyone in the three strongholds, and in the last year, those duties had taken precedence over everything else.

And strained Lina and Zara's already tricky relationship even further.

It was too much to hope for that the late meeting meant the war was over, but maybe there'd been some new development. Something that meant there was an end in sight.

Something that would bring Zara back to her.

Whatever was happening, Lina knew she wouldn't learn anything standing outside the council building. Luckily, there were better ways to get information. The building's extensive network of ventilation shafts, for example.

Lina smiled, though her grin quickly faded as she

considered what she was about to do. Sneaking through abandoned cave tunnels was one thing, but getting inside this place to eavesdrop was something else entirely. She would need all her skills to pull it off. She wasn't worried, exactly. "Focused" was a better word. If she wasn't focused, she could be caught, and if she got caught— well, she didn't want to think too far down that path.

Lina tried to be nonchalant as she approached the building. Formal sculpted gardens of blue and green moss flanked the steps leading up to the entrance, and stone staircases on either side of the double doors led to the public galleries on the second level. Usually, the doors stood open, and any of the archivists, apprentices, sarnuns, or chamelins could sit in and observe the council meetings, though no one was allowed to speak without the council's permission.

The first thing Lina decided to do was take stock of how heavily guarded the meeting was. A slow circuit of the building, blending in with the crowd, would tell her what she needed to know. At most, she thought there would be someone standing at every entrance to turn people away. Lina confirmed this when she saw that the double doors at the front were closed. Nirean, one of the chamelin guards, stood watch in front of them.

A thin layer of dark fur covered Nirean's body, stopping short of her throat and the membranous edge of her leathery brown wings, which curled over her arms and chest like a bat's. Her face closely resembled a lizard's, with a long, scaled snout and lambent yellow eyes. When Nirean caught sight of Lina, the chamelin inclined her head and, with a flick of her wings, began the transformation that would shift her back to her human form.

Lina felt a tremor of apprehension. She hadn't expected to be noticed in the crowd, but Nirean and Zara were good friends to her. Now that she'd been spotted, she had no choice but to talk to the chamelin. She walked up the short flight of steps and stopped in front of the double doors as Nirean's wings shrank and disappeared into her back. Her snout drew in, and her face turned round and wrinkled as scales became skin. Fur lightened and receded. The dark green dress robe she and the other chamelins typically wore fell in loose folds around her as her body became more slender and she lost several inches in height.

When the transformation was complete, Nirean pushed her long grayish-brown hair out of her face and tightened the belt on her robe to accommodate her new girth. "Hello, Lina," she said politely, and even as she spoke, the tenor of her voice changed from rough and gravelly to smooth and deep. "It's nice to see you out and about in the main corridors. I heard from several teachers that you missed your afternoon classes today."

"Hello, Nirean." Lina bit her lip, her mind racing. Word traveled fast in the stronghold. And judging by the chamelin's stern expression, she wasn't going to let this unapproved absence pass. Lina sighed. She would have to pay Zara a visit to try to explain herself—if Zara was even in her office when Lina came calling. Often, her teacher was just as hard to find as Lina was, and if Zara did need to tell her something or reprimand her for some infraction, usually she slipped notes under Lina's door or passed the lectures along through Nirean.

"Sorry, I wasn't feeling well earlier." That was certainly true. "I'll talk to Zara and explain everything right after the meeting," she promised, and started backing down the steps. The last thing she wanted was for Nirean to pepper her with questions about where she'd been or what she was doing in the Heart of the Mountain that evening. Questions led to suspicion, and Nirean was better than most people—chamelin or human or sarnun—at sniffing out when Lina was up to something.

Nirean opened her mouth as if she meant to stop Lina, but luckily, at that moment, a pair of sarnun archivists came up the steps to try to get into the meeting, and Nirean was forced to step in front of them and explain that it was off-limits. With a sigh of relief, Lina took the opportunity to sidle off through the moss gardens. She was just out of sight of Nirean and the front entrance when a different voice brought her up short.

"Hey, what are you doing?"

The voice made Lina's skin crawl. With a groan, she

turned, and her heart sank when she saw Simon smirking at her. Where had he come from? He was like a cave snake: you never noticed him until he was leaving a slimy trail right next to you. Encountering Simon was much worse than being spotted by Nirean.

"Wait, is that you, Winterbock?" Simon asked, adopting a tone of mock surprise. "Sorry, I thought you were one of the refugees. Have you been crawling around in the trash bins again?" He waved a hand in front of his face and made a show of backing away from her.

Lina knew she didn't stink, but she could only imagine how she must look after the cave-in. Her hair was probably full of rock dust. She was surprised Nirean hadn't mentioned it. Then again, the chamelin was probably used to her odd appearance by now. Simon just enjoyed mocking it.

"You guessed it," Lina said, pretending to smile sweetly at him. "I rolled around on your bedsheets afterward. You don't mind, do you?"

For a split second, Simon's face blanched, as if he didn't know whether she was kidding. The reaction gave Lina a warm feeling in her chest.

"Very funny," he said. "Do you even know what bedsheets are, Winterbock? I always thought you slept in a hole in the ground."

"Oh, I do," Lina said without missing a beat. "Sleep in holes, eat garbage—all that fun stuff you constantly remind me about."

If Simon noticed her sarcasm, he didn't comment on it. He was too busy looking her up and down suspiciously. His gaze lingered on her hands, and Lina noticed a flash of disappointment cross his face when he saw they were normal again. She hadn't thought it was possible to hate him more than she already did, but with that look, he made it easy for her.

"What are you doing lurking around here anyway?" he asked. "The council meeting's off-limits."

"So I heard," Lina said, crossing her arms over her chest and pretending to look bored. "Tolwin didn't tell you what it was about?" Like Zara, Tolwin served on the ruling council, but Lina doubted he'd give his apprentice, even a senior one like Simon, the details of any secret meeting. Still, never hurt to ask.

"Of course he did." But Simon's face reddened, and Lina knew he had no idea what the meeting was about. "If you think I'm going to tell you, you're crazier than I thought."

"Oh, come on, Simon," Lina said, unable to suppress a chuckle. "We both know you're lying. Must be big news, though, if they called the meeting this late."

"That's none of our concern," he said, sniffing. "You should be more worried about when you're having your next bath."

"Fine." Lina rolled her eyes. Trust Simon to think of nothing beyond pleasing his teacher—the two of them were inseparable in a way that made Lina want to vomit—or insulting her every chance he got. "As much fun as this has been, I'm tired, and I'm going back to my room now." She started to move away, tossing a wave over her shoulder. "By the way, next time we get together, how about you make fun of my hair or something? The bath and garbage jokes are starting to get a little stale."

She spoke casually, but inside, she was trying to push down the anger and embarrassment burning in her chest as Simon's snickers echoed behind her.

When she was far enough away, Lina darted into the shadows behind a stone column. She was determined that no one else would see her. Running into both Nirean and Simon had been bad enough. Self-consciously, she reached up and wiped at a bit of dirt crusted on her cheek. So what if she got a little dirty crawling through the tunnels and ventilation shafts? She had no idea why Simon hated her as much as he seemed to, but he never wasted an opportunity to give her a hard time.

Lina shook her head. She was letting herself get distracted, and that was dangerous. She had more important things to think about than Simon. The council meeting had started, and she was missing it.

Moving along the side of the building, Lina spotted what she was looking for behind a patch of dusky purple cave mushrooms. The hinged grate covering the ventilation shaft was rusty and secured with four equally rusty screws.

Lina turned and put her back to the building. Fumbling in her apron pocket, she removed a screwdriver and her small metal pry bar. These tools were among her particular favorites, and she usually carried them with her. Torque was the greatest thing in the world, as far as Lina was concerned.

Clutching the worn grip in her hand, she fitted the screwdriver to the screws and loosened them one by one behind her back, all the while keeping an eye out for anyone who might venture too close and see what she was doing. A few minutes later, she had four rusty screws safely tucked into her apron pocket. She fitted the pry bar between the grate's edge and the wall and carefully levered it open. Thankfully, the hinges only squeaked a little bit. No one had noticed her either.

Easy as breathing, Lina thought.

She put her tools away and squeezed headfirst into the shaft. "A little bit of light would be good here," she told the lumatites, and put her hand out when they started to glow brightly. "Not too much. We really, *really* don't want anyone to know we're coming."

⋙ THREE ⋘

"**Y**ou asked for one last vote to reaffirm that we are in agreement on this matter," Councilwoman Zara declared as Lina moved with agonizing slowness through the dusty, cobwebbed ventilation shaft—almost directly above her teacher's head. "You have your answer, Councilman Tolwin: the archivists are and shall remain neutral in this war. However, we will not prevent any man or woman—human, chamelin, or sarnun—of sufficient age from joining the fight for either side, provided they first sever their affiliation with us."

"I acknowledge the council's vote, Zara." Tolwin's smooth, deep voice gave Lina as much of a crawly feeling on her skin as Simon's did. "Nevertheless, I wish to reiterate my misgivings about this course of action." Lina heard the faint sound of shuffling papers. "The Merrow Kingdom's forces have established a large military outpost in the city of Tevshal and are now moving southwest from there. Every day they draw closer to our borders. Just last night, our scouts reported seeing campfires from the top of Previs Peak. Twenty miles, my friends, is all that separates an army from our doorstep."

"That's a bit of an exaggeration, Councilman," Zara observed. "Twenty miles of snowbound foothills and subzero temperatures lie between them and the bridges spanning Gazer's Gorge, where our defenders from each mountain stronghold can decimate their armies as they try to come across. They won't risk it."

"Agreed," spoke up Councilwoman Vargis. "We have discussed this before, Tolwin. Merrow's target must be Kalmora. It's the largest city in the western Dragonfly territories and a hub for the iron trade. But Merrow will need thousands more troops if they have any hope of capturing it."

"At the rate they're mustering, by the end of the month they may well have thousands of soldiers in place," Tolwin pointed out. "And whatever the outcome, one day the war will end, and neither the Merrow Kingdom nor the Dragonfly territories are likely to forget that we refused to choose a side. They may punish us for it in ways we haven't foreseen. Once the war is over, the Merrow Kingdom may refuse to let us set foot in the meteor fields to collect artifacts. Can you imagine how devastating that would be to our nation, our way of life?"

Councilwoman Vargis scoffed. "We have made important concessions to the Merrow Kingdom to ensure that that does not happen, Tolwin. Don't create problems where none exist."

Lina paused at the councilwoman's words. Well, that explained why the archivists were still able to ship in objects from the meteor fields without interruption. They'd come to some kind of agreement with King Easmon. Though, if they were neutral in the war, what "concessions" could there be?

"Kings can change their minds, Vargis," Councilman Tolwin continued in an ominous voice. "Worse, if the Dragonfly territories were ever to discover the deal we struck—"

"The issue has been decided, Councilman," another voice, that of Councilman Davort, interrupted Tolwin. "Can we move on, please?"

So there *had* been a deal, one that secretly put the archivists on the Merrow Kingdom's side, or at least favored them highly. Lina hated to admit it, but Tolwin had a point. The archivists were taking a big risk if the Dragonfly territories were to find out.

Sweat poured down Lina's face as she continued to inch forward. As juicy as all this information was, the meeting was taking forever, and she needed to get out of the shaft.

She was prepared to admit that she'd encountered a

few wrinkles in her eavesdropping plan. For one thing, she'd forgotten that this shaft veered to the left and had taken her right through the center of the room and above the council table. She'd thought the shaft went around the outside of the room, which would have allowed her to listen in from a safe distance—the last thing she wanted was a front-row seat. By the time she'd realized where she was, she'd figured it was too late to turn back.

She also hadn't expected this part of the shaft to be so old and . . . well, "shoddy" was the nicest word she could think of for it. Every time Lina moved, the shaft made ominous creaking and groaning sounds. If it hadn't been for the council members occasionally breaking out into impressive shouting matches to cover the noise, she never would have made any progress at all through the shaft. Now she was stuck waiting for the meeting to end so she could get out without anyone hearing her.

The most disappointing part of all was that, as far as she could tell, there'd been no new developments in the Iron War. Lina had hoped to hear good news, but the council only seemed interested in rehashing an old argument.

"Who is in command of the Merrow Kingdom's armies in the west?" one of the other council members was asking. "Is it the princess Elinore?"

"Technically, yes," Zara answered. "But as far as our

scouts can tell, she's being kept away from the front lines. The king won't want to risk her safety, so the western forces are being led by Commander Cartwell."

Worried murmurs swept through the council room, and Lina caught her breath. News from the front lines was often slow to trickle down to the apprentices, but even *she* had heard of Commander Cartwell. He had a reputation as a brilliant—and brutal—field commander. Knowing he was at the head of an army marching in the direction of the strongholds was not a comforting thought.

"Enough, enough," Tolwin said, and the room gradually quieted. "My concerns have been recorded, but let me offer one last proposal."

Just one *more?* Lina resisted the urge to bang her head against the wall of the shaft. *I should be so lucky.*

"If we would reconsider our position of neutrality and throw our support to King Aron of the Dragonfly territories, I am convinced they would be willing to provide us not only with a contingent of troops to help protect our borders but also with significant monetary resources. In exchange, we can offer them vital technological support in their campaign. I'm certain King Aron would greatly value our combined expertise."

Zara's angry voice echoed in the chamber. "That has never been our way, Tolwin, and you know it! We're preservationists. We're not in the business of developing weapons of war and destruction. That you even suggest such a thing offends me."

"Not to mention it would destroy any goodwill we have established with the Merrow Kingdom," Councilman Davort added more calmly. "Tolwin, you said yourself you were afraid of being cut off from the meteor fields. How quickly do you think King Easmon would block us from collecting artifacts if we threw our support to the Dragonfly territories?"

"If Dragonfly wins the war—and I believe, with its strategy and its iron, it can—it won't matter," Tolwin said. "In exchange for our support, we can ask that Dragonfly annex the meteor fields to us. We would *own* the scrap towns and everything in them. Consider it, friends. That's all I ask," Tolwin said in a smooth voice. "For the good of our nation, when the war is over, I want to be able to say I supported the winning side."

For a moment, silence reigned in the chamber as the council considered Tolwin's words. Lina held her breath, her heart thumping hard in her chest. She knew what Zara's reaction to Tolwin's proposal would be: fury.

Then, into the silence came a soft creaking sound. She hadn't noticed it when the council members were talking, but now it grew steadily louder. For one blissful second, Lina thought it was the sound of a door opening in the room below her. Maybe the council members were leaving, or maybe Zara was storming out in a rage to end the meeting.

Until Lina realized with a dawning horror that the source of the creaking was actually the rusty metal plate she crouched on—bending, bowing under her weight.

Oh, you have got to be kidding me.

The rusty plate broke loose. Lina flailed her arms wildly, trying in vain to find a handhold on the sides of the shaft, but there was nothing to grab. She started to fall but at the last second caught the edge of the next plate in front of her, so that she was hanging out the bottom of the shaft by her fingertips. She glanced down as the broken plate crashed to the marble floor in front of the council table. Her legs swung back and forth, and she was already slipping. She knew she wouldn't be able to pull herself back into the shaft.

The game was up. With a wince, Lina let go and dropped the six or seven remaining feet to the floor, landing in a crouch next to the traitorous piece of metal, facing the long oak table where the nine council members sat staring at her, eyes wide and mouths in various stages of falling open.

This is one of those moments. The thought flitted through Lina's mind as she stood up and plucked a cobweb—and what looked like part of a mouse's nest—out of her hair. One of those moments when she wished with every fiber of her being that she could melt into the floor and disappear, as if she'd never been born.

Whatever you do, don't make it worse by trying to come up with some flimsy excuse for why you were in the ventilation shaft, Lina told herself.

That's right. Just keep quiet.

But when she glimpsed those nine pairs of eyes pinning her to the spot, she couldn't help herself. "Wow, see now, I suspected that that shaft needed replacement parts," she blurted out. "I said to myself, 'Lina, you should go up there and test it to make sure it won't rot away and fall apart,' and it's a good thing I did, because, well, look what just happened. And you know, you would not believe how dirty it is up there, so if you want me to clean things up a bit—"

She stopped the flood of words when her gaze fell on Councilman Tolwin's face, which was turning a deeper shade of red than Lina thought she'd ever seen on a person. Even worse than that, though, was the disappointment that shone clearly in Zara's eyes when Lina turned to look at her teacher. Lina's stomach churned with guilt.

This is going to be bad. Bad like the time she'd tried to dig a tunnel underneath the library and made a whole section of the floor collapse.

And the explosion of anger, when it came, was—unsurprisingly—from Tolwin.

"Lina Winterbock—I should have known!" he

cried, leaping to his feet so quickly that for a moment, Lina thought he might jump across the table at her. He slammed his fist on the tabletop. "This is a closed council session, apprentice!"

"Are you hurt, Lina?" Zara spoke up, ignoring Tolwin's tirade.

Lina shook her head. "I'm fine," she said, even though it wasn't true. She'd scraped her shoulders on the rough metal edges when she fell out of the ventilation shaft, and they were already stinging fiercely, but she didn't think she'd get much sympathy from the council.

"How did you get in here?" Tolwin demanded. When Lina didn't immediately reply, he slammed his fist on the table again. "Look at me, girl!"

"I think it's fairly obvious how she managed the feat," Councilman Davort interjected. Lina thought she detected a flicker of amusement in the old man's voice, but it was gone too quickly for her to be sure. At eighty-two, Davort was the oldest member of the council. He had a thin ridge of white hair at the back of his head, and his hands shook slightly when he reached for the water glass on the table in front of him. "The real question is: why is she here, and who should have been looking after her?" He turned his gaze to Zara as he spoke.

"I hear you, Davort," Zara said, accepting the rebuke with a bow of her head. "Lina is my responsibility. I apologize to the council for her intrusion."

Lina squared her shoulders. She couldn't allow Zara to be lectured for something she had done. "Zara didn't know where I was," she said, realizing after she spoke that that bit of information wouldn't help either of them. "I mean, this is my fault. I shouldn't have eavesdropped. I'm sorry."

"Lina, leave the council room now and go to my office," Zara commanded. "I'll be along in a few minutes to discuss your punishment."

"I object. The council should decide her punishment," Tolwin snapped. He turned to glare at Lina. "We all know you, Lina Winterbock, and I say you've played these tricks too many times. My suggestion to the council is that, effective immediately, Lina Winterbock be stripped of her apprenticeship. That she no longer be allowed access to the archivists' workshops, and any artifacts she is currently studying be confiscated and redistributed to the other apprentices."

Lina swayed on her feet as panic seized her. "No, you can't!" she cried. This couldn't be happening. Yes, she shouldn't have eavesdropped, but she hadn't done any real harm. They couldn't just take away her rank, her projects—could they? She thought of her workshop. At least the *Merlin* would be safe, but the idea of losing everything else made her sick.

Lost in her misery, Lina jumped when Zara's hand came to rest on her shoulder. She hadn't noticed her teacher rise and walk around the table to stand beside her.

"Due respect, Councilman Tolwin," Zara said, squeezing Lina's shoulder, "but this is not a matter worthy of the council's attention. If you wish to issue a formal reprimand to me as Lina's teacher, I accept that. But I request that the council allow me to punish my apprentice in the manner *I* deem appropriate."

"Seconded," said Davort, and two of the other council members nodded. "Stripping her of her apprenticeship is too extreme, Tolwin," the elder councilman added.

"And you are too quick to forgive," Tolwin shot back. He turned to glare at Zara. "For years, we've tolerated your letting her run wild through Ortana, but it's time to put an end to it. The child needs to be assigned a new teacher, one who will supervise her properly and restrict her movements within the stronghold."

"No!" Lina felt Zara's grip tighten on her shoulder to silence her. She couldn't believe what she was hearing. True, it was better than losing her apprenticeship, but not by much.

"I agree she must have supervision," Davort said, ignoring Lina's outburst, "but with the refugees taking up more of our attention and resources, now is hardly the best time to be reassigning apprentices."

"And it is not necessary," Zara interjected firmly. "I

apologize again for Lina's intrusion, but Councilman Tolwin overestimates the seriousness of the situation."

Tolwin gave Zara a calculating look that Lina didn't like. "Do I? And would my reaction seem so extreme if she had overheard certain information that could jeopardize—"

"But she did not." This time, Councilwoman Jasanna stood up, her work apron clinking with tools. "Let this go, Tolwin, before you say something that all of us will regret."

For the first time, Lina noticed the strained looks on the faces of the other council members. They were uncomfortable, anxious, but some instinct told her that those feelings weren't caused by her. Curiosity overcame some of Lina's misery. What was going on here? What had Tolwin been about to say?

"I promise you, Lina will be adequately punished for what she did," Zara said. "Will you allow me this, friends, and call the meeting adjourned? It's been a long night, and our tempers are already short."

"Agreed," murmured Davort and several of the other council members. Then the elder councilman turned to address Lina directly, his expression grave but not unkind. "You've been given a reprieve, child. Use it wisely. If you wish to remain under Councilwoman Zara's tutelage—and I can tell by your passionate response that you do—you must learn to temper your curiosity. If you can't do that, you will be reassigned to another teacher."

"If that action does become necessary, know that *I* would be willing to take on the task," Tolwin offered, "so as not to burden the other archivists with extra duties. And I feel certain that I could correct the child's behavior."

Dread clawed at Lina's stomach. She hated the tone of smug satisfaction in Tolwin's voice. And be Tolwin's apprentice? Spend every day studying with him and Simon breathing down her neck? It was unthinkable. She might as well give up her apprenticeship at that point. She would lose all her freedom.

Davort stood up and struck the bell in the middle of the table to signal the end of the meeting. One by one, the council members stood and began filing out of the room, until only Lina and Zara were left. Tolwin was the last to storm out, slamming the double doors behind him.

"I think he's starting to like me," Lina said, smiling feebly at Zara.

"Please tell me you don't really think any of this is funny," Zara said, but she sounded more tired than angry, which surprised Lina. She'd been prepared for shouting, but instead, Zara walked to the table and sank into a chair. "I never expected you to do something like this, Lina," she said, shaking her head. "I know that you love to explore and hide—"

"I'm not hiding," Lina interrupted—and immediately regretted it when Zara glared at her. "Right, sorry, I should let you talk," she said.

"I thought the reason you did it was to avoid people," Zara said, "not to eavesdrop on a group of men and women who believe they're speaking in confidence about matters that impact our entire nation."

Lina felt her cheeks flush with shame. Shouting would have been easier to take. "I know I messed up," she said. "I'm sorry."

"So why did you do it?" Zara pressed.

"When I saw the meeting was off-limits, I thought there'd been some news about the war," Lina said. "I thought maybe you'd heard something good."

Zara shook her head, and for a moment, she seemed distracted. Her face took on a faraway expression. "Nothing like that, I'm afraid. We called the meeting because we'd gotten word from some of Ironstar's archivists who are traveling in the Merrow Kingdom—and this will be common knowledge soon, but for now, keep it to yourself—that old King Easmon has been ill. We're not sure how serious it is."

A mixture of excitement and trepidation went through Lina. She loved it when Zara confided in her, but she didn't like the look of worry in her teacher's eyes. "What does that mean for the war?" she asked.

"I don't know, but if there's going to be any hope of a peaceful end to it, the last thing we need in either

kingdom is instability," Zara said. "The Merrow Kingdom has an impressive military, but King Aron has
more money and resources. And Easmon's ambition has
him sending troops far across Solace—maybe too far.
I don't know how his illness will affect his campaign,
especially in the west. He's been very active there lately,
and though I truly don't think he'd attack us, he's still
closer to our borders than I or anyone on the council
is comfortable with. And Tolwin, no matter how much
I hate to admit it, makes some valid points about the
archivists' position. This won't be the last late-night
meeting," she added, but it seemed to Lina that she was
speaking mostly to herself.

"Maybe I can help you," Lina said. If Zara was willing to confide in her, maybe she would consider other
changes to their relationship. Like a fresh start. "If you
take up my lessons again, eventually I could share some
of your workload. You haven't been able to go any further with your translation of those stone tablet pieces
since the war started, have you?" she pointed out.

It was Zara's turn to be surprised. "How did you
know that?"

*Because I've been keeping track of you, hoping that you
would see me, have time for me.* But Lina was too embarrassed to say it. Instead, she plowed ahead: "If you gave
me your notes, I'm sure I could catch the thread of your
research and continue the translation. Or if you don't

want to do that, I could help with the refugees, bring messages back and forth quickly from the dormitories. Whatever you need." She tried not to sound overeager, but she couldn't help it. This was a chance to make Zara proud of her and maybe erase some of that disappointment from her eyes.

Zara stood up and came to stand in front of her. Her dark curly hair was shot through with thick gray streaks, more than Lina remembered her having a year ago. The creases around her brown eyes were deeper too. Zara rested her slender hand on Lina's shoulder again.

"I believe that you could help, Lina," her teacher said, smiling sadly, "but with the war and the refugees swelling our population, the council is stretched too thin just trying to keep order. I'm sorry, but I don't have the time to spare to start teaching you again. You'll have to keep studying independently and attending all your regular classes. Once the war ends, things will be different."

The hope that had begun to build inside Lina vanished, replaced by a hollow ache. And a flash of anger. She knew it was wrong—Zara had just stood up for her in front of the council—but she couldn't hold it in. "Fine," she said curtly, "but don't keep blaming the war."

Zara blinked in surprise, but then her eyes narrowed. "Excuse me?"

"My lessons stopped before the war started," Lina said. "There's always something that drags you away."

Zara threw up her hands, at last losing patience. "We've had this discussion many times. You know that my work with the council must come first. I found you three different teachers, men and women who were willing to be involved with you on a day-to-day basis. Keep you from pulling stunts like this one," she added sternly, gesturing at the hole in the ventilation shaft.

Lina shook her head stubbornly. "No."

"Exactly," Zara said, her voice rising. She was inching closer to shouting. "You refused to accept any of them, until they all gave up and sent you back to me. I've tried to be patient, but believe me, my girl, that patience is quickly running out. And now you've got the council involved!" She sighed and shook her head. "Perhaps they're right. Maybe it's time for a new, permanent teacher, whether you want one or not."

"So you'll break your promise, is that it?" Lina clenched her fists at her sides. "Toss me off to Tolwin or whoever else you can find? Mom and Dad wanted you," she insisted, clearing her throat to hide the tremor in her voice. "They wanted *you* to teach me—no one else. You made a promise, and you're breaking it!"

"Lina . . ." Zara sighed again, and suddenly she looked exhausted. "That was a long time ago."

"No, it wasn't," Lina whispered. She tried to swallow the lump that had risen in her throat. It might as well have been yesterday, it still hurt so much. But talking about it never got them anywhere; it just made things worse. "Can I go now, Zara?" She cast a longing glance at the door. "I'm sorry about ruining the meeting. You can tell me my punishment in the morning."

For a second, it looked as if Zara was going to argue. Lina braced herself, but then her teacher simply said, "Fine, you can go. We'll talk tomorrow, but there will be a hefty punishment for this, Lina, I assure you. Sleeping on it won't change anything."

Lina didn't like the sound of that. "How hefty?" she asked.

Zara was unsympathetic. "Let's just say you won't have time for any of your own projects for the next several weeks. You'll have work every day, all day, and I expect to know where you are at all times. You'll also show up promptly for every meal in the dining hall and be in bed an hour after the evening one."

Lina's shoulders slumped, but she knew there was no getting out of this. So much for stealing away to her workshop to try to knock those boulders loose. Tonight would be her last night of freedom for a long while.

"Come to my office early tomorrow," Zara continued, "and go to the medical wing tonight before you go to bed and get those scrapes on your shoulders tended to. I can see that they hurt."

Lina nodded, not trusting herself to speak. She was tired, aching, and angry. Casting one last look above her at the sizeable hole she'd made in the ventilation shaft, she turned and crossed the meeting room to the double doors.

Thankfully, Simon was nowhere in sight when she exited the building. He and Tolwin were probably sitting in Tolwin's office plotting more ways they could strip her of her apprenticeship. Lina winced at the thought. In that terrifying moment back in the council room, she'd really thought she was going to lose everything.

The truth was, Tolwin and Simon could despise her all they wanted. Zara's dismissal was what was harder to take, but Lina forced that sting aside too.

What were you thinking anyway, offering to help her? Lina chided herself. She didn't have time to work on Zara's projects. She had the *Merlin,* and no one could take that away from her.

Only tonight would be the last night she could visit it for several weeks. Surely, she had time to sneak down to the workshop just one more time before she went to bed. She'd be exhausted tomorrow, but it was a small price to pay for a few more minutes with the beautiful airship.

As she stood on the steps outside the council building, Lina was surprised to find the large cavern dark and deserted. The people who'd been milling around earlier were all gone. Then she remembered that it must be after midnight by now. She'd lost track of time while she'd been crouching in that ventilation shaft—and her stomach reminded her with a sharp pain that she'd also skipped dinner.

Most of the lumatite clusters arranged along the walls had been removed for the night, and the few that remained cast long, ominous shadows in the cavern. Lina had her own wristband of light to guide her, and she'd never been particularly afraid of the dark, but it was still unsettling to be so suddenly and surprisingly alone. She had started to walk down the steps when she heard voices echoing from within the council building behind her.

That was odd. Hadn't she and Zara been the only ones left in the room? Zara had stayed behind after dismissing Lina, but someone must have come in through the rear entrance after Lina left. Lina stopped, listening out of habit, even though the last thing she needed was to be caught eavesdropping again. The voices were muffled by the doors, but Lina thought she recognized Zara as one of the speakers. First, a secret meeting, and now Zara was talking to someone who had slipped in the back door to the building in the wee hours of the night. What was going on here?

Then Lina heard the soft click of the door handles turning. She was going to be caught again! When it came to sneaking, she was having no luck at all tonight.

Down the steps from the council building, the cavern's sculpture garden was only a few yards away. Lina sprinted for the closest statue: an elaborate carving of the extinct servoya tree. She ducked behind its thick stone trunk and tried to get her breathing under control so no one would hear her. Then the double doors to the council building creaked open, and a voice echoed in the quiet cavern.

"When did this happen? Is Nirean searching for him?" a woman's voice asked.

Lina perked up. She'd been right. That was Zara, but who was she meeting?

"She's looking in the refugee areas right now," said a second voice—one of the councilmen, though Lina couldn't remember his name. "The search would go faster if we asked more of the chamelins to assist."

"No," Zara said firmly. "It's too great a risk."

There was a beat or two of silence before the other councilman replied. "I'm sure I don't have to remind you that the chamelins would give their lives to protect this community. They have proven themselves worthy of trust time and again."

Now Lina knew who the man was. His name was Lantric, and he was a chamelin archivist—one of three who sat on the council. His clipped tone suggested that Zara's words had offended him. What was going on here?

"Lantric, please let me apologize. I know how important you are to Ortana," Zara said. "But there's a great deal at stake here, and the need for secrecy is as much for your protection. We want as few people involved as possible."

"Nirean will find him," Lantric said, his voice softening. "He's unfamiliar with the layout of the stronghold. There are only so many places he can hide."

"I hope you're right," Zara said, but she didn't sound convinced.

Their voices moved away across the cavern. After a moment, Lina could no longer make out what they were saying. When it was silent again, she stepped out from behind the statue.

They must have been talking about one of the refugees, someone who'd wandered off into an area where he wasn't supposed to be. It happened often enough. With so many refugees roaming around the dormitories, they were bound to get restless, curious about their temporary home. And Ortana was certainly unique, as homes went.

But if that was the case, why all the secrecy surrounding the search? Why didn't Zara want to get the other chamelins involved? Something didn't feel right.

Lina was torn. Part of her wanted to slip back down to her workshop to visit the *Merlin* one more time, and then get herself off to bed before she got into any more trouble. But another tantalizing voice whispered that she could take the secret passage along the refugee corridor and maybe find Nirean or this mysterious person she was looking for. It was a newer ventilation shaft, so she wouldn't have to worry about someone hearing her moving around in a creaky old tube, or wonder whether it was about to collapse under her. She could find out what was going on, and no one would even know she was there.

Yes, and remember the last time you planned something like this? she scolded herself. *It was only hours ago, and it almost cost you your apprenticeship.* No, whatever was happening here, it was the council's business, not hers.

But she was part of this community too, and the council's decisions affected everyone. What if this was important?

Lina sighed. *All right, a quick detour, long enough to find out what's going on, and then back to the original plan.*

Her decision made, Lina was about to make a move when she caught movement out of the corner of her eye. A second later, a shadow emerged from an alcove on the east side of the cavern. Her heart leapt into her throat. Instinctively, she crouched down behind the stone tree, hoping that whoever it was hadn't seen her. Then, very slowly, she peeked around the statue.

The shadowy figure moved fast across the cavern toward her. It *had* seen her! Lina clutched the sculpture. Heart pounding, she cast around for a better hiding place in the garden, but she couldn't move anywhere now without being tracked. The figure was too close.

She was about to make a break for it in the opposite direction when she realized the shadow wasn't coming toward her any longer. It had slowed and was now moving in a zigzag pattern across the hall, as if whoever it was didn't know exactly where he was going or maybe couldn't see very well in the dimness.

Or both. Was this the refugee Zara and Lantric had been talking about?

As the shadow approached, Lina realized the figure was much shorter than he'd seemed from across the room. He stepped into a pool of lumatite glow, and Lina got her first glimpse of his face.

Her breath caught in surprise. He was just a boy, no older than she was. Dressed in tattered, dirt-stained clothes, he had thick bandages wrapped around his head, covering part of his cheek and nose. One end of the bandage had come loose and fluttered behind his right shoulder. Lina's heart clenched at the sight of the injuries, and she made a decision. She stood up and stepped out from behind the statue. She hadn't wanted anyone discovering her here, but she also didn't want the boy falling in the dark and hurting himself further.

She stepped forward, intending to touch his shoulder to stop him as he ran past her, but suddenly, the boy made a sharp turn and dashed forward. His eyes widened an instant before he plowed straight into her.

The air rushed out of Lina's chest when the boy hit

her. She thought she was going to go flying through the air, but then instinct took over, and she grabbed at the boy, searching for something to stop her fall. She wasn't picky: shirt, hair, arms, neck, whatever was handy. She ended up latching onto the boy's shoulders, and they fell together. Lina's butt hit the ground first—this had to be some kind of record for most scrapes and bruises in a single night—and then she fell on her back with the boy sprawled on top of her so that they formed a human X.

Gasping, Lina fought to return air to her lungs. To be fair, she'd done her best to stay out of trouble this time. She'd been trying to help, yet here she was, lying on the ground again with scraped shoulders *and* a sore backside. She hoped the boy had fared better.

Uh-oh. Lina tamped down the beginnings of panic. *He's not moving.* The boy was lying on his stomach across her legs, his face turned away from her. *Please tell me I didn't knock him out,* she hoped. *Or worse.*

"Um . . . hello?" Lina said, nudging him gently with her knee. "Are you all right there?"

"Mmphus," the boy replied, which he followed by a prolonged groan.

That didn't sound good. Lina's worry intensified. What was she going to do now? "Please say something," she implored the boy. "I, er, didn't mean to knock you out."

"I'm . . . fine . . . I think," the boy said, his speech becoming somewhat clearer, even though his face was still pressed against the floor. "Wow, you . . . I mean, you came out of nowhere. One minute, I was running . . . I was running, and then . . . there was this wall right in front of me. You. Wall. I was *not* expecting that." He was still a little disoriented. Then, to Lina's relief, he rolled off her and onto his side so they were face to face. "Oh, hello," he said, smiling weakly.

"Hello." Relieved that he seemed to be all right, Lina mirrored his smile and raised her hand in greeting. "I'm Lina—or, you know, the wall."

"I'm . . . uh . . . Fredrick," the boy replied. His grin widened. "Or, you know, the crazy person running through the dark."

Together they sat up. Lina rubbed her lower back and wondered how many black-and-blue spots she would have there tomorrow morning. Crawling through the ventilation shafts was going to be a chore for the next few days.

"I didn't hurt you, did I?" Fredrick asked, watching her. The darkness and the bandages made it difficult to read his expression, but she could hear the concern in his voice.

"I'm fine," Lina assured him. "I was more worried about you."

"Me?" The boy looked confused.

Lina pointed to his bandages. "You're already hurt,"

she said. She hoped whatever injuries lay beneath the bandages weren't too serious.

"Oh, these." The boy reached up and touched the bandages. His lip curled in disgust. "Don't worry about them. I'm all right."

But Lina could tell by his reaction that she'd hit on a sore subject. "Hey, listen," she said, eager to make amends, "are you hungry? Because I'm starving. We could make a raid on the kitchens for a late snack, and then I could take you back to your room—"

"Thanks," the boy interrupted, getting to his feet, "but I'm not hungry." He started to limp away from her.

Lina's mouth fell open. "Where are you going?" she demanded, automatically raising a hand to stop him, even though he was already too far away from her. "You're limping. You might really be hurt!"

"I'm fine!" the boy assured her, moving faster. "I have to get going—got, umm, important things to do!"

"Important things? But it's the middle of the night! And you're going the wrong way," Lina added. "The refugee dormitories are that way." She pointed, but the boy didn't look back.

Then, from across the chamber, there came a babble of voices moving fast toward them from one of the adjacent corridors. Once again, Lina crouched behind her statue just as light spilled into the room. It came from a lantern held by Zara. Nirean followed close at her heels.

The chamelin spread her wings and leaped into the air, soaring across the cavern in pursuit of the boy.

So they were after Fredrick? But why all this fuss over a refugee boy? Lina pressed herself against the stone tree trunk, but Nirean's attention was on Fredrick. She never saw Lina. The chamelin caught up with him just as he was about to enter the hallway to the museum. She glided over his head and banked, folding her wings so she could drop into a crouch in front of him, effectively blocking his escape.

Fredrick let out a choked yelp and skidded to a stop before he ran into the chamelin's chest. Good thing too—it would have been a much harder impact than running into Lina. When they were shape-shifted, the chamelins' bodies were hard as granite.

The boy's shoulders drooped as he realized he was caught. Nirean shifted back to her human form and crossed her arms as she stared down at him, disapproval etched on her aging features.

Shooting a quick glance across the room, Lina noticed that Zara had remained in the far corridor with the lantern. She appeared to be watching the other entrances into the chamber. Lina wondered what—or whom—she was looking for, but then Nirean's voice distracted her.

"You should go back to your room, Fredrick," Nirean said, her deep voice carrying across the chamber. "You can get lost wandering around by yourself at night."

"You know, that is an *excellent* point," Fredrick said brightly, as if it had never occurred to him before. "It's a good thing you found me when you did. I might have ended up running into a wall in the dark."

Lina covered her mouth to keep from chuckling. She recognized what the boy was trying to do, but unfortunately for him, all the charm in Solace wasn't going to work on Nirean. Lina knew because she'd already tried that tactic at least a dozen times.

"What I really wanted was a breath of fresh air," Fredrick continued. "I don't suppose I could step out for a few minutes, run around in the snow, maybe get a look at the stars?" By his tone, Lina could tell that the boy already knew what the answer to his request would be.

"You know I can't let you do that. Now come with me," Nirean said, laying a hand on his shoulder. "We can discuss this when you're back in your chamber."

The boy's sigh was loud. "Sure, why not," he said, and Lina thought he was working hard now to sound cheerful. "Back to my room—that's much more exciting anyway."

They moved across the chamber, and Lina couldn't help noticing that the boy subtly steered Nirean's path away from her hiding place. Fredrick may have been caught, but he wasn't going to give her up. Lina smiled to herself in the dark.

After they'd disappeared down the corridor from

which Zara and Nirean had come, Lina stood up, stretching her cramped legs. Her gaze fell on an object lying on the ground near the statue. She knelt down and picked up what looked like a wad of cloth. Turning it over in her hands, she realized it was a large bandage. It had to be Fredrick's. It must have come off his cheek when they collided and fell. But if it was Fredrick's bandage, why was it perfectly clean? There was no blood, or even medicine for his wound.

Lina clenched the bandage in her hand as the memory came back to her, of that moment when the two of them had been lying on the floor facing each other. She'd looked right at the boy, and even though it had been dark and hard to see his features clearly, she remembered now that there hadn't been a wound on his face. Did that mean there was nothing under the other bandages as well?

But if not a wound, what were those bandages covering?

⇒ FOUR ⇐

Lina crawled through the ventilation shaft as fast as she dared, hoping to catch up to Zara, Nirean, and Fredrick before they turned down one of the side corridors and she lost them. She'd mapped all the man-made ventilation shafts that paralleled the largest corridors in the east wing of the stronghold long ago and knew them by heart, but once she reached an intersection, she had to listen for voices to tell her where to go next. There were only so many grates along the ceiling where she could get a look down into the corridor to see if she was on the right track. And she couldn't move too fast, or Zara and Nirean would hear her. She needed to avoid that at all costs.

Maybe it was the mysterious boy and the bandages hiding his face, or the fact that Zara and Nirean didn't seem to want anyone to know what they were up to, but Lina had a sinking feeling that if her teacher caught her snooping around again, she might be in very real danger of losing her apprenticeship. Only Zara would be the one tossing her out this time. The thought weighed heavily on her, and for the tenth time since she'd crawled into the ventilation shaft to follow Fredrick and the others, Lina told herself she was being monumentally stupid. Yet she kept going anyway.

Something was happening here, and Lina wanted to know what it was. She knew it had nothing to do with helping a lost refugee who snuck out of his bed in the middle of the night. Zara and Nirean were trying to hide the boy. Lina could tell from the corridors they traveled through that they were keeping him in a separate area from the rest of the refugees, and they'd gone so far as to wrap fake bandages around his head. Lina couldn't begin to imagine why.

Did it have anything to do with the council's closed session? Was that why the council members had looked so anxious when she'd crashed into their midst, why Tolwin had been so furious? Had they been afraid Lina would overhear an important secret, something to do with the boy?

Voices echoing from below and ahead of her made Lina pause. If she pressed her ear to the floor of the shaft, she could just make them out.

"I'll let you take it from here, Nirean," said Zara's voice. "We'll talk in the morning, Fredrick."

Lina bit her lip in sympathy for the boy. She

recognized Zara's tone. It looked like Lina wasn't the only one who would be getting a lecture and a punishment in the morning. Then she heard footsteps moving in opposite directions down the corridor.

No! Up ahead was an intersection. She had to choose to go right or left. She wanted to follow Nirean and the boy, but what if she accidentally trailed Zara instead? The footsteps were moving away. She only had a second to decide. Then the footsteps moving left stopped, and she heard Fredrick's voice coming from the same direction.

"Councilwoman Zara," he called after her, and the footsteps moving to the right stopped. Lina went very still, listening. She thought that surely the three of them could hear her heart beating a frantic rhythm in her chest.

"Yes?" Zara replied.

"You would tell me if anything . . ." The boy's voice trailed off, and Lina wondered what he was thinking. He was much more subdued than he had been earlier. "You'll let me know if you hear anything—any news?"

No, Lina realized. He sounds sad. Sad and lonely.

"I promise I'll tell you," Zara said, her voice softening. "Try not to worry. Good night, Fredrick." Her footsteps moved away again down the corridor to the right.

Lina waited for Nirean and Fredrick to resume their

walk before following. After a few more twists and turns, their footsteps stopped, and Lina caught the sound of a door opening and closing.

Now came the tricky part. Surveying the intersection before her, Lina had to guess which of the smaller ventilation shafts led to Fredrick's room. And she had to see if she could fit down the shaft. The archivists' quarters were notoriously stuffy because the ventilation shafts were so narrow that they never cleaned the air properly or circulated it enough.

In the end, Lina chose a shaft that angled downward slightly, and she wiggled through it. She was pleased that her hips fit in the narrow space, though every now and then she rubbed her injured shoulders against the sides of the shaft and had to bite back a hiss of pain.

She crawled up to one of the metal grates and peeked through, hoping to get a good view into Fredrick's quarters. The room was slightly larger than the typical archivists' quarters, certainly bigger than Lina's modest room. She could make out a bed pushed against the far wall, with a wooden nightstand next to it stacked with books. A candle burned beside the bed; Lina smelled the beeswax as the smoke drifted up to tickle her nostrils. She clamped a hand over her nose. She'd come too far to let a sneeze give her away.

Fredrick stepped into view then and sat on his bed. He perched on the edge with his hands resting on his knees, shoulders slumped. Lina didn't see Nirean, but she heard the chamelin's deep voice soon enough.

"You can't ever do that again, Fredrick. Do you understand?" she asked. "That was incredibly reckless. What if you had been seen?"

There was a long pause before the boy spoke, but when he did, he'd once again adopted a cheerful tone. "You're right, of course," he said. "I was just feeling a little cooped up, and I wanted to get away by myself for a while. Nobody saw me," he assured Nirean.

"By sheer luck. Half your bandages are gone. What happened to them?"

"I tripped and fell," Fredrick said. "I'll put new ones on tomorrow."

Nirean moved into view beneath the grate, then moved away. She was pacing, agitated. "You can't leave this room, not until I do a search of the area. We have to be sure no one saw you. After that, you can go to Zara's office or my quarters if you need something, but you *have* to stay out of the common areas."

"For how long?" The cheerfulness in the boy's voice was gone.

"I don't know," Nirean said. "But we have to—"

Suddenly, the boy jumped to his feet as if he'd been stung. "You can't keep me in here forever!" he burst out.

"Lower your voice," Nirean commanded.

"You can't speak to me that way!" Anger made the boy's voice unsteady. "I'm a prince of the Merrow Kingdom. True, I might be the least important prince that ever lived, but I'm still part of the royal family, and you can't keep me locked away like this!"

Up in the shaft, Lina had to cover her mouth to keep from releasing a shocked squeal. She dug her fingernails into her cheeks, clasping her face tight as she let Fredrick's words sink in.

Oh boy. Oh boy, ohhhh boy. This was big. Huge. A prince of the Merrow Kingdom? Here, in Ortana? No, it had to be a terrible mistake. The archivists didn't take sides in the war. They would never hide a prince of the Merrow Kingdom here. Doing that would be as good as declaring they'd sided with King Easmon.

With an ominous feeling in her gut, Lina wondered just what she'd stumbled into this time.

"You can't ever do that again, Fredrick. Do you understand?"

For a second, Ozben didn't respond. He thought Nirean was addressing someone else. Fredrick. Who had come up with that name, anyway? As fake names went, it was uninspired. If his family was going to force him to conceal his identity, they could have at least let him pick his own name, something grand like Titan or Nicodemus. But that would defeat the whole point of blending in. Not that he'd been doing a great job of it so far.

Pretending to be a refugee with his head wrapped up

in fake bandages. Ozben shook his head in disgust. It was an insult to the refugees who really had been hurt, and the soldiers, like his sister, who were out there in the field right now fighting for their kingdom.

Ozben realized then that silence had fallen in the room. He'd barely been listening to what Nirean, his bodyguard, had been saying. Guilt tugged at him. He hoped the chamelin wouldn't get in trouble with Zara for letting him slip away from her. "You're right, of course," he said. "I was just feeling a little cooped up, and I wanted to get away by myself for a while. Nobody saw me," he assured her.

Except for that mysterious girl, he didn't add out loud—the one who'd left a girl-sized dent in his chest when they'd collided in the Heart of the Mountain. What had she been doing there so late at night? He hoped he hadn't hurt her when he'd knocked her down.

"Half your bandages are gone," Nirean was saying. Ozben heard the worry and annoyance in her voice. "What happened to them?"

Ozben reached up and touched his bare cheek. He hadn't even realized the bandages had been ripped off. "I tripped and fell." That was true enough. "I'll put new ones on tomorrow."

Tomorrow. Of course, he'd have to rethink his plans now. First, he would apologize to Zara, and he'd have to be on his best behavior for a while as he planned his next escape attempt. But it would have to be a good one. When he ran off earlier that night, he'd claimed he just wanted to be alone, and that excuse would only work once before his hosts caught on to his true intention.

Zara was already suspicious of him, Ozben thought ruefully. They'd be watching him closely for the next several days. The best thing he could do was lie low, explore the stronghold, and look for a better way out than the museum entrance. It was too far from his quarters, and he got turned around easily in the dark.

"You can't leave this room," Nirean said then, snapping Ozben's attention back to the chamelin. His stomach plummeted. "Not until I make a search of the area. We have to be sure no one saw you. After that, you can go to Zara's office or my quarters if you need something, but you have to stay out of the common areas."

"For how long?" he asked. She had to be joking. Stay here, trapped in this tiny, freezing room, buried in tons of rock, while thousands of miles away his parents and sister fought a war without him? No, they couldn't do that. Waves of helpless anger bubbled up inside him.

"I don't know," Nirean said. "But we have to—"

Ozben couldn't listen anymore. He jumped up from the bed. "You can't keep me in here forever!" he shouted. He was shaking, all the emotions he'd been trying to suppress these past few days pouring out in a mess.

"Lower your voice," Nirean told him sternly.

"You can't speak to me that way!" Ozben tried his best to sound imperious and commanding like his grandfather, but his voice trembled. "I'm a prince of the Merrow Kingdom. True, I might be the least important prince that ever lived, but I'm still part of the royal family, and you can't keep me locked away like this!"

He'd expected Nirean to shout back at him, as his grandfather might have, so Ozben was surprised when a flicker of fear passed over the chamelin's face. Seeing it, Ozben immediately regretted losing his temper. Nirean was just trying to protect him.

"I'm sorry," he began. "I didn't mean to—"

But Nirean raised a hand. "Be quiet," she snapped. Her fear was gone, replaced by wariness. She glanced around the room, head cocked as if listening. "Did you hear something?"

Confused, Ozben looked around. "I didn't hear anything. What's wrong?"

Nirean didn't reply. After another minute, she said, "I think it's all right." Then she glared at him. "Are you trying to get yourself killed?" she asked tersely.

"Of course not!"

"Do you know," Nirean continued, speaking slowly, as if she were trying to contain her temper, "how many people have risked their lives to keep you safe these past few days? All our careful planning, the lengths we went to in order to get you here, keep you hidden, and protect your identity? Tonight, you threw all that away on a reckless whim, and now you're shouting your secret to the world."

"There's no one here," Ozben said, circling the tiny room and gesturing to the four empty corners. "No assassins are going to follow me here."

"Your mother and father thought the same thing about the palace in Ardra. They were protected by a dozen of the best-trained guards in Solace," Nirean said quietly. "Four of those guards are dead now."

"I know. I was there when they died." Ozben hated to think of that day, when his world had been turned upside down. His anger drained away, and worry filled his gut. "You're right," he murmured. "I shouldn't have exposed myself like that. I'm sorry."

"I know you feel like a prisoner here, Fredr—" Nirean stopped. Ozben gave her a small smile, grateful that she hadn't finished the name. "If you want to help your parents, the best thing you can do is to stay hidden and stay safe. This war can't go on forever," she said.

Tell that to my grandfather, Ozben thought. He wished he could share Nirean's hope. "You should go to bed," he said. He tried to make his voice light. "I promise to be less of a pain in the neck tomorrow."

"I'd appreciate that," Nirean said dryly. She moved to the door and paused, casting one last glance around the room. "I'll check the area to make sure everything's quiet. Remember, my quarters are just down the hall, and I'm going to put a guard at the end of the opposite hall. Call on either of us if there's trouble."

Ozben watched the door close behind Nirean, then sat on the edge of his bed and stared at the floor. Guilt and frustration churned inside him. He knew Nirean was right. His family owed the archivists an incredible debt for the risks they'd taken on his behalf. But he hadn't asked for any of it, and he'd certainly never wanted to put anyone in danger. His father and mother hadn't given him a choice. He missed them and his sister so much, but at the same time, Ozben was furious with all of them. He picked up his pillow and clenched it in his hands. Being locked away like this was making him go crazy. He sat day after day with nothing to do but stare at the walls, imagining the worst happening back home.

"Careful, you're going to rip that pillow in half."

Ozben didn't know quite how it happened, but when the disembodied voice suddenly filled the quiet room, he found himself on his feet, halfway to the door, the hairs on the back of his neck all standing on end. His heart pounded hard against his ribs, and he whipped around, looking for the source of the ghost voice.

Then he happened to look *up*.

The girl he'd clobbered in the Heart of the Mountain was hanging upside down out of a ventilation grate in the ceiling. Her short, curly brown hair flopped around her head in a wild halo, and her dirt-smudged face was already turning red as the blood rushed into it. She looked at him with one eyebrow cocked curiously.

"Sorry, didn't mean to scare you," she said.

Ozben raised a shaky hand, waving it off. "Oh, don't worry, you didn't scare me."

Her eyebrow arched a bit more. "You looked pretty scared."

"That's just my face," he assured her.

"You're kinda pale," she observed.

"Again, just my face."

"You let out this weird yowling noise when you jumped off the bed. Sounded like a carnelian cat."

"I don't know what that is, so I'll have to take your word for it." He looked up at her, smiling sheepishly. "Okay, you did scare me a little bit, but let's be honest, I wasn't expecting anyone to pop out of the ceiling like that. You turn up in the oddest places."

And then a cold hand of dread clamped on Ozben's heart, and he swallowed hard. The oddest places. She'd been in the ventilation shaft. Directly above him.

Listening.

"How long . . . have you . . . been up there?" he asked, hoping, impossibly, that she would say, *Oh, I was just passing through, didn't hear a thing, not a thing, well, goodbye now*, and everything would be all right.

The girl bit her lip, and her eyes shifted away from his face. Ozben was all too familiar with that kind of guilty look. His heart sank.

"Well . . . I guess I'd curtsy if I wasn't hanging upside down," the girl said. "Um, Your Highness."

Hearing the title, Ozben broke out into a cold sweat. This was bad. Very bad. How could he have been so stupid, shouting out his identity like that? Nirean was right. He was reckless. Now he had to deal with it and make sure the girl didn't tell anyone else.

He put his shoulders back, trying to look serious and confident, and crossed the room to stand underneath her. "All right, so, you already know who I am," he said. "What's your name?"

The girl's guilty expression melted into a tentative smile. "I'm Lina," she said. "Lina Adelia Winterbock." She reached her hand down to him, and the whole situation seemed suddenly so ridiculous that, despite his worry, Ozben couldn't help matching her smile. He reached up and shook her hand.

"Well, Lina Adelia Winterbock, why don't you let me help you down from there?" he said. "I think we have a lot to talk about."

⇒ FIVE ⇐

"This tastes amazing," Lina said, taking another sip of the kelpra juice. She had to drink it slowly, but once she'd gotten used to the face-puckering tartness, she'd discovered that the thick, pulpy liquid was rich with flavors that reminded her of cherries and grapes mixed together.

Ozben swirled the red liquid in his own glass and looked at her in surprise. "You don't have kelpra juice here?"

They sat on the floor of Ozben's room, the glasses of juice between them. At first, Lina had been worried that Ozben would be furious with her for discovering his identity, but he hadn't looked angry, nor did he shout at her. That was a good sign. Lina was even more shocked when he invited her into his room and offered her juice. That wasn't the sort of behavior she would have expected from a prince of the Merrow Kingdom. She'd never met one, of course, but she pictured princes and princesses as being haughty and cold. Ozben wasn't like that at all.

He did seem preoccupied, though. His eyes kept darting warily from her face to the door and back again. Lina wondered what he was thinking.

She shook her head in answer to his question. "It's too expensive to get enough juice for everyone in the stronghold. Did you bring yours with you?" she asked curiously.

"My mother sent it," Ozben said. "Back home, whenever I was upset or got in a fight with Elinore—my sister—she'd pour me a glass to make me feel better. I keep it in the ice chest so I can make it last."

"You miss your family a lot, don't you?" Lina asked.

"I'm all right. Listen, Lina," he said, frowning, "you can't tell anyone about my being here. It's important. I know I should never have said who I was, but I didn't know anyone was listening. I should have been more careful."

"I'm not going to tell anyone," Lina assured him. Was that what had made him so preoccupied? That she would tell other people he was here? Lina bit her lip. Ozben had no idea that if she told anyone she'd discovered him by listening in the ventilation shafts, then she'd be in as much trouble as he was. She kept that part to herself.

"Why are the archivists protecting you?" she pressed. "I thought we were supposed to be neutral in the war."

"You still are," Ozben said. He swallowed the last of his juice and laid his glass aside. "I don't know all the details, but my mother and father made some kind of deal with your ruling council. You protect me until the war is over, send me home, and the Merrow Kingdom will never tell anyone that I was here."

And in exchange, the archivists would still be allowed to ship in objects from the meteor fields, even with the war going on. Lina put the details together from what she'd overheard in the council meeting. But if something went wrong and King Aron found out that the archivists were hiding a prince of the Merrow Kingdom—even if it was just for his own protection—they might decide to declare war on the archivists too. *Why would they take such a huge risk?* Lina wondered. Dozens of questions burned inside her, but she didn't want to make Ozben more nervous.

There was one thing she was desperately curious about, though. "Were you really attacked by assassins?" she asked. "That's why your family sent you away?"

Ozben's expression darkened. "Yes. Someone from the Dragonfly territories hired them—maybe King Aron himself, for all we know. There were two of them—they took my family by surprise one night while we were sleeping. I never saw them—the guards killed one before they could get to our rooms, and the other escaped. But I heard they were dressed all in black, with their faces covered, except for their eyes." He toyed with his glass, then plunked it down hard on the floor, making Lina jump. "I told my parents I wasn't afraid, but they wouldn't listen to anything I said. They're convinced that the other assassin will come back and try again. Grandfather was the only one who stood up for me, said I was old enough to make my own decision."

At the mention of his grandfather, Lina again felt a jolt of apprehension. Ozben had assassins after him. Ozben was important. He was *royalty*. Lina crawled around in cave tunnels and regularly got mouse nests stuck in her hair. Should an apprentice like her even be talking to him like this? Yet it felt so natural, and for the most part, Ozben seemed like an ordinary boy. Because he was so normal, it had made Lina forget that his grandfather was King Easmon, the one who'd provoked the Iron War to begin with.

When the war began, Lina told herself that since the archivists hadn't picked a side, she wouldn't either. And in many ways, she blamed *both* kingdoms for the conflict that had caused so many innocent people to lose their lives and brought suffering to all of Solace. The Merrow Kingdom's aggression and stockpiling of weapons had made the people of the Dragonfly territories afraid it was going to launch an invasion, and Lina didn't blame them.

Nobody should have to live with the constant threat of an attack looming. But King Aron's response to the threat—cut off trade and hoard all the iron for his own kingdom—had just made the situation worse.

Both sides were to blame, but Lina couldn't get over the fact that the Merrow Kingdom had *started* the fight. They'd thrown the first punch, so to speak, launched the first attack against the Dragonfly territories. Maybe if they hadn't, the two kingdoms could have eventually solved their problems peacefully. But King Easmon had been too greedy and heartless. He'd wanted to conquer Dragonfly, to take its land and iron by force. Lina had just assumed that the rest of his family would be equally cruel.

Yet Ozben was polite and kind, at least to her. True, she'd only just met him, but somehow she sensed he didn't have a cruel heart. The difference threw Lina into confusion. How could a man like King Easmon have a grandson like Ozben?

"So, if you don't mind my asking," Ozben said, interrupting her thoughts, "why were you spying on me up there?" He pointed to the ceiling.

Lina blushed furiously. "Spying" was such a harsh word. "I found your bandages," she said. "I realized you were trying to disguise yourself, and I wanted to know why. It was curiosity."

He raised an eyebrow. "Most people I know wouldn't

be curious enough to crawl around in a dirty ventilation shaft. Speaking of which, you have a smudge on your cheek," he said, pointing to the left side of her face.

"Oh, but I do that all the time." Lina licked her palm and scrubbed at the dirt on her face. "Can't say I've used the shafts in this part of the stronghold much, but once you've seen one ventilation duct, you've pretty much seen them all."

"Um, okay." Ozben smiled wryly. He shifted on the floor and stretched out his legs. "So you're an apprentice?"

Lina swallowed the last of her juice before replying. "That's right." She fiddled with her glass, striking her fingernail against the rim to listen to the ringing sound. "You know, it's not that bad here," she said.

"What do you mean?" Ozben asked.

"Earlier, Nirean said you felt like a prisoner, but you shouldn't," Lina said. "This is a good place."

"I'm sure it's great," Ozben said. He shivered then and rubbed his hands up and down his arms. "Maybe a little cold. Really cold. Look, I don't mean to be rude, but what has it got that the Merrow Kingdom's capital doesn't? Besides being its own ice chest?"

"What does it—" Lina couldn't believe what she was hearing. "Do you know what the archivists do here?"

Ozben shrugged. "They study the junk that comes down in the meteor storms."

"Junk?" Lina repeated, incredulous. Oh, she wasn't about to let that pass. "You think we collect a bunch of junk and pick through it for fun? Three strongholds, thousands of people working together, and you think we just play with meteorite rubble all day long?" If that was what he thought of the archivists, no wonder he felt cooped up here.

"I didn't mean it in a bad way," Ozben said, raising his hands in defense. "It's just, isn't that stuff all broken and smashed when you find it?"

"Some of it is," Lina said. Thinking of the *Merlin*, she flashed him an enigmatic smile. "But not all of it."

And then an idea began to take shape in her mind, an idea that made the hairs on the back of her neck prickle with excitement and trepidation.

Lina studied Ozben. He was small, just as she was—maybe an inch taller but easily as skinny. His shoulders were slightly broader—he might have a rough time of it at the beginning of the passage, though she thought he would fit. But once she got him to her workshop, would he be strong enough to help her move the boulders? It would be tricky, but with two pairs of hands instead of one, they could use certain tools Lina hadn't been able to try before. Yes, they might just be able to pull it off.

I'll offer him a trade, Lina decided, her heart thumping excitedly in her chest. A secret for a secret.

She stood, dusted off the seat of her pants, and

motioned for Ozben to get up too. "Come on," she said. "I want to show you something."

For an instant, Ozben's eyes brightened, but then he frowned and shook his head. "I can't," he said. "Someone might recognize me, and I can't let Nirean catch me outside my room again tonight. If she does, she really will lock me up."

"That's why we're going to use my way of getting around," Lina said, pointing to the ventilation shaft. "And anyway, it's the middle of the night. Where I'm taking you, there won't be any people."

"That's what I thought, too, but then you turned up." Ozben hesitated. "Why do you want to show me around anyway? Shouldn't you be busy—I don't know—being an apprentice?"

"This is part of what the archivists do," Lina said, smiling at him. "We share the things we've discovered." Though in her case, that wasn't strictly true. Ozben would be the first person with whom she'd ever shared her secret. "Trust me, there are things in this mountain that will make your jaw bounce off the floor."

Ozben's brows lifted. She'd made him curious. "All right," he said finally. He stood up and went over to the bedside table, where there was a roll of fresh bandages. Lina thought he intended to repair his disguise, but instead he turned to her and motioned to the bed. "First you need to let me clean and wrap those scrapes on your shoulders," he said. "They look awful."

In all the excitement, Lina had completely forgotten about the injuries, though now that Ozben mentioned them, she realized the stinging had gotten worse. Much worse. Lina twisted her arm to get a look at the scrapes and saw that Ozben was right. If they weren't cleaned and bandaged soon, she risked an infection.

"I have some medicine you can put on the bandages," she said, fishing in her pocket. She pulled out a tube of ointment and handed it to Ozben before walking over to sit on the edge of the bed. "I can show you how to put the bandages on," she said. "I get banged up a lot, so I'm getting pretty good at patching myself up."

"So am I," Ozben said, measuring out a length of gauze. "Not for myself, though. Back home, I'd treat my sister's wounds all the time when she was training to be a soldier." He stood up and went over to the small wash-room adjacent to the bedchamber. A moment later, he returned with a bowl of water.

"So your sister's fighting in the war?" Lina asked. She scrunched up her face against the pain as Ozben dipped a washcloth in the water and began cleaning dirt from the scrapes.

"She's a general," Ozben said. "I don't know exactly where she's stationed, but I don't think she's seen much fighting. She can't, really, being second in line to the throne."

"I'm glad she's not in danger," Lina said.

"I'm sure Elinore hates it," Ozben said, chuckling.

He applied the medicine and carefully wrapped the first bandage around Lina's arm. "She always wants to jump into the middle of a fight. Makes my parents crazy."

Ozben moved to Lina's other side to bandage her left arm. He seemed to be concentrating awfully hard on his work. Lina angled toward him so he could wrap the bandage, and for a second their eyes met. He tried to hide it, but Lina saw the pained expression in Ozben's face. And who could blame him? His parents were far away, his sister was fighting in the war, and his grandfather was ill, maybe seriously. If he died, it could cause dangerous instability in the kingdom. Ozben was here alone while the rest of the world went on without him.

"Done," Ozben said, pulling Lina out of her thoughts. "The bandages aren't too tight, are they?" he asked.

Lina flexed her arms and rolled her shoulders back and forth experimentally. The bandages held, and the ointment was already taking away the sting. "Perfect, thanks," she said, and stood up. "So, how about it? A late-night tour of Ortana? I promise it'll be worth the lost sleep—and the cold," she said, grinning. "You'd better wear the heaviest coat you have."

Ozben glanced up at the ventilation shaft above their heads and laughed uneasily. "Good thing I'm not claustrophobic," he said, then added, "at least, I don't think I am."

On hands and knees, Ozben crawled through the narrow tunnel and tried to ignore what sounded like a large rat scratching at the other side of the wall. "Did you hear that sound?" he asked Lina, who crouched a few feet in front of him. She'd poked her head out of the hole at the end of the tunnel and was looking around to see if anyone was in the hallway.

"Probably a poscil rat," Lina whispered, pulling back from the hole. "They can be pretty loud."

"Loud because they have strong voices," Ozben asked, "or loud because they've grown to an unusual size?"

"Just their teeth," Lina said brightly.

"Oh, well, if that's all." Then Ozben heard her soft giggle echoing in the tunnel. She held up her arm, which glowed with a strange silver light, and allowed him to see her grin. He shook his head. "You're kind of diabolical, you know that?" He considered for a moment. "I like it."

She grinned wider. "Come on. The path's clear ahead."

"Right behind you."

Truly, this was the last thing Ozben had expected to be doing at this hour of the night. Earlier, his best hope had been that he would escape the stronghold and bribe his way onto a caravan headed for the nearest city, where he could then catch a train to Ardra. He'd never dreamed he'd be crawling around secret tunnels with a strange girl.

Strange but fascinating, he had to admit. He'd been skeptical at first, but she seemed to know exactly where she was going, as if she'd done this kind of exploring every day of her life, just as she'd claimed. She talked about animals he'd never heard of and wore a bracelet of light that he was dying to ask her about. This whole night had been one surprise after another.

Was it possible she knew a secret way out of the stronghold itself? A tingle of excitement ran down Ozben's spine, and his mind spun with the possibilities. If she could sneak him out of the stronghold in the middle of the night, he'd have a solid four- or five-hour head start before anyone found out he was gone. Maybe it was fate that had brought her out of nowhere in the Heart of the Mountain. Fate smacking him in the chest like a club, but still. He could take a hint.

Ozben crawled out of the hole behind her and stood up. By the light of her bracelet, he could see they were in what looked to be a small closet. Lina crouched down and shoved a large box full of cleaning supplies and old filthy rags in front of the hole.

"Won't whoever cleans this place eventually find the hole when they come back to get their supplies?" Ozben asked.

"Nope," Lina said confidently. She stood up and wiped her hands on her pant legs. "The cleaning stuff's mine. It's good for covering up the hole, but nobody uses this closet anymore anyway. Come on." She headed for the door. "We're on the fourth floor of the museum—Special Collections. It's my favorite wing."

"Why's that?" Ozben asked as Lina opened the closet door a crack and peeked into the hall beyond.

"Because of the staircase," Lina said. Ozben thought she sounded a little awed.

She led him out the door and left down a short hallway that spilled out into a large circular room. Evenly spaced along the walls were colorful murals of stained glass, each one standing about ten feet tall and as wide as the span of his arms. Lanterns burned behind them, illuminating the room in a soft, vibrant rainbow. Ozben stopped to examine the closest picture. It depicted a forest of lush green trees with leaves in shapes he'd never seen before. They looked like oversized clovers. In front of the trees was the figure of a sarnun woman.

During his short time in the stronghold, Ozben had seen several sarnuns among the archivists, though there were even more in Ardra, the capital city of the Merrow Kingdom. Unlike humans or chamelins, the sarnun species communicated telepathically, exchanging thoughts with each other instead of words spoken aloud. Their form resembled that of a human, but like the woman in the mural, they had blue skin and chalk-white eyes, and in place of hair, they possessed long, thin, filament-like feelers that they used to express emotion and recognize scents. The woman in the mural was bent at the waist, pointing her feelers at a row of white flowers growing at her feet.

"It's a scent window," Lina explained. "A sarnun artist named Kessel makes them. He donated a set to the museum. If you lean in close, you can actually smell the glass flowers."

"I've heard about these," Ozben said excitedly, "but I've never seen one in person." He bent closer to the mural. He didn't have a sarnun's keen sense of smell, but he detected a faint whiff of sweetness, like a lily, coming from the glass panes. "That's amazing," he said. "I know the sarnuns lock the scent into the glass during the foiling process, but I never understood how they make it last so long." Etched in the bottom right corner was the name of the piece. " 'Forests of the Mind,' " he translated. "Good title."

"Wow, you can read the sarnuns' language?" Lina asked, sounding impressed. "I could never manage that—the vowels are too complicated."

Ozben laughed. "Not as complicated as the chamelin tongue," he said. "I've been studying that one for years, and I still can't understand it, but then I've heard that most humans can't."

"How many languages do you speak?" Lina asked curiously.

Ozben looked up as he tallied them in his head. "Five—six, if you count the dead languages and the chamelin tongue. Nirean doesn't, though. She says my accent is terrible." He chuckled again.

But Lina didn't laugh. Her mouth had dropped open. "You're full of surprises," she said. "What else have you studied?"

He shrugged. "Odds and ends like geography, political history, and economics. Bit of sword fighting. The usual stuff."

"Usual sword-fighting stuff?" Lina said, laughing. "I like your kind of classes. The archivists don't offer courses in actual sword fighting, only theory."

"It's not as exciting as it sounds," Ozben said. "I never wanted to be a soldier, but I asked my sister to teach me to fight anyway, just to keep ahead."

"Ahead of what?" Lina asked.

"Just *ahead*. I don't know." Ozben felt a little flustered. He wasn't used to talking about himself like this, but Lina looked at him with such an earnest expression, as if she genuinely wanted to know. Most people weren't that interested in him. "It's hard to explain," he said, "but when you're the spare heir, like me, you have to find ways to make yourself stand out, to be important. Someday I want to be able to contribute to the family legacy—that's what my grandfather calls it. So I've tried to learn as much as I can about as many things as I can."

"Sounds like that could be exhausting," Lina said, "especially if you'd rather be doing something else."

"It's not so bad," Ozben said, "and the sword fighting is kind of fun, at least the way Elinore teaches it." He glanced up at the mural, memorizing the vivid colors of the forest scene and the faint scent of the white lilies. "This is better, though. Thanks for showing me," he said. "So not everything in the museum comes from another world?"

"Most of it does," Lina said, "but we're in a unique part of the museum, one that's off-limits to the public. Apprentices aren't allowed either, but I like to come here."

"Of course you do," Ozben murmured, smiling to himself. He had a feeling that no amount of locked doors and OFF-LIMITS signs could keep Lina from going wherever she wanted to.

"Come on. There's a lot more to see," she said, tugging gently on his arm. He allowed himself to be led away from the murals and across to the center of the room. A staircase led down to another level of the museum.

"The archivists sometimes call this area The Art of the Unknown," Lina explained as she guided him down the stairs, which curved slightly, revealing a series of alcoves set into the left-hand wall. "Mostly we call it Special Collections."

Ozben stopped at the first alcove. A sphere of interlocking metal rings covered in holes enclosed what looked like a tiny candle flame, no bigger than his thumbnail. The flame appeared to float in midair. A plaque beneath the piece read SUN SPHERE. "What's holding up the flame?" he asked.

"We don't know," Lina said, "but it never goes out, even if you touch it or squeeze it in your fist. It just stays. Go ahead, try it."

Fascinated, Ozben reached out a hand and flicked his finger at the edge of the hovering flame. A flash of heat caressed his skin, and the fire trembled for an instant before stabilizing. Then it burned on like a tiny star.

"I've never seen anything like that before," he said in a hushed voice. "This comes from another world—it has to, doesn't it?"

Lina nodded. "All these artifacts were scavenged from the meteor fields. And *none* of them are junk," she added significantly.

Ozben wasn't about to argue. He followed her down the stairs to the next alcove, where a large leather-bound book rested open on a stone pedestal. Dividing the book's two halves was a tattered green ribbon. The pages themselves were gold-leafed and looked as if they had once been very fine, but age and water damage had made them crinkled and brittle, so that in some places the text was unreadable.

"This is one of my favorite books," Lina said. "It's called *The Ever Story*. The pages are so old and fragile, the archivists turn only one each month. But the book is amazing. It tells a different story for each person reading it, and the words appear in their native language. Isn't that wonderful?"

Ozben blinked. "A different . . . Wait a minute, what?" He must have misunderstood her explanation. He squinted at the tiny writing on the page closest to him and read the first couple of lines aloud: " 'Delia woke up with her cheek pressed against burning hot sand. Salt water dripped from her hair. *The Gauntlet* had sunk in the storm, but what had happened to her friends? Had they perished?' " He stopped reading and glanced up at Lina. "Is that what your words say?"

Lina smiled and shook her head. "Nope. My story's about a magic wardrobe—can you believe that, a magic closet?—that's a portal to another land. I didn't think I was going to like it, but now I can't stop reading. It's hard getting to read only a page a month, but at least it makes the story last."

"But how?" Ozben said, flabbergasted. How could one book contain a different story depending on who was looking at it?

Lina shrugged. "Maybe it alters the story to fit the

person reading it. The archivists think it makes a weak telepathic connection to the reader. They were consulting with a sarnun who lives in Tevshal about it—I think her name was Raenoll—but then the war started, and they lost contact with her."

"That's too bad. I'd love to know how the book works." Ozben's head was still spinning as Lina moved down the stairs, gesturing for him to follow.

"This one you have to lean in and smell, like the stained-glass murals," she instructed him at the next alcove. "It doesn't have a name, but I call it a memory jar."

Ozben moved up beside her, eager to see this latest wonder. He gazed into a square glass vase about six inches tall. In the bottom of the vase swirled a thin pink mist. He bent forward and sniffed. The scent tickled his nose with hints of cinnamon mixed with something else he couldn't identify. It was a nice smell, though, and it reminded him of something. What was it?

A memory popped into his head then, so vivid and sharp that it made him jump. Ozben felt Lina's hand on his arm, steadying him, but in his mind, he was suddenly back in Ardra at the royal palace.

He was five years old and playing at sword fighting with his sister, just as he'd described to Lina. Elinore's straight black hair flew around her face as she moved, dodging his clumsy sword swipes and leaping backward over their mother's petunia beds. She was almost fourteen and so much taller and more graceful than him, but it didn't matter. He was laughing, having a good time, and so was she.

They danced and dueled through the palace gardens while bees buzzed around the flowering ivy growing thick on the walls. Once, Elinore tripped and fell backward, sprawling on the lawn. Ozben ran over and dived on top of her, squealing with laughter. Elinore let out a big "oof" noise and flopped on the ground, pretending he'd crushed her.

"Enough, both of you!"

The angry shout came from somewhere near the garden gate. Elinore scrambled to her feet, helping Ozben up with her. The speaker was their grandfather. Ozben's joy shriveled into fear—he'd always been a little in awe of his grandfather—but his sister had stood beside him with her hand on his shoulder, and that made him feel better and worse at the same time. He'd wanted to be the one to step in front of her and protect *her* from the king's anger.

When King Easmon strode across the garden, the sunlight reflected off his silver hair and the epaulets at his shoulders. Ozben stared, thinking how equally noble and frightening the king appeared. At that age, Ozben's head barely came up to the man's waist. He knew the cuts and facets of the emeralds in the sword swinging from the king's belt better than he knew the cracks and wrinkles in his grandfather's face.

"Go inside, Elinore," the king instructed sternly. "Your mother wants a word with you."

"As you wish, Grandfather." Elinore bowed to the king, shot Ozben a wink and an encouraging smile, and left the garden. Ozben started to follow—his grandfather rarely paid attention to him, so he didn't expect any different treatment now.

But this time, the king reached down and seized him painfully by the arm.

"You're the least of all of us, you know," his grandfather said softly, staring into Ozben's eyes. "The most unimportant."

Ozben's stomach clenched. He was suddenly cold all over, except where the king held on to his arm. A grip like iron, and his hand was hot, so hot Ozben imagined it might burn him if he held on long enough.

But it was his grandfather's tone of voice that was more painful than anything. He didn't sound angry or even disappointed, as Ozben's father and mother did when he got into trouble. No, it was because the king sounded *resigned*, as if there was no hope for him.

"I'm sorry, Grandfather," he said haltingly. Whatever he did, he would not let the king see the tears that stung his eyes. He stared into his grandfather's grim face, not daring to blink in case they fell.

"It does neither me nor your family any good to hear you say you're sorry, boy," the king replied. "You won't be a child forever. Soon you'll have to decide what you can contribute to this kingdom. Earn the privileges you've been given, or I'll see them taken away."

"Ozben?"

His sister was calling to him. *Of course I'm not all right,* Ozben thought miserably. He wished more than anything that Elinore would dash back into the garden and rescue him from his grandfather.

"Ozben, say something!"

Wait, that wasn't his sister calling to him. It was Lina's voice. His grandfather's face swam in Ozben's vision, melting and reshaping into a jar of mist resting in an alcove.

Ozben came back to himself with a jolt. The memory had seemed so real. In fact, he could have sworn he still felt his grandfather's hand squeezing his arm. Ozben rubbed the feeling away and suppressed a shudder.

"What was that?" he asked, his voice trembling.

"What did you see?" Lina asked. She laid a gentle hand on his shoulder, just as his sister had done.

"It was . . . the clearest dream I've ever had," Ozben said, fighting for the words to describe how he felt. "Except it wasn't a dream. It happened." He remembered that day in the garden, sword fighting with Elinore, but the rest of it, the conversation with his grandfather—

he'd forgotten all about that part, blocked it from his memory.

Until now.

"It's the mist," Lina explained. "Its scent conjures a memory you've lost. Only the one, though. I've tried it about a dozen times to see if I can remember something different, but it doesn't work that way."

"If you knew how it worked, then you might have warned me," Ozben said, his temper flaring. He'd been unprepared for the memory jar's effect on him, and his grandfather's hurtful words still rang in his mind. *The least of all of us.* That was what he'd said. His grandfather had always been strict, yet Ozben never remembered his being cruel.

But beyond the hurt and confusion in Ozben lurked also a hint of fear. Why and how had the mist conjured that memory out of all the others in his past? This was more than just a candle flame that wouldn't go out, or a book that told telepathic stories. This artifact seemed much more powerful to him. It had reached deep into his mind to conjure that lost memory. Ozben looked from the curling mist to Lina's face, his brow furrowed in consternation. "Is the mist . . . it can't be . . . some kind of magic?"

Lina frowned. "The archivists never use that term," she said. "Saying something is 'magic' just means we don't have a scientific explanation for how and why it works. But there's nothing here to be scared of. All these artifacts have been tested and retested a thousand different ways to make sure they're harmless."

"I don't believe you," he said curtly, unwilling to let his anger go. The memory of his grandfather had been anything but harmless. But Ozben didn't want to tell Lina what he'd seen. "How can you really know if they're safe if you don't understand how this stuff works?" he asked, gesturing to the alcoves.

"Well . . ." Lina stared at the mist, and her eyes took on a faraway glaze. She leaned forward and closed her eyes as she breathed it in. After a moment, she opened her eyes and looked at him. "You're right," she admitted. "We can't know for sure that these things won't hurt us. Kind of like with people," she added quietly, as if she were speaking to herself. "No matter how much you think you know someone, you don't always understand why they do the things they do."

She looked so sad all of a sudden that Ozben's anger drained away. He wondered what memory the mist had conjured up for her. If it was anything like the vision he'd just seen, he could understand why she'd tried dozens of times for a different one. Maybe it was just the nature of the thing to bring up bad memories, though he couldn't imagine why that would be useful. "Will you show me more?" he asked, hoping to distract them both. As much as he feared some of these artifacts, he was equally fascinated by their mysteries. He was beginning to under-stand why the archivists were so dedicated to their work.

And Lina did show him more. By the time they'd reached the bottom of the stairs, Ozben had seen a plant that chimed the faintest notes of a song when he touched its leaves, a clock with seventeen numbers on its face, and a sculpture of a ballerina that looked so real, he'd expected it to dance right off its platform at any minute. He wanted the alcoves and their mysterious wonders to keep going on forever.

"Elinore would love this place," Ozben remarked as they continued through the museum, walking down a hallway flanked by lifelike statues. "So would my parents. I wonder why they never came here before."

A pang of homesickness hit Ozben, and he had to pause in front of a statue of a man on a charging horse. He'd gotten so caught up in seeing the museum that he'd forgotten to ask Lina if she knew a secret way out of the stronghold. Time was running out if he wanted to be away before dawn.

So what if you do escape? whispered a voice in the back of Ozben's mind. *What then?* Hope that he had enough coin with him to buy passage on a train or caravan, if one existed that could navigate the snow-covered roads out of the mountains and take him all the way to Ardra. What if he ended up having to walk for miles with no food and water? Was he truly brave and resourceful enough to make it all the way back home, or was he just fooling himself? Maybe his grandfather was right.

A few steps ahead of him, Lina stopped and turned around. "Something wrong?" she asked.

Ozben shook his head. "Nothing. I'm all right."

"Good," Lina said, and her eyes lit up. "I saved the best for last."

There was more? "Um, all right." Maybe it would distract him from the dark direction his thoughts had taken. Besides, Lina looked so excited, Ozben found himself wondering what she had up her sleeve that could possibly top all the things he'd seen so far. "Is it in this wing of the museum?" he asked.

"It's not in the museum at all," she said. "I'm taking you to my workshop." She hesitated and seemed suddenly nervous, clasping and unclasping her hands. "I've never shown it to anyone before," she said. "It's a secret. No one can know about it. Do you understand?"

Ozben smiled wryly. "I have some experience with secrets," he said. "Don't worry. I won't tell anyone."

She nodded, but Ozben sensed she wasn't quite convinced. Now he was really curious about what she might be hiding in this workshop.

"It's a bargain, then?" she said. She walked over to him and held out her hand. "I'll keep your secret, and you'll keep mine?"

She looked so serious that Ozben's grin faded. He

took her hand and shook it firmly. "I swear on my honor as a prince of the Merrow Kingdom, I'll keep your secret."

"All right, I believe you," Lina said, and her serious expression melted into a smile. "Come on. I know you're going to love this."

≈ SIX ≈

Lina stood next to Ozben, watching him out of the corner of her eye as he stared at the *Merlin*. She was tempted to point out that his mouth was quite literally hanging open, but she decided not to, especially since it was likely she'd worn the same dumbfounded expression when she first clapped eyes on the airship. And Ozben was seeing not only the airship for the first time but its strange wings as well. He had to be overwhelmed.

"This is"—Ozben turned to her as he spoke, his eyes enormous—"the most amazing thing ever!"

Lina grinned hugely. "See, I knew you'd be impressed."

"Impressed?" Ozben made a slow circle around the ship as he spoke, looking at it from every angle. "It's an airship buried inside a mountain! How did it get here?"

"Same way the other artifacts do," Lina said. "Someone found it in the scrap fields, brought it here, and the archivists rebuilt it. I think a cave-in must have buried the chamber a long time ago, so the archivists thought it was gone."

"Do you think it flies?" Ozben asked, pausing beneath one of the wings to examine the ship's rigid frame.

Lina walked over to join him. "It's possible," she said. "I tested one of the engines, and it worked fine, but without getting inside the ship to look at the controls, there's no way to know for sure. Though even if we did get it to fly, it wouldn't go very far in this chamber."

"So there's no other way out of this cave?" Ozben asked, gazing around the room. He appeared to be lost in thought.

"Not that I've seen," Lina said, but then again, she'd been concentrating all her efforts on digging out the ship and getting inside it. "You see those stones wedged in front of the ship's door there?" She waited for him to look, but Ozben was still staring intently at the cavern walls. Impatient, Lina grabbed his arm and, ignoring his yelp of surprise, towed him over to the door. "Those four large, incredibly annoying boulders are keeping me from opening the ship," she explained. "I need your help to move them."

"Oh?" Ozben went over to the closest stone and nudged it with his foot. It didn't budge. He crouched down and shoved his weight against it, trying, Lina assumed, to scoot it across the ground. His face turned red, and he broke off with a gasp. He glanced up at her with a raised eyebrow. "Yeah, that's not possible."

"Of course it is," Lina said, smiling brightly. "You're exactly what I need."

Ozben's skeptical expression didn't change. He stood up and gestured to himself. "I don't know if you've noticed this or not, and believe me, I'd rather not mention it at all, but I'm not exactly the biggest or the strongest prince that ever lived. Although what I lack in strength, I make up for in strategy," he added quickly.

"Even better," Lina said. "I've been thinking it over, and it's all a matter of tools, not strength. I've tried using a pry bar and fulcrum by myself, but it isn't enough. I need another pair of hands running another tool." She surveyed the cavern. "Right . . . there," she said, pointing to a large stalagmite jutting up near the rear of the ship. "And there." Next she pointed to Lumpy, the most rectangular-shaped of the four boulders. "If we hook up a hand winch at those two points, and you run the thing while I lever the boulder with the pry bar, it should be enough to dislodge it and knock loose the other three rocks. Simple as that."

Ozben rubbed his chin while his gaze darted between the stalagmite and Lumpy. Slowly, he nodded. "All right, I can see how that might work," he conceded. "Let's give it a try. Where's the hand winch?"

Lina grinned sheepishly. "Well, that's where your strategizing is going to come in really handy," she said.

"Uh-oh," Ozben said, his eyebrow shooting up again. "You don't have a hand winch, do you?"

"Not even close. But I know exactly where to get one."

She grabbed his arm and led him over to her work-table. She selected one of her large maps of the stronghold and unrolled it. Ozben looked at the map and then studied Lina's face. He pursed his lips. "Go ahead and correct me if I'm wrong, but I'm starting to get the impression that this 'late-night tour of Ortana' was actually an elaborate plan to get me down here so you could embroil me in a different but equally elaborate plan to help you break into your airship. Am I close?"

Lina blushed. "Yep, you're pretty much on the nose," she said. She looked at him hopefully. "Did it work?"

"Did I mention you're diabolical?" Ozben asked, but he smiled as he said it, and Lina felt a surge of hope. She'd come this far—it was time to sell him on the rest of the plan.

She turned back to her map, which showed a general layout of the entire stronghold. "See, the Heart of the Mountain is here, in the center of everything," she said, tracing her finger around the large circular chamber in the middle of the map. "If you go out the south passage from there, you end up in the museum. What we want are these six areas to the east and west. Those corridors lead to the archivists' workshops." She tapped her finger on each of the six rooms as she named them. "There's the Flora and Fauna divisions, but we call them the Garden and the Menagerie. Then there's the medical wing, the library, and the Gears and Steam room, which is where we need to go to get our hand winch."

"And since you're showing me all this in the same way my grandfather shows his commanders a battlefield map," Ozben said, "I'm guessing we're not going to be able to just stroll up to the Gears and Steam room and ask for the hand winch."

Lina patted him on the shoulder. "You're quick," she said. "Technically, the archivists' tools can be used by anyone, but if I ask for the hand winch, it'll attract attention and questions I don't want to have to answer. We need to do this in secret," she said.

"Makes sense." Ozben traced a finger across the map, studying the pathways she'd drawn. He glanced up at her curiously. "But what I don't understand is, why me? Not that I don't enjoy the idea of a challenge," he added hastily, "it's just, why haven't you asked one of your friends to help you before now?"

The question caught Lina off guard, and she felt her face get hot. She tried to hide her embarrassment by turning away to rearrange her tools. "You said it yourself. You know what it's like to have a secret—something you can't trust to anyone else. And I don't have any friends . . . I mean, I don't have anyone else who understands that."

"I see," Ozben said quietly. "Well then." He clapped his hands together. "We'd better get started. We have a lot of planning to do."

Lina sneaked a glance at him to make sure he wasn't teasing her. He was staring intently at the map, biting his lower lip as he studied the tunnels. A thread of excitement worked its way through her. They were really going to do this. She'd been right: Ozben was the perfect partner.

Then, as quickly as her excitement had built, it faded. Nirean had said Ozben was in danger here. He might be perfect for her task in some ways, but there was also a large obstacle where he was concerned.

"If we're going to do this," Lina said, tapping on a section of the map near where Ozben's room was, "we need to figure out how we're going to handle the assassins."

Ozben's brow scrunched up in confusion. "What do you mean?" he asked. "There are no assassins coming after me. Not here."

"Of course there are," Lina said, exasperated that Ozben could be so smart one minute and so dense the next. "Assassins don't just give up on their targets. In fact, they might already be here disguising themselves as refugees just like you are, waiting for a chance to strike. If we're going to work together and move around the stronghold without Nirean or Zara watching out for us, we have to be prepared to deal with these people on our own."

"So, let me get this straight." Ozben crossed his arms and looked at her askance. "You crawl around in hidden tunnels, you're keeping a secret airship in storage, and now you're telling me you're also an expert on assassins?"

"I study a lot," Lina said. She grinned, rubbing her hands together. "Besides, I've always wanted to thwart an assassination attempt." When Ozben's eyes widened, she laughed. "Kidding. But we do have to be prepared."

"All right—whatever you say." Ozben raised his hands in surrender. "What do you suggest?"

Lina thought for a moment, then she began ticking things off on her fingers. "First, when you go back to your room tonight, I want you to make a note of where every object is—I'm saying the *exact* spot. That way, if someone sneaks into your room to lay a trap, you'll know about it if they leave anything out of place. Second, don't eat or drink anything unless it comes from someone you know. Assassins love to use poison. Third, don't go anywhere by yourself—wait for me or Nirean to go with you."

Ozben nodded, though Lina thought he still looked a little skeptical, as if the only assassins were in her own imagination. "I can do all that," he said. "Let's talk about this hand winch."

"Getting the hand winch is going to be difficult," Lina admitted. Ozben wasn't the only one who came to this scheme with problems. Lina had to figure out how she was going to work around the punishment Zara would assign her for eavesdropping on the council meeting. According to her teacher, she would be too busy to sit down for the next few weeks, let alone work on breaking into the airship. And even after she dealt with her punishment, her troubles still weren't over. "We have a Simon problem," Lina said, plopping down on her stool beside the table.

"What's a 'Simon problem'?" Ozben asked. "Is that code?"

Lina laughed. "I wish it were. Simon's one of the senior apprentices. He goes from workshop to workshop supervising the younger apprentices. He doesn't like me very much on account of what I did to his teacher, Councilman Tolwin."

"Oh?" Ozben said. "This I have to hear."

"It wasn't a big deal," Lina said, but she flushed guiltily. "A couple years ago, I was studying dralfa moss, which is this thick purple cave moss that thrives in cold, dark places and actually doesn't like the light. It used to grow all over the cave walls, but as more people came to inhabit the mountain, they generated more light and heat, so the moss started to wither and die off. I was experimenting to see how much cold and darkness it would take to make it grow back, and I needed an empty room close to my teacher's workshop. When I found one, I planted a little patch of moss in the corner of the room." She winced at the memory of what had happened next. "The room I chose turned out to be Tolwin's private study—but he hadn't been in there for a month, I swear!" Lina said when Ozben started to laugh. "I thought he wasn't using it. How was I supposed to know he took private meetings there with potential donors to the museum?"

"Oh no." Ozben's face was turning red from laughing so hard. "What . . . happened?" he wheezed.

"Well . . ." Lina had intended to leave the room sealed and dark for a couple of days to see how much the moss would grow in that time, but then she got distracted by her other projects, and it ended up being more like three weeks. "I slightly underestimated how fast the moss would grow," she admitted. "It was pretty spectacular by the time Tolwin saw it."

"I'll bet," Ozben said, wiping tears from his eyes. "How far had it grown?"

"Pretty far," Lina said, "and pretty much all over everything in the room. It covered his desk, his chairs, the bookshelves—you name it, it had a coat of fuzzy purple moss on it. But the worst part was—"

"It gets *worse?*" Ozben said.

Lina scowled at him. "Even after I'd scraped all of it off, the moss left behind this weird purple stain. I never could get it out of the furniture. Tolwin was furious. He really loved that desk," she said, sighing. "He's hated me ever since, and because he hates me, Simon does too."

"All right, then, so we have a Simon problem to deal with," Ozben said, still chuckling. "Why don't we just sneak up there now while everyone's asleep and get the winch?"

Lina shook her head. "Tools like that are locked up at night in the Haystack," she said. "It's this huge messy storeroom right next door to the Gears and Steam room." She pointed to it on the map. "I've tried to sneak in before, but the locks are unbreakable, believe me. The best we can do is sneak in during the day while the storeroom's open. There are so many tools and machine parts and so much scrap lying around, chances are no one will even notice the winch's gone."

"Which brings us back to needing a plan." Ozben glanced at the little clock on the worktable, and his eyes widened. "Wow, it's almost dawn," he said. "I didn't realize that I'd . . . I mean, I'd better get back up to my room before Nirean comes to check on me." He stood straight and stretched. A thoughtful expression crossed his face.

"We'll work on it—give it a week maybe. We can't act now anyway—I've already made Nirean suspicious by running off once. She'll be watching me closely."

"All right," Lina said, stifling a yawn. She didn't like the idea of waiting, but maybe after a week she could persuade Zara to let her out of the rest of her punishment. She rolled up the map and held it out to Ozben. "Here, you take this. Study it; memorize every landmark you can. And sorry about my messy writing."

"Thanks," Ozben said, taking the map. He looked at her for a moment as if he wanted to say something. Lina waited expectantly, but in the end, he just gave her a brief smile and said, "I can't wait to get started."

After Lina had guided him back to his room and left, Ozben sat on the bed, the rolled-up map resting on his knees. Sleep would be a long time coming. He lifted one of the blankets and draped it over his shoulders to banish the chill of being in Lina's workshop. His thoughts raced with everything that had happened that night.

He had missed his chance to escape the stronghold. He berated himself for that, but on the other hand, he'd been completely unprepared for the amazing secret Lina had shared with him and the opportunity it had created.

Lina had an airship. Lina Adelia Winterbock—that beautiful, wonderful, dirt-smudged girl. In Ozben's wildest dreams, he couldn't have come up with a better solution to his problem of how to get home than what she had just presented to him. Sure, there were several monumental obstacles between him and his vision of flying an airship to Ardra. The two biggest ones: Ozben didn't know if they could get the ship to fly, and even if they did, how would they ever get it out of that cavern? For the former, he had to rely on Lina. He didn't know the first thing about steam engines or piloting. As for the latter, Ozben was convinced that if somebody had gone to the trouble of reconstructing an airship inside a mountain, they had to have thought up a plan for how to get it out again. A hidden door or a secret tunnel leading out of the mountain that Lina just hadn't found yet. He would work on that angle.

But Ozben frowned as a new thought occurred to him. His plans sounded great in his head, but all of it relied on Lina's cooperation. For the first time since he'd seen the airship, his excitement faltered, replaced by a pang of guilt. What would she say when he told her he wanted to fly the ship all the way to the Merrow Kingdom? She'd been so vehement about not letting the archivists take the ship away from her. But surely, she couldn't argue with what he intended to do with the ship. He needed to get back to his family. Wasn't that worth her giving it up?

But she might not see it that way, and Ozben couldn't

take that risk. *I won't tell her,* he decided, *not until the time's right.* He tried to push aside his guilt. He was getting ahead of himself, anyway. They had a lot of work to do, and neither of them could do it alone. More than anything, Lina wanted to get inside that ship, and Ozben would help her make that happen. He was doing the right thing.

His decision made, Ozben stood and shoved the map underneath his mattress to hide it from Zara and Nirean. Then he started to shed his clothes to get ready for bed. While he struggled with the laces on his boots, his gaze fell on the flask of kelpra juice on the table across the room. He'd left it there after pouring him and Lina each a glass. Except, he was almost sure he'd left the stopper out of the flask.

Ozben stopped fiddling with his bootlaces and walked over to the table. The hairs on the back of his neck prickled, and the room seemed suddenly much colder. He picked up the flask, sniffed the contents, and swirled the liquid around in the bottom. Lina's warning about assassins and poison rang in his mind. Was it possible someone had been in his room?

No, it couldn't be. Nirean or the other guard would have seen them. He was just tired, and Lina's imagination had him seeing invisible enemies. Assassins would never risk coming after him here. What would be the point? He was the spare heir, the backup—his father and mother and Elinore were far more important to the kingdom.

Ozben shook his head. He really needed to get some sleep. He put the flask back on the table and finished changing into his nightclothes.

And yet the last thing he did before climbing into bed and blowing out the candle on his nightstand was pour out the kelpra juice in the washroom sink. The juice was getting stale, Ozben told himself. That's all.

≈ SEVEN ≈

Lina mopped the sweat from her forehead with her sleeve and turned to skewer another pitchforkful of hay. To say it had been a long three weeks was the understatement of understatements.

Ozben had predicted it would be a matter of days before Nirean and Zara began to trust him again, enough to let him wander around the less crowded common areas of the stronghold in disguise. Lina had predicted that Zara would let her out of her punishment early also. As it turned out, they'd both underestimated the councilwoman.

It took two weeks for Nirean to stop watching Ozben's every move like a hawk, and Zara made it very clear that she wasn't going to go easy on Lina. She was to work in the Menagerie every day for three weeks, cleaning up after the animals and helping the archivists with whatever they needed. There were worse jobs, but, as Zara had promised, the task would keep her too busy to do much of anything on her own during the day. And she still had to attend all her regular classes.

Although, as it turned out, the extra time was good for their plans. In order to throw off Nirean's suspicion, Lina encouraged Ozben to develop a daily routine. He'd get up in the morning, take breakfast in his room, and then don his disguise to take a walk along the corridors between his room and Nirean's. By staying out of sight and behaving himself, Ozben eventually persuaded the chamelin to let him wander farther, edging into the common areas. As the days passed, his disguise held, and despite Lina's caution, no assassins materialized. On the strength of that—and possibly the fear that he would revolt if he was watched twenty-four hours a day—Nirean allowed Ozben more freedom, and he eventually ended up in the stronghold's library. There he had the perfect excuse for long absences from his room.

The library spread out across two huge caverns, shelves upon shelves built into the cave walls, soaring out of sight toward the stalactites clinging to the ceiling. A series of bridges and spiral staircases connected the various levels of the library, and there were dozens of tiny study rooms where the archivists could hide away and work undisturbed.

Testing the limits of his freedom, Ozben took to

spending long hours each day in the library, reading books on a variety of subjects, so that when Nirean came to look for him, he was never in the same place twice. When it became clear that the secret of his identity was safe, Nirean checked on him less frequently, until finally there came a day when Ozben didn't see her at all until dinnertime, when he returned to his room. Lina was relieved. She'd been worried the chamelin would never let the prince out of her sight.

During those weeks, the only time Lina and Ozben could talk to each other was late at night, when Lina used the ventilation shaft to sneak into his room. When she wasn't with him or in the Menagerie cleaning the animal pens, she spent her limited time spying on Simon and the other senior apprentices to see what their routines were during the day. As she'd feared, Simon spent an awful lot of time watching out for her, looking for an excuse to assign her some menial task in addition to her punishment from Zara. But it was better than the alternative, she'd told Ozben.

"If you think about it, it's actually kind of your fault that I almost lost my apprenticeship," she'd told him calmly.

"My fault?" Ozben said, incredulous. "What did I do?"

"You were the reason Tolwin and the other council members looked so upset that night," Lina explained. "I mean, I know Tolwin and I aren't exactly best friends, but I thought it was a little harsh of him to want to kick me out just for eavesdropping. But what if they'd mentioned you and I'd overheard? They almost gave away the whole game, and I think it really shook them up."

"And then I went and gave the secret away anyway," Ozben said glumly.

"That's true," Lina said with a grin, "but only to me."

They'd decided to implement their plan as soon as Lina's punishment ended, and even though today was her last day, the day of liberation, she felt as if time had slowed to a crawl just to spite her.

She jabbed her pitchfork into the hay impatiently, then suddenly the whole pile shifted and Ozben poked his head out at her.

"Gah!" Lina fumbled the pitchfork, catching it by the handle. "You scared me to death! I could have stabbed you in the eye!" A wide grin spread across Ozben's bandaged face, and Lina looked around to make sure no one was watching them, but the closest archivists were intent on their inspection of a horse's hoof over by one of the barns. "What are you doing here?" she asked.

"Taking a lesson from you," he said cheerfully. "I can see how you manage to get so much eavesdropping done around here. Ortana has a million places to hide, if you take the time to look for them."

"Yeah, as long as you make sure you don't end up

getting stabbed," Lina said dryly. She stuck the pitchfork into some loose hay on the ground and leaned on the handle. "Nirean's not looking for you, is she?"

"She thinks I'm in the library right now," Ozben said. He flicked a piece of hay out of his eyes. "I've been meaning to tell you, I had no idea you had such an amazing collection of books. And this Menagerie . . ." He looked around the cavern at the grazing animals and gardens. "Wow, you know, I wouldn't mind living here, if only I could see the sun. Living underground is cold and creepy."

"*Creepy?*" Lina repeated, aghast. Had he really just called her beautiful mountain home creepy? Now she *was* tempted to poke him with the pitchfork. "We can see the sun whenever we want to," she informed him stiffly. "There are four towers built into the side of the mountain with glass turrets where you can go and get as much sunshine as you want. And we have a huge outdoor terrace that overlooks Gazer's Gorge. The astronomers go there with their telescopes to study the stars. Not that you really need one—a telescope, I mean," she said. "You can see millions of stars from up there. Sometimes the archivists hold parties out there too. Everyone bundles up in thick coats, and they serve hot punch, and there's music and sometimes dancing. The apprentices aren't allowed to go, but I snuck up there once with a blanket and watched. Oh, and then there are the aeries," she went on, juggling the pitchfork from hand to hand as she got more excited. "They're open to the sky so the chamelins can fly in and out whenever they want. So we get plenty of sun."

Ozben listened, but he didn't look convinced. He picked at a strand of hay, twisting it around his thumb. "That all sounds great, but I still think it'd be lonely, being inside so much, away from the rest of the world. Just look at the way you are with the war."

"What's that supposed to mean?" Lina asked, narrowing her eyes.

"Nothing bad," Ozben said quickly. "I always wondered why the archivists didn't choose a side in the war, but I can sort of see it now. You're so far away from everything. It's like you're in your own world."

"That doesn't mean we don't care about the rest of Solace," Lina argued. Her face flushed. Ozben didn't know what he was talking about. "We've followed everything that's happened in the war from the beginning."

"Well, then what do you think about it?" Ozben asked.

Some of Lina's anger faded, replaced by sadness. "I wish it were over," she said. "It's disrupted everything here, and it's all anyone can talk or think about." She thought of the refugees in the dormitories. "I've seen little kids who lost their parents. They come here from the Merrow Kingdom and the Dragonfly territories. The archivists keep the refugees in separate areas so the two sides won't go after each other, but if you ask me, by the time they get here, hungry, sick, and wounded, the last thing they want to do is fight. Everybody's suffering, so why not end it already?"

"You sound like my dad," Ozben said. "He wants to make peace with King Aron, but grandfather says it's impossible, because the Dragonfly will never give us iron again."

"So what does that mean? Your grandfather thinks he should just take it?" Lina asked, annoyed.

"It's not like that," Ozben said defensively. "Not having iron has put a ton of our people out of work. Blacksmiths, factory workers—all because King Aron wants to use it for his inventions. He's being selfish."

"But people say King Easmon wants to use it for weapons," Lina pointed out. "They say he wants to conquer all of Solace."

Ozben scowled. "So what you're saying is, you do side with the Dragonfly territories," he accused. "You think the Merrow Kingdom's wrong."

"I think you're *both* wrong," Lina shot back. "But King Easmon is the one who's attacking in the west, getting closer and closer to our border every day." She remembered the concerned expression on Zara's face when she'd told Lina this. If Zara was worried, Lina knew there had to be a good reason.

Ozben shook his head. "Grandfather would never attack the archivists while they were neutral, even if they're taking in refugees from both sides," he said. "He just wants to protect his people."

"Are you sure?" Lina asked. "You said your father wants peace with King Aron. What does your grandfather say about that?"

Ozben's expression faltered. "Yeah, they argue about that a lot. Grandfather thinks father's being too trusting. He doesn't think King Aron will stop his attacks for any peace talks. And when the assassins invaded the palace, you should have seen how furious he was. He accused Father of putting his family in danger. But Grandfather's always been protective of his family, especially my sister and me. Well, more so of Elinore," he said with a strained smile. "I'm just an extra heir; I'm not that important."

"Don't say that." Sadness squeezed Lina's heart. "I'm sure your parents don't feel that way," she said, crouching down so she could look him in the eyes.

"I know they don't, it's just . . ." Ozben trailed off as he picked at the hay. "It's not that I want to be king or anything. Elinore was born for it, and she'll make a great ruler after Father, but I just wish that I was needed for something, you know? That I was important to someone the way she is. I mean, she's the commander of our entire forces. What have I got that can compete with that?"

"Well, for one thing, you've got a really hard head," Lina joked, hoping to lift his mood by making him laugh. She tapped him gently on the forehead with the pitchfork handle. "I found that out when we ran into each other in the Heart of the Mountain."

"That's a comfort," Ozben said. His eyes were still sad, but he smiled at her. "Your head wasn't exactly a pillow either. I think I still have bruises and cracked ribs."

They laughed, and then one of the archivists called over to Lina to stop talking to herself and get back to work. Ozben ducked deeper into the hay so he wouldn't be seen. Lina made a face when the archivist turned away. "Guess I'd better keep scooping," she said, wrinkling her nose. "I still have to clean out the barns after this." Zara was nothing if not thorough in her punishments. "At least princes don't have to clean cow pens all day long."

"Nah, but I had to shovel plenty of horse dung whenever I got in trouble at home," Ozben said. "The royal stables in Ardra have to be twice as big as this cavern. And I'm not sure what they feed the horses, but the smell is bad enough to make your eyes water."

"Ugh," Lina said in sympathy. "Well, I think another two hours of work here should do it. As soon as I'm finished, I'll come and get you. Be ready when I do," she added.

"Don't worry. We've been planning for weeks. We're

more than ready." Ozben saluted her and grinned before ducking back into the hay pile.

True to her word, almost exactly two hours later, Lina stuck her head through the grate in Ozben's bedroom and said it was time.

They made their way back to the Menagerie, where they would put the first stage of the plan into motion. Lina led him along the edge of the cow pens, ducking low so the archivists wouldn't spot them.

Lina had explained that the Menagerie and the Garden were technically separate divisions but that physically they tended to overlap. The plants that needed sunlight were grown in greenhouses built into the side of the mountain, and what the archivists didn't need for themselves from the harvests was brought down to help feed the animals. In return, the animal dung helped fertilize the plants. The whole area was set up like an underground farm. Sheep and cows grazed alongside flocks of small white flightless birds with red beaks that made low cooing sounds as Lina and Ozben passed by. Ozben slowed to look at the birds, and the closest one ruffled up its feathers and squawked at him. As it did so, its plumage flashed from white to bright yellow and back.

Ozben blinked and slowed down to see if the bird would change colors again, but it didn't. It just stared at him with eyes shining like black onyx. Ozben marveled at how much there was to see around here. Shaking his head at the strange bird, he hurried to catch up with Lina.

"How many of these animals come from other worlds?" he whispered.

"Four mammals, two amphibians, two species of flightless bird, one reptile, about a dozen insect species, and I can never remember how many plants," she whispered back. "There's a chalkboard up on the back wall that lists every species that's come down in the meteor storms."

"It's hard to believe," Ozben said. Though he'd never seen one, he'd heard stories about how violent the meteor storms were. "How could anything survive the trip from one world to another?"

Lina shooed a goat away from the fence when it reached out to chew on her sleeve. "Some archivists believe that the objects are shielded somehow and that the shield dissolves sometime during the object's descent. Maybe some objects are more protected than others? Animals don't come through very often, or we'd have a lot more of them here." She stopped in front of a small pen that had a high fence of chicken wire. "The ones we do have, the archivists study thoroughly to see if they can be released safely into Solace's ecosystem."

"Is that what you're doing with the bugs on your wrist?" he asked, pointing to her leather band.

Lina looked down at her leather bracelet and smiled sadly. "The lumatites." She nodded. "Before my parents died, they were studying the lumatites' light-producing capabilities and trying to develop a communication system. They're actually very intelligent. I've gotten a little bit further with their theories, but the communication is still rudimentary."

"I see," Ozben said. He didn't, really, but he was distracted by what she'd said about her parents. She hadn't mentioned them in the last few weeks, but Ozben had assumed they were alive. It stunned him to find out they weren't. "Do you have any brothers or sisters?" he asked abruptly.

"Nope, it's just me." Lina glanced at him. "I thought you wanted to ask about the animals," she said pointedly.

Ozben could take a hint. Obviously, she didn't want to go into detail about her family, but his mind was still spinning. No parents or brothers and sisters—surely she must have some friends, people she spent time with besides him. He started to ask her about it, but she was crouching down next to the chicken wire fence. She put her fingers in her mouth and let out a low whistle.

"Come on out, kitties," she called softly, snapping her fingers. "Come on."

A trio of hairless cats spilled out of a little metal barn at the back of the pen. Lina had described them to Ozben a week ago as they finalized their plan, but that description hardly did them justice. They were without a doubt the ugliest creatures he'd ever seen in his life. Slightly larger than house cats, they had huge orange eyes that seemed to swallow up the rest of their faces, and long, spindly necks covered in fleshy ridges. Still, what they lacked in cuteness, they more than made up for in personality. They pranced over to Lina and meowed eagerly, crowding one another to rub their smooth heads against her hand through the gaps in the wire.

"You can pet them," Lina said, motioning him to crouch down beside her. "They don't bite."

Ozben eyed the cats warily, but he got down on his knees and tentatively reached his fingers into the pen. Immediately, one of the cats broke off from the pack and trotted over to rub his neck against the boy.

"Whoa!" Ozben pulled his hand back, rubbing his fingers together. "They're . . . warm. Really warm."

"That's a carnelian cat for you," Lina said. "Their internal temperatures run about ten degrees hotter than a human's, and they can raise and lower their skin temperatures according to their environment." She reached up to open the door to the pen a crack, waited for one of the cats to come over, and then scooped him up, cuddling him against her chest with one hand while she shut the door to the pen with the other. "They're pretty great, like holding a blanket that's been left in front of the fire," she said.

"Amazing," Ozben breathed. It seemed like he was constantly saying that word, but he meant it every time. Lina's world was unlike any place he'd ever been before. Despite what he'd said earlier about not wanting to live underground, if things had been different—and there were no war going on—he was beginning to think he wouldn't want to leave. He'd be happy to spend his days exploring, as Lina did.

Lina held the cat securely in her arms and glanced around. Ozben noted that there were several archivists in the cavern, feeding the animals or checking on the mushroom gardens, but nobody was paying any attention to them. He followed Lina as she stood up and moved away from the pen to the far side of the room. They slipped out of the cavern through a side passage. They had their distraction, now they just had to put the little guy into place in the Gears and Steam workshop.

"I'm going to turn him loose in one of the workrooms, wait a few seconds, then run in after him as if I've chased him there all the way from the Menagerie," Lina said as they made their way down the hall. "It should cause a big enough commotion that you'll have time to slip into the Haystack and find the hand winch. But you'll have to be quick," she warned. "I'm only going to let this guy run around for a minute or so before I grab him. I don't want him to get hurt."

"I'll have enough time," Ozben assured her. He'd

been studying Lina's maps and had taken notes when she told him where the winch would be in the storage room. "Third row on the left, halfway down the aisle, bottom shelf." He had it all memorized. "I sneak in, grab the winch, and we meet back in your workshop."

"Easy as breathing," Lina said, grinning at him.

Lina stood outside the doorway of Gears and Steam's main workroom, stroking the cat's smooth skin as he wriggled in her arms. His soft purr vibrated against her chest, but all Lina was aware of was the pack of weasels wreaking havoc in her stomach. She petted the cat reflexively, just to have something to keep her hands occupied.

She'd been waiting so long to put her plan into action that, now that it was time, she found herself hesitating, and she had no idea why. The plan would work. She'd thought it out a thousand different ways, gone over everything twice with Ozben, and he'd agreed they were ready.

Lina forced herself to relax and take a breath. When she did, she felt some of her confidence return. It would work, she told herself. It wouldn't be long now.

A few minutes later, the clock on the wall of the workroom struck the hour. That was the signal for Ozben to be ready to move and for her to let the cat loose.

"Okay, boy," Lina whispered, setting the cat on the ground just outside the doorway. "Go make a little noise and have some fun. Go!"

To Lina's surprise, the cat didn't need any urging. He took off as soon as his paws hit the floor, darting inside the workroom. She waited outside and counted to ten, then, pretending to be out of breath, she tore into the room, ready to shout, "Hey, did anyone see a cat run in here?"

Before she could even open her mouth, one of the archivists cut her off, screaming, "Grab it! It's heading for the forge! Block the forge!"

The forge? What was going on? Lina tried to make sense of the chaotic scene in the workroom. About a dozen archivists were there, and every one of them had scrambled up from their worktables, knocking over benches and scattering tools all over the floor in their haste to make a grab for the carnelian cat. The creature hopped from table to table and then back down to the floor, moving steadily toward the blacksmith forge in the back of the room.

And then, as Lina looked more closely at the cat, her stomach plummeted, and she realized what had the archivists so panicked. The animal was glowing bright orange—not just his eyes but his entire body. The closer he got to the forge, the brighter he glowed.

"Oh no," Lina whispered. This was without a doubt

the worst miscalculation she'd ever made. That was her last thought before she took off running, leaping over tables just like the archivists, scrambling to reach the cat before it got too close to the open flames of the forge.

None of them made it in time.

Reaching out helplessly, Lina watched as the cat streaked between an archivist's legs and hopped up on the ledge in front of the fire.

And burst into flames.

Several facts clicked into place for Lina at that moment. Why the carnelian cats were kept separate from the other animals in the Menagerie. Why their enclosures had no wood, fabric, or other flammable materials anywhere nearby. And the most important revelation: why the archivists were studying their body temperatures so closely.

The cats' body temperature regulation was linked to the air temperature in the room, but Lina had no idea it could be taken to this extreme. As this cat got closer to the forge fire, some unknown biological mechanism activated, and the result was a living, breathing fireball sitting calmly on the ledge of the forge, scratching himself behind one ear as flames licked harmlessly along his skin.

The archivists in the workroom had formed a rough semicircle on either side of Lina, fencing the cat in. "Don't scare him," one of the men to Lina's right murmured tensely. "We need to coax him away from the fire."

Easier said than done. Now that he was bathed in orange flames, the cat seemed perfectly content to sit in front of the forge all day. But they had to do something to put that fire out before he decided to make a run for it through the stronghold, lighting fires along the way.

Suddenly, Lina heard the sound of footsteps coming up behind them, and a familiar voice yelled out to her from the doorway.

"What's all the noise in here? Winterbock, what happened?"

It was Simon. As if the situation couldn't get any worse.

"Shh!" Lina said, whirling toward him and pressing her finger to her lips.

Then Simon saw the cat, and his eyes got so big, Lina thought they would pop right out of his head. "Emergency!" he yelled. His voice carried up and down the hallway. "Technology division—emergency! We need to contain that cat!"

"Simon, don't!" Lina tried to shush him again, but it was too late. The cat, startled by the noise, bunched himself up into a ball, launched himself from the forge's ledge, and was off, streaking across the room before anyone could react.

Lina turned and sprinted across the room after the cat, tripping and bumping into the archivists as they all tried at once to cut him off from the open doorway. If they couldn't grab him barehanded, maybe they could at least turn over one of the large tables and shove it across the entry, closing off the cat's escape route. The workroom had no door to close.

But as he ran, the cat brushed against a towel hanging from one of the worktables. The fabric ignited into a ball of flames, forcing two of the cat's pursuers to break off and work to put the fire out before it spread.

This isn't good, Lina thought, trying to push down the panic that threatened to overwhelm her. She needed a plan. Wildly chasing the cat was just going to start more fires, but they couldn't let him get out of the room either.

Simon was still at the back of the room, but he'd moved into the doorway. He held a small crossbow—he must have picked it up from one of the tables—and was aiming it at the cat.

"No!" Lina screamed, horrified. "You can't kill him! Simon, don't!"

He ignored her and fired. Lina screamed again, but to her relief, the bolt went wide, skipping off the stone floor and coming to rest harmlessly under one of the tables. Simon reached for another bolt on the table, but the cat had already darted past him into the hall, leaving a streak of flames that caught the boy's pant leg. The archivists ran out of the room in pursuit.

When Lina reached Simon, he'd dropped the crossbow and was squealing and slapping the fire out. His pant leg was singed brown around the ankle, and he wore a murderous expression.

"I'm going to get that stupid cat," he growled. "Stay here, out of the way."

"What are you going to do? You can't kill him!" Lina cried. How could he even think it? She snatched the crossbow off the floor before Simon could reach for it and hurled it across the room.

"Are you crazy?" Simon made a grab for Lina's arm as if he meant to shake her, but she dodged out of the way. "If we don't stop that thing, the whole stronghold will go up in flames!"

"He's not lighting the fires on purpose," Lina shouted, "He's just scared!" And it was all her fault. She ran out into the hall and took off in the direction the cat had gone, leaving Simon shouting angrily after her.

She had to fix this before the cat got hurt or hurt someone else. So far, Simon had been the only one to try to use deadly force to stop the cat, but if the situation got any more desperate, the archivists would have no choice but to put him down for the safety of the stronghold.

With a sinking heart, Lina realized as she ran that the cat was heading for the library, the worst possible place he could choose to go. She followed a trail of small fires eating at the wall hangings in the corridor, and she passed more of the archivists who had pulled off from the chase to put them out. By now, the rest of the divisions must have been alerted to what was going on—Lina heard doors slamming up and down the corridors as the archivists tried to seal the cat off from as many rooms as they could. But the library's front entrance, like Gears and Steam's main workshop, had no doors, just an open archway of chiseled stonework. Surely, the archivists would have time to block the entryway. If only there was something in the library or the corridors leading to it that Lina could use to trap the cat or at least entice him to calm down.

Then, suddenly, she had an idea.

Lina took the next left and pelted down the corridor toward the Heart of the Mountain. If she used the tunnel she'd taken Ozben through the night they met, she could get to the museum's Special Collections wing and back in a few minutes. She just prayed that she had enough time.

≈ EIGHT ≈

Ozben had just exited the Haystack when he heard the panicked shouts of the archivists. At that moment, they were probably chasing the cat around the Gears and Steam room. Lina's distraction was working perfectly. Ozben smiled. He hadn't encountered a single person in the Haystack, and the winch was right where it was supposed to be. So far, the plan was working perfectly.

He followed the path Lina had made him memorize on her map, turning left, then right, then right again, until he finally came to a small, out-of-the-way corridor. He ran his hand along the wall, and Ozben's smile grew wider when he encountered a patch of loose stone. Right where Lina had said it would be. She really did know this place like the back of her hand.

Casting a furtive glance around, Ozben crouched

down and carefully removed the loose stones to reveal a hidden pocket in the wall. He stashed the hand winch inside it and arranged the stones back in place. They would come and get the tool later that night, when there were fewer people around.

Ozben stood up and dusted his hands off on his pants. Now all he had to do was return to the library to make sure Nirean wasn't looking for him, then meet up with Lina in his room. The plan had gone off perfectly.

"Fire! Fire!"

Ozben's heart stuttered when he heard the shout. Fire? Fire was bad. Fire was definitely not part of the plan. What was happening? Where was Lina?

It sounded as if the shouts were coming from the direction of the library. Ozben checked his disguise to make sure the bandages covering his face were secure, then moved quickly down the corridor back the way he had come. The passage eventually opened up into a larger hallway, where dozens of archivists had gathered.

"The workshops and private quarters all along this hallway have been sealed off," a woman was saying as Ozben came within earshot. "Everybody out here, fall back to the library before they barricade the entryway. I've sent five apprentices to the Garden for buckets of water if they're needed. Let's move!"

The small crowd scattered as everyone rushed to do as the woman ordered. Ozben wanted to go in the opposite direction, to the Gears and Steam workshop where he knew Lina would be, but a pair of archivists had planted themselves in the middle of the hallway to keep people away. He had no choice but to blend in with the crowd headed for the library. He slipped through the entryway with the archivists and ducked behind a nearby bookshelf. Looking up, he saw that most of the bridges connecting the bookshelves on the upper levels were deserted. Ozben ran up the closest set of stairs to the second level and looked down over the railing. From this vantage, he could see most of the main floor, but there was no sign of Lina.

The archivists had said there was a fire, but he hadn't smelled any smoke out in the corridor. And why would they barricade themselves in here? Wouldn't it be better to try to get the people outside the mountain before the fire spread?

As Ozben stood watching the archivists block the library entrance, a prickling sensation teased the back of his neck, and with it came the strong feeling that he was being watched. He spun around, but there was no one behind him in the aisle of books. He gripped the railing with one hand and rubbed the back of his neck with the other, but he couldn't banish the uneasiness that had swept over him.

And then—maybe it was instinct, or maybe he caught movement at the edge of his vision—he happened to glance up at the bridge that crossed the chamber several stories above him. There, in the shadows by the metal railing, a figure crouched. Ozben swallowed hard as a sudden rush of blood pounded in his ears, drowning out the shouts of the archivists and the bustle and chaos below him.

The figure was dressed from head to foot in black and was nearly invisible where he crouched on the bridge. Ozben might not have seen him at all if not for the sudden gleam of the lumatites on the wall reflecting off the silver tip of a crossbow bolt. It was pointed right at his chest.

Time stood still.

Run. Run! Ozben screamed at himself, but his feet wouldn't move. Somehow, he managed to turn his head and saw at the end of the bridge a table situated against the far wall. The chairs around it had been pushed aside by the last people to sit there, leaving a little gap underneath.

A tiny space of safety.

Ozben's body reacted before his mind had fully formed an intention. He broke into a run and dove under the table just as the twang of the crossbow filled his ears.

Lina pounded down the corridors toward the library, legs aching, the breath burning in her lungs. In her hands, she clutched the Sun Sphere she'd taken from the Special Collections wing of the museum. Its flame flickered and danced as she ran, but it never went out.

One of the archivists, Edlind, had caught her taking the sphere from its alcove, but she'd managed to outrun him in the Heart of the Mountain. For that stunt, she was likely going to land back in the Menagerie scooping cow dung for the rest of the year, but at the moment, Lina didn't care. All she cared about was getting back to the carnelian cat before Simon and his crossbow.

Lina slowed when she heard the voices of some archivists up ahead of her. Rounding the corner, she saw what she'd been dreading: two archivists had cornered the cat in a small alcove near the library entrance, which by now had been blocked off from the inside. One of the archivists had a crossbow, and the other had a net that looked as if it was made out of some sort of soft wire. The cat crouched in a corner, still on fire, hissing and spitting sparks off his tail.

"Wait!" Lina cried, trying to stop them before they could move in on the frightened animal. "I have an idea."

The two archivists exchanged doubtful glances. The one with the net said, "Better stay back, apprentice. If he jumps at you, he'll burn you. There's no way to get him calmed down."

"Yes, there is," Lina said. With shaking hands, she held up the Sun Sphere. "Remember, he's drawn to fire."

The flaming sphere wasn't nearly as hot as the forge, but Lina reasoned that it would be at least as enticing as a cat toy.

"Where did you get that?" The archivist with the net squinted at the sphere. "Hey, is that from—"

"Never mind where it came from!" Lina snapped. "I don't want the cat to be hurt. At least let me try to calm him down. If it doesn't work, you can use the net. *Please.*"

The archivists exchanged another look, but Lina didn't wait for permission. She moved forward until she was standing directly in front of the carnelian cat.

Heat radiated from the alcove, making Lina wince. If anything, the cat had gotten hotter than when he had first jumped up on the forge. But if that was true, it had to mean the environment wasn't the only thing that could change his body temperature. *It must be the stress of being chased*, Lina thought, and a fresh wave of guilt washed over her. How could she have been so stupid? She should have researched the cats much more thoroughly before going and grabbing one to use as a distraction. She shook her head and forced the guilt aside. She needed to focus on getting the cat out of this safely.

"Easy, boy," she said, trying to make her voice as soothing as possible. The cat wasn't having any of it. He continued to hiss and spit sparks as Lina went down on one knee in front of him. "I know you're upset, but it's all right. There's nothing to be scared of now." Once she was on her knees, she stopped moving, but she kept right on talking to the cat, letting him hear her voice.

Beside her, the archivists watched, tense and ready with net and crossbow. Lina wanted to ask them to move back so they weren't crowding the cat, but she knew they wouldn't do it. They couldn't take the chance that he would bolt again.

Footsteps bounded up the corridor behind her. Lina glanced over her shoulder and saw Simon, his crossbow at the ready. Well, she was ready for him too.

"Simon, if you take another step or point that cross-bow anywhere near this cat," Lina warned, keeping her voice calm, "the next time you leave Ortana with Councilman Tolwin, I'm going to plant dralfa moss all over your room."

She was gratified to hear him let out a small gasp. "You wouldn't," Simon growled.

"Oh, you better believe I would. Every crack and crevice will be filled with the stuff," she promised him. She kept up her soothing tone of voice so she wouldn't scare the cat. "All of your clothes—bright purple stains forever. Now, stay still back there and keep quiet."

Lina could practically feel the older boy's anger, like a second wall of heat at her back, but he didn't come any closer. In fact, he took a few steps backward down the hall. Lina breathed a quiet sigh of relief, though she knew it was only a temporary reprieve. He'd given her some space to work, but his patience wouldn't last, even under the threat of dralfa moss.

As Lina turned her attention back to the cat, she thought she detected a break in the heat. The animal was still balled up in the corner, eyeing her warily, but he wasn't hissing anymore. Flames danced around his face and neck, making his big orange eyes glow like twin bright suns.

Then, Lina noticed that the cat was no longer looking at her. His attention was instead fixed on the Sun Sphere she clutched in her hands. His head bobbed back and forth as it followed the hovering flame inside the metal rings, completely enthralled.

"That's it," Lina whispered. "Look at that sparkly light. Pretty great, huh?"

Slowly, the cat relaxed its arched back and took a hesitant step out of the alcove. His eyes never strayed from the sphere. Lina shuffled backward to give him some room, but he didn't seem to notice. He reached out a paw and took a swipe at the metal sphere. Hope surged in Lina. Carefully, she passed the sphere back and forth between her hands, letting the cat paw at the hovering flame.

That's it. Just a game between friends. No need to be afraid.

Silence reigned in the corridor as she, Simon, and

the archivists held their collective breath. Lina imagined the whole stronghold standing still. She was so focused on distracting the cat with the Sun Sphere that minutes passed before she noticed that the flames enveloping him were beginning to diminish. The more they played with the sphere, the calmer the cat seemed. Soon there were only a few fitful sparks coming from his tail. Lina decided it was now or never. Carefully, she reached out a hand.

"Come on, boy," she said, coaxing him to her. "That's enough excitement for one day, don't you think? Time to go home."

Alternating between watching her hand and the sphere, the cat ambled forward and nudged at Lina's fingers. His head was still warm from the heat but not uncomfortably so. Lina scratched him under the chin and was rewarded with a soft, contented purr. Then the cat began rubbing his whole body against her, and Lina knew it was time to make her move. Trembling a little, she wrapped her arms around the cat and scooped him up in her arms.

And just like that, the danger passed. Lina allowed herself such a sigh of relief that it made her dizzy.

"Well done," the archivist with the net said, patting her gently on the shoulder. In all the excitement, Lina hadn't recognized him, but now she realized it was Feldwon, one of the senior archivists, who was in charge of the Menagerie. He was a tall, thin-faced man in his late thirties, with bright blue eyes and big lumpy calluses on his hands. He bent down and picked up the Sun Sphere, handing it to his partner with the crossbow. "I don't know how he got out of the pen," Feldwon said to Lina, shaking his head. "He must have found a hole somewhere in the enclosure fence."

Hearing the words, Lina felt a mixture of relief and shame churning in her stomach. No one had seen what she and Ozben had done. It looked like the cat had only damaged a few wall hangings and some towels in the Gears and Steam workshop, but it could have been so much worse. If he had managed to get into the library, he could have devastated the stronghold in a matter of minutes. And Simon, in his anger and panic, had almost killed the cat to keep that from happening.

Never again, Lina vowed. Trying to understand the mysterious artifacts the archivists collected was difficult enough, but she would never again be so careless with a living thing.

"I can take the cat back to the Menagerie for you," Lina offered. Up and down the corridor, doors were opening as Simon and the archivist with the crossbow called out that all was clear. Lina didn't want too many people crowding around and scaring the cat further.

Feldwon nodded. "Come on, then." He led the way back past the Gears and Steam workshop. Lina walked past Simon, ignoring the glower he threw her way.

"Winterbock!" he called out to her.

Lina stopped and turned to face him, careful to keep a secure grip on the cat. "Leave me alone, Simon," she said curtly. She wasn't in the mood to play their usual game of insults.

An unfamiliar expression crossed the senior apprentice's face then, a mixture of anger and some other emotion that Lina couldn't read. Was it— No, she was surely imagining things. If she didn't know any better, she'd say Simon almost looked ashamed.

"I didn't want to . . ." He trailed off and bit his lip, not meeting her eyes. "I wasn't going to kill the cat," he finished in a rush. His face was turning bright red, and he stared at the floor. "I fired at him in the workshop, but I wasn't really aiming for him. I just knew we had to stop him somehow."

His words caught Lina completely off guard. Why was Simon telling her this? Why would he care what she thought of him? He'd never shown anything but contempt for her before.

"None of this is the cat's fault," she said.

Simon looked up and managed to meet her eyes. "No, it's not," he agreed. "But you caught the cat. So everything's all right."

Lina nodded, but she was too shocked to respond. Simon had never given her anything resembling a compliment before, yet it sounded as if he'd come close just now. Maybe the smoke from the fires had made his head fuzzy.

As the silence stretched between them, Simon's face got even redder. "All right, then, what are you still standing there for?" he snapped. "Get going, and don't let go of that cat for anything, even if it lights you on fire."

Now, that was more like the Simon she knew. Still puzzled by his behavior, Lina turned and resumed walking down the corridor.

When she arrived back at the Menagerie, the archivists were examining the pen as the two other cats watched the proceedings curiously. Lina tried not to look guilty as she walked over to them.

As Feldwon reached for the latch on the door, the two cats suddenly let out a loud yowling sound and started hissing at her. Lina took a step back, even though Feldwon hadn't yet opened the door.

"What's wrong with them?" she asked, shocked by the sudden change in the cats' behavior. Did they smell something on her, a scent from the Gears and Steam room that they didn't like? No, it couldn't be that. The cat in her arms was calm and happy, purring as it laid its head on her shoulder.

Feldwon's brow wrinkled in consternation as he looked from Lina to the other cats. He shook his head. "I was afraid of that," he said. "The cat's scent has changed. He's out of alignment."

"What do you mean?" Lina asked. "They sound like they're mad at him." She stroked the cat in her arms.

"We don't fully understand the science involved," Feldwon said, frowning, "but it has something to do with the cats' body chemistry. We know that keeping their temperatures regulated is important not just to prevent them from the self-immolation you witnessed but also to keep harmony within the group."

"You mean because this one's body temperature got out of sync with the others, they don't want him around anymore?" Lina couldn't believe what she was hearing. "Maybe they just need time to adjust to him, like getting used to a new scent or something."

Feldwon shook his head. "I'm afraid if we put him in there now, the other two will attack him. I can't take the risk. I'll have to arrange a separate pen for him from now on."

"But he's always been in a pen with other cats," Lina said, her voice rising. She stroked the cat's neck, holding him protectively against her chest. "He won't like being by himself."

"I realize that, but it's better than the alternative," Feldwon said sadly. "If you wouldn't mind holding him for a bit longer, I'll go and see about cleaning out one of the transport cages. He can sleep there until we get a new pen built."

Now they were going to put him in a *cage*? Lina was

too stunned to do anything but nod as Feldwon moved off, calling out orders to the other apprentices within earshot.

No, she couldn't let this happen. The cat shouldn't have to suffer because she'd been a selfish idiot. There had to be a better solution than putting him in a cage off by himself. He just needed a place to live where there were no huge sources of heat like the forge and no rooms full of flammable objects.

Lina looked down into the creature's huge orange eyes as he meowed in her arms. An idea came to her. A place where there were no large fires. Her workshop. Of course. She should have thought of it immediately.

"Feldwon," she called, hurrying over to the archivist just as he was finishing giving instructions to an apprentice. "I know what we can do with the cat," she said. "Please, will you let me speak to Councilwoman Zara?"

Ozben landed hard on his stomach and rolled until he banged against the bookshelf. He flopped onto his back, staring up at the underside of the library table. Instinctively, he looked down at himself, running his hands frantically over his chest, arms, and legs, making sure that no crossbow bolts were sticking out of him. It took him a full minute to realize he was fine. The assassin had missed him.

When his breathing steadied and he could start to think clearly again, Ozben shifted onto his side, careful to stay under the protection of the table. He listened for the sound of approaching footsteps. Was he trapped? Would the assassin come down to hunt for him? There was only one way to know.

Ozben leaned forward and cautiously peeked out from under the edge of the table. His heart stuttered in his chest. A crossbow bolt was stuck in the wooden bookshelf nearest the bridge where he'd been standing only seconds ago. If he hadn't turned around and seen the assassin when he did, the bolt would be protruding from his chest right now.

His mind raced even as he tried to quell the panic that rose inside him. How could this be happening? He'd been so sure he was safe here. His parents and the archivists had been so careful to keep his identity a secret, giving him a disguise and hiding him away in the last place anyone in Solace should have ever thought to look for him. Yet here he was, hunkered down under a table, a hairsbreadth from a crossbow bolt skewering him.

The assassin had not only seen through his disguise; he'd known exactly where Ozben would be—in the library. That meant he'd probably been watching him for some time, waiting for the perfect opportunity to strike. And what better moment than in the midst of a crisis that had all the archivists running around distracted? As frightened as he was by these revelations, the question remained: how had the assassin found him, and what was Ozben going to do now?

He couldn't stay under this table; that much was certain. He had to find some better cover or a place to hide in case the assassin tried to come down to finish the job. But when he risked another glance out from under the table and toward the upper levels, Ozben saw that the man in black was gone. The assassin had disappeared.

"We're all clear!" called a voice from the doorway. "The cat's contained. They got him back to the Menagerie. The danger's past."

Ozben crawled to the other side of the table and looked down toward the library entrance. Some of the archivists were taking down the barricade while others clustered in the foyer, talking excitedly about what had just happened in the hallway. From what Ozben could tell, it involved Lina, one of the carnelian cats—and the Sun Sphere.

At least it meant Lina was safe. He had to find her, tell her she was right all along about the assassin, and find out what was going on. But first he had to go to Councilwoman Zara and Nirean. They needed to know that an assassin had invaded their home, and no one was safe.

Ozben crawled to the edge of the table and checked the upper bridges again. The shadows there were just shadows. No crossbow bolts pointed at him. Still, Ozben couldn't calm his racing heart. He told himself the assassin probably wouldn't risk trying to kill him a second time today, not when things were starting to settle downstairs. One of the archivists might see, and the chances he'd be caught were much greater.

No, the assassin—or assassins, if more than one had infiltrated the stronghold—had learned from the attack on the palace. He would be patient and bide his time until Ozben was alone again.

With that grim thought, the sense of safety Ozben had felt within the stronghold's cavernous halls vanished. He was terrified and furious at the same time. Assassins had threatened his family, chased him from his home, and now they'd destroyed the small bit of happiness he had carved out for himself in Lina's world.

Lina. Just by being near him, she was in danger too. All the more reason for him to leave the stronghold as soon as possible. They had to carry out Lina's plan to get inside the *Merlin*. Somehow, he would find a way to use the ship to get home.

Galvanized, Ozben scurried out from under the table, pausing only long enough to retrieve the assassin's crossbow bolt from the bookshelf so he could show it to Zara and Nirean. A shudder coursed through him when he closed his fingers around the bolt's shaft. He didn't want to think about how close he'd come to having it sticking out of him.

Making his way down the stairs, Ozben joined

a crowd of archivists waiting to get out of the library. He heard the people standing closest to him murmuring that some of the tapestries hanging in the corridors had caught fire. The archivists wanted to make sure they were out before they let people back into the halls.

For fifteen agonizing minutes, Ozben waited at the back of the crowd and kept watch for any sign of the assassin. He didn't want to draw attention to himself by getting impatient, but he wished they'd hurry up. Sweat ran rivers down his back. Every second he was exposed in the large, open room he expected to feel a crossbow bolt bury itself in his back.

Finally, one of the librarians, a middle-aged man with a thick gray beard and reading glasses sliding down his nose, made the announcement that all was well. People could return to their workshops and dormitories whenever they wished.

Ozben forced himself not to run as he exited the library and moved along the corridor in the direction of Councilwoman Zara's office. The whole way, he clutched the crossbow bolt in front of him as if it were a poisonous snake, and watched the shadows for hidden enemies.

NINE

"You have to let me do this," Lina insisted. "I know I can take care of him."

Zara stood behind her large oak desk, holding a stack of papers in her hand. Her office was sparsely furnished, containing just the desk, a white stone fireplace in the corner, and bookshelves flanking the door. The whole room smelled of wood smoke and old paper.

"Mucking out the stalls in the Menagerie doesn't qualify you to care for a dangerous animal," Zara said.

Lina had expected to meet with resistance when she told her teacher her plan to care for the carnelian cat herself, especially when she left out a key detail. She hadn't wanted to tell Zara about her workshop, so she'd been vague about where exactly she'd be keeping the cat, only that it was someplace safe and fireproof. She hadn't counted on Zara being quite so immovable.

"He's a cat," Lina said, as if it weren't obvious. "He'd never intentionally hurt anyone."

"Intent doesn't matter when you can turn into a fireball," Zara said. "What if he gets away from you? He could destroy the stronghold." She laid aside the stack of papers and sat down. "Speaking of fireballs," she said, folding her hands on the desk, "what possessed you to take the Sun Sphere from the Special Collections wing? I've already had Edlind in here screaming at me that you tore up his whole department."

"He's exaggerating," Lina said indignantly. "And I would have asked to borrow it, but there wasn't time. I had to get back before the cat reached the library—and before Simon got to him," she added. She was still angry with Simon for trying to kill the cat.

"And it never occurred to you that it might be extremely dangerous to bring the cat into contact with an artifact we don't fully understand?" Zara asked sternly. "That's why we keep them separate from the rest of the museum."

"I'm sorry, but I told you, I didn't have time to come up with a better plan. And those artifacts have been tested a hundred different ways," Lina argued. "There's nothing dangerous about them."

Zara shook her head, still wearing that implacable expression. "Learning respect and care for the things we don't understand is at the core of our principles. You'll never become a proper archivist until you understand that."

As her teacher lectured, Lina couldn't help remembering what Ozben had said the night she'd shown him the Sun Sphere, the changing storybook, and the memory jar. How could she really know that those artifacts were harmless, he'd asked her. He'd been right, of course. She couldn't know. Just as she hadn't known that the carnelian cat was a potential threat to the stronghold. In her ignorance, she'd inadvertently put him and the whole of her community in danger.

Mistake after mistake—they were piling up in a great heap of misery inside Lina. She didn't know what she was doing anymore.

"Is that why you stopped teaching me?" she asked abruptly, her face turning red with shame. "Because I'm reckless, and you think I won't make a proper archivist?" It was the question she'd been secretly wanting to ask Zara for a while but hadn't had the courage to. She stared at the wood whorls in Zara's desk, unable to meet the older woman's eyes.

Zara made a noise of surprise. "Of course not. I've never thought that. Well," she amended, "reckless, yes—I've thought that on many occasions. But I've always believed you'd make a wonderful archivist."

She said it so firmly that Lina almost thought she was telling the truth, but doubt still nibbled at the back of her mind. Then why had Zara stopped her lessons and pulled away from Lina? She still didn't believe it was all because of the war.

Lost in thought, Lina jumped when the door to Zara's office banged open. She turned in time to see Ozben burst into the room and hastily shut the door behind him. He leaned against the wood, chest rising and falling rapidly. Even with the bandages covering parts of his face, Lina could see that he was in a panic.

Before either Lina or Zara could react, Ozben spoke. "Sorry," he said. "The door was unlocked, and I needed—" He stopped when he caught sight of Lina, and surprise registered on his face.

"It's all right," Zara said quickly. "Lina, we'll discuss this later. For now, I want you to go back to your room. Lina, do you hear me?"

But Lina wasn't paying attention to Zara anymore. Her gaze flicked from the crossbow bolt clutched in Ozben's hand to her friend's face. A knot of cold dread formed in her stomach. "What is it?" she demanded. "What happened?"

"Lina." Now there was a note of warning in Zara's voice. "I told you to leave."

Ozben tried to summon a grin, but it wavered and fell away. "I had some trouble in the library," he began. "There was someone—" He paused, swallowed, and tried again. "An assassin came after me."

"No!" Lina crossed the room to Ozben and put a hand on his shoulder. "You were alone," she said in a choked voice. "I didn't even think about someone trying to attack you." She blinked back tears. Goddess. Mistake after mistake.

"I'm all right," Ozben assured her, again trying to summon a grin, this time with a little more success. "I should have listened to you about the assassin, though—to all of you," he added, looking at Zara.

With a jolt, Lina realized that Zara was now aware that Lina knew Ozben's identity. But right now she didn't care. She was more worried about her friend.

For her part, Zara seemed momentarily stunned. She stared at Ozben, Lina, and the crossbow bolt. Shock and disbelief spread across her face, but she quickly gathered herself and came out from behind her desk, striding over to where they stood. She took the crossbow bolt from Ozben.

"Are you sure you're all right?" she asked. "You're not injured?" Without waiting for Ozben to reply, Zara took him by the shoulder and turned him, examining the back of his head and neck, as if she expected to find some hidden wound.

"Really, I'm fine," he said. "He only fired at me once, and he disappeared right afterward."

"Where?" Zara said sharply. "Where did this happen?"

"The library," Ozben said. "I think he knew I'd be there."

"He must have been watching you these past few weeks," Zara said, her eyes narrowed. "He knows that's where you've been going. Both of you stay put." She walked over to the door and opened it, looking up and down the hallway before calling out to someone they couldn't see. "Apprentice, a moment," she said, beckoning with her hand. "I need you to go find Nirean and bring her here immediately. Hurry, now!"

Lina heard a muffled reply and then footsteps running off down the corridor. Zara shut the door, locking it from the inside.

"What are you going to do?" Lina asked.

Zara looked up at her absently, as if she'd forgotten Lina was still in the room. Then her gaze sharpened. "How much do you know?" she asked. "Don't lie to me, Lina. Not now."

"Everything," Lina said, glancing at Ozben. "I know who he is and what he's doing here."

"I suppose I don't need to ask how." Zara sighed. "Eavesdropping again, were you?"

"It was my fault," Ozben said, coming to Lina's defense. "I said my name and—"

"But you didn't know I was listening in," Lina interrupted. She faced her teacher and braced for a storm. "I'm sorry. I did exactly what you told me not to."

"We'll address that later," Zara said. "What I want to know right now is: did you tell anyone?"

Surprise and hurt heated Lina's cheeks. "Of course not!" she said. How could Zara think that? "I shouldn't have eavesdropped, but I'm not sorry I met Ozben. He's my friend, and I would never betray his secret."

"She's right. And I don't regret it either," Ozben said. He smiled at Lina, and she felt a bit of her misery slip away.

"All right. That's good." Zara nodded. She turned to Ozben. "Your Highness, I apologize. We were complacent, and you almost lost your life because of it. That won't happen again. We're going to put more guards with you, which means we'll have to tell more of the chamelins your secret." She scowled. "We'll have to bring some of them back from their scouting patrols. Goddess, this couldn't have come at a worse time."

"Why?" Lina asked, suddenly worried. "What are the chamelins out scouting for? Are the Merrow Kingdom's armies getting closer?"

"They are, but that's not what the chamelins are looking for. The weather's taken a turn for the worse," Zara explained. "We've had more snowfall and storms in the last week than we've seen all year. It's making it difficult for the refugees to reach us. If they can't find the bridges to get to our gates, more often than not they end up lost in the mountain passes, and that's no place to be during a blizzard. The chamelins are out looking for the lost ones to guide them to us."

Ozben's brow furrowed with worry. "If the weather's that bad, you can't bring the chamelins back here just to protect me. I'm only one person, and there are hundreds of refugees out there. They could freeze to death if they get lost."

Zara shook her head. "Don't worry, we won't bring all the scouts back, just enough to cover you. You'll need to stay in your room from now on so we can ensure your safety."

"What?" Ozben cried. "But—"

"It will be fine," Zara cut him off. "We'll move you to a more secure area, and Nirean or one of the other chamelins will be with you all the time. No assassins will be able to get near you, I promise."

Ozben looked at Lina helplessly. She knew what he was thinking. They would never be able to open the airship if the chamelins were with Ozben day and night. The risks they'd taken, and that pile of mistakes—it had all been for nothing in the end. Lina wanted to protest, but Zara was right. They had to keep Ozben safe.

But was Zara right about surrounding him with guards? Lina had lived in the mountains all her life, and she knew they were an unforgiving place in a storm. The fewer eyes there were out looking for the refugees, the greater the risk that the people trying to reach the stronghold would be lost and freeze to death in the cold.

Besides that, would the extra guards do any good against the assassins? She remembered what Ozben told her about the night they'd broken into the palace in Ardra. There had been plenty of guards then, and it hadn't stopped the assassins. Would the chamelins really be able to protect Ozben, or was there another way?

"Zara, wait," Lina said as an idea formed in her mind. "I think I may have a better plan to protect Ozben."

But Zara wasn't listening. "When Nirean gets here, she can escort you to your new room," she said to Ozben. She walked back to her desk, examining the crossbow bolt in her hands. "I'll study this bolt myself. It might lead us to the assassin."

"Zara," Lina repeated, louder this time. "You have to listen to me."

"Lina, I don't have time right now," Zara said tersely. "Didn't I tell you to go back to your room?"

Lina shook her head stubbornly. "If you put Ozben in a room and stack guards outside his door, the assassin's going to know exactly where he is," she said. "He won't be safe at all."

Zara was still examining the crossbow bolt, her lip curled in disgust as she touched its wicked point. "It doesn't matter if he knows where Ozben is," she said. "The best assassin in the world will think twice before taking on a group of chamelins while they're shape-shifted."

"Oh, really?" Lina looked at Ozben. "Weren't you

surrounded by skilled fighters at your palace? And people still got killed."

"It's true," Ozben said. His voice dropped. "I don't want anyone else to die, Zara—not Nirean or any of the other chamelins."

"I understand, and your concern does you credit, Your Highness, but you're our responsibility," Zara said. "The archivists promised your parents we would keep you safe."

"That's what I'm trying to do," Lina insisted. "All I'm asking is that you listen."

"All right, all right." Zara sighed loudly and raised her hands in surrender. She laid the crossbow bolt on her desk. "What are you proposing?" she asked, sounding reluctant.

"That we hide Ozben," Lina said, "with me." She fidgeted, clasping and unclasping her hands as she spoke. Explaining the plan was going to be the tricky part. She didn't want to reveal too much to Zara. "I know a place," she continued, "somewhere the assassin won't be able to go."

"Where?" Zara asked, and frowned when Lina shook her head. "You have to tell me where, Lina."

"I can't," Lina insisted. "Besides, the fewer people who know, the better. Isn't that the best way to guarantee Ozben's safety?"

"This is different," Zara said, crossing her arms. "I can't let you take him somewhere when I don't know where you're going. You'll both be in terrible danger, with no one to protect you."

Ozben glanced at Lina, and the two of them shared a look. His eyes brightened, first with surprise and then excitement as he guessed the hiding place she was hinting at. "We won't need protection," he said. "Lina's right. No assassin will be able to get to us there. It's the best hiding place in the whole stronghold."

"You've seen this place, Ozben?" Zara's eyes narrowed in suspicion. "How long have you been sneaking off under our noses, then?"

"Just the once," Ozben assured her. "But it's a good place. Think about it. If I'm hidden, you'll be free to help the refugees and hunt for the assassin at the same time he's looking for me. Sooner or later, he'll show himself."

Zara didn't reply, but she looked thoughtful, which Lina took as a hopeful sign. Maybe she really was considering the idea.

But after a moment, Zara shook her head. "I can't agree unless I know where this hiding place is," she said.

Lina's shoulders slumped with disappointment. "Why won't you trust me?" she asked, trying to keep the tremor out of her voice.

"Trust has to go both ways, Lina," Zara said calmly. "If you want me to trust you with the huge responsibility of hiding Ozben, I have to know where, in case something goes wrong."

"But . . ." Torn, Lina looked to Ozben for inspiration. He knew better than anyone what she risked by confiding in Zara. Even if she couldn't take her teacher there through the tiny Hourglass passage, revealing the location of her workshop brought the archivists a step closer to her hidden world. But if she didn't tell, she lost the chance to keep Ozben safe.

Ozben smiled at her sadly and lifted his shoulders in a helpless shrug, as if to say, *It's up to you.* Lina nodded and tried to push down the fear churning in her gut. There was no choice. She had to convince Zara that this was the right thing to do.

"I want to take Ozben to my workshop," Lina said. "It's in a hidden cave near the museum. I'll show you and Nirean the access tunnel—*only* the two of you. It's too small for anyone bigger than me or Ozben to get through."

"All right," Zara said. "And this is where you've been going all those times you disappear?"

Lina nodded. "I like to be alone down there, that's all."

Looking closely at Zara, Lina could tell she didn't quite believe that was Lina's only purpose, but for whatever reason, she didn't press the point. Instead, she said, "And you're sure no one bigger than you and Ozben can get down there?"

"You'll see for yourself," Lina said. She hesitated.

Might as well go all the way with this plan. "That's where I want to take the carnelian cat too," she added.

"Don't push it," Zara said, a warning in her voice.

"They'd be away from everything dangerous, I promise you," Lina said. "No forge fires, no flammable objects, and no assassins. And if anything happens, I can come out and tell you and Nirean. The assassins aren't looking for me, so I can still move around the stronghold freely. It's the perfect situation."

Zara sighed again and rubbed her hand across her forehead. Lina would have given anything to know what she was thinking in that moment, but she could only wait, her heart pounding, as Zara considered her plan.

Finally, she looked at Lina and Ozben and held up her index finger. "First: the cat. Feldwon is in charge of the Menagerie, so he gets to decide," she said. "Make your case, and if he says no, that's the end of it. But if you can convince him, I'll agree to let you care for the cat temporarily until he can go back to living with the other animals. All right?"

Lina nodded vigorously. "I'll talk Feldwon into it," she said.

"I imagine you will," Zara said dryly. She held up another finger. "Second: Ozben. In light of the situation with the storms and the refugees, I'm willing to try your hiding plan for a few days, but with conditions. I'm assigning a guard to patrol the area around the entrance to the workshop to watch for trouble." She looked at Lina, and her severe expression thawed a bit. "Your idea is a good one. If Ozben's safe and hidden, Nirean and I can track this assassin, maybe even set up a trap using a decoy. But if there's any sign of trouble, we're pulling you out and putting Ozben under lock and key—no argument. Is that understood?"

Lina and Ozben both nodded. Lina could hardly believe it. She'd convinced Zara, and more than that, her teacher had actually *liked* her idea.

But now that it was settled, questions and fears filled Lina's mind. At least one assassin was out there in the stronghold right now—in her home—and he was stalking her friend.

"I still don't understand how the assassin found Ozben," Lina said. "He must have had help, someone to tell him where Ozben was going." Her expression turned grim. "Or someone at the stronghold told him." Her stomach clenched. She didn't like to think that one of her own people would betray them.

"I don't know how he discovered that Ozben was here. It doesn't do us any good to speculate until we know more," Zara said. But Lina could tell by her teacher's face that she was worried. If there was a traitor somewhere in the stronghold, they were all in danger.

And they couldn't trust anyone.

⇒ TEN ⇐

Four days later, Lina stood at her worktable, inspecting the hand winch that she and Ozben had risked so much to acquire. She'd removed it from the hidden pocket in the wall where Ozben had left it and brought it with her to the workshop when the two of them had gone into hiding. They'd spent the next few days settling into their new, temporary home and recovering from the turmoil of the assassin's attack.

Lina knew how lucky she was. She and Ozben were safely hidden in her workshop, they had the hand winch, and they were free to use it. It looked as if they were on the verge of clearing the boulders blocking the airship's door. The carnelian cat wound himself through Lina's legs, purring contentedly and leaving little trails of heat in his wake.

Feldwon had been skeptical of her plan at first, but

he had a soft heart, and Lina knew he didn't want to put the cat in a cage by himself any more than she did. He'd given her a mesh screen to block the entrance to her workshop so the cat wouldn't wander back up the tunnels, and he'd made her promise to let him know at once if the cat became too much to care for. She'd lit a small fire in the fire pit to keep her and Ozben warm, but nothing that would cause the cat to burst into flame if he walked near it.

Everything had worked out the way Lina had hoped. Yet she felt awful.

Lina reached down to stroke the cat's smooth flank. When she stood up, she banged her fist down on her worktable. At the sound, the cat darted under the table.

"Sorry, Aethon," Lina said, abashed. The name had been Ozben's suggestion, from a book of collected mythologies he'd been reading in the library.

Ozben, who'd been looking at the boulders wedged against the ship's door, called out to her, "What was that for?"

"Nothing. I'm fine." She turned and leaned against her worktable, hugging herself and pulling her heavy coat closed to ward off the chill she felt in the absence of the cat's heat. "I'm sorry," she said. "I should have come up with a better way to get the hand winch."

"What do you mean?" He stood up and walked over to her, his brow furrowed. "The plan worked, didn't it? We got the winch, and the assassin missed his target."

Lina shook her head. "As an apprentice, the first lesson I learned is to never take anything for granted when dealing with things from other worlds. Don't assume anything, and be three times as careful as you think you need to be. I should have made sure I knew everything there was to know about the carnelian cats, but I didn't. I just rushed in and took advantage of them, and look what happened. Aethon might never be able to go back to be with the other cats, and I created the perfect opportunity for an assassin to go after you."

"The assassin isn't your fault," Ozben said firmly. "He would have found me no matter what. As for Aethon—well, I'm no expert, but he doesn't look all that unhappy to me."

"That's not the point." Lina tried to extricate herself from Aethon, who'd wandered back over to her and was enthusiastically brushing against her legs and making loud purring noises that echoed through the quiet cavern. "I should have been more careful. Remember that night on the staircase in the museum? You asked me how the archivists knew those objects weren't dangerous if they didn't fully understand how they worked."

"I remember," Ozben said, nodding. "You told me it was because they'd been tested over and over."

"For *years*," Lina confirmed. "But we're even more cautious with living things. Most of the time, they don't survive the passage from their world to ours, but when they do, there's a chance they could upset the balance of Solace's ecosystem, so the archivists try really hard to make sure any living things that survive the meteor storms end up here." To do that, the archivists routinely sent expeditions to the scrap towns to watch out for people selling plants and animals at the trade markets, and they made it known that they'd double any offer made for them by a potential buyer.

"I never knew that," Ozben said, surprised. "I guess it's hard to imagine what would happen if the carnelian cats were running around free in Solace." He reached down and petted Aethon. "I mean, did this little guy really catch on fire?"

"Sort of," Lina said. "Feldwon's theory is that the cats originally came from a world with a lot of volcanic activity and that, over the centuries, they developed adaptations to allow them to survive the extreme temperatures while at the same time developing a defense mechanism against predators. So when they're exposed to extreme heat, they're able to self-immolate—it's a protective instinct." When she'd put Aethon down outside the Gears and Steam workshop, in the unfamiliar environment, he was drawn to the fire to create a defense in case something came after him. Once he was away from the fire and finally calmed down, the flames went away.

"Amazing," Ozben said, letting out a soft whistle. "I would never have guessed he had that kind of power inside him." He looked thoughtfully at the cat. "You know,

I've always wondered why it happens," he said. "How do these things end up in Solace? Do the archivists know that?"

"Not for sure," Lina said. "Some people believe that when the goddess left the world after she created Solace, she tore a hole in the sky, and that's where the objects come from. Other people think the objects are things that were forgotten in their own worlds, lost by the people who used to own them, so they fell out of those worlds and into ours."

For her part, Lina believed the second theory, and her work with the otherworldly artifacts was also a promise: *I will restore you and care for you. I won't ever let you be forgotten.*

She gazed at the *Merlin* as she spoke. Here was another artifact that was full of mysteries, something to treat with great care. But for the first time since she'd found the ship, Lina wondered whether she was doing the right thing, keeping its existence hidden from the archivists. What if it turned out to be dangerous and unpredictable too, like the carnelian cats?

No, she couldn't believe that. True, the ship was a mystery, but it wasn't dangerous. She had no proof, but she felt it deep in her bones.

Silence fell in the cavern except for Aethon's constant, rhythmic purring as he sauntered back and forth between them, bumping their legs to get attention. With an effort, Lina pushed aside her doubts and anger at herself. She couldn't change what had happened, but at least she could make the sacrifice count for something. They had the hand winch. It was time to use it.

"Come on," she said, "we're wasting time. We have a ship to open."

Ozben's face split into a wide grin. "Now you're talking. And you said we can use Lumpy—that's the boulder with all the bumps and dents in it, right?—to attach the winch. It should be secure."

"Let's do it." Lina carried the hand winch over to the ship, and together they began looping the thick metal wire around the boulder. When she was sure it was fastened tightly enough, Lina handed the crank part to Ozben. "Fasten it to the stalagmite over there," she said, pointing across the chamber.

"Got it," Ozben said, moving to do as she instructed.

While he worked on the other end, Lina ran back to her worktable and retrieved her pry bar and fulcrum. She put the fulcrum in place as best she could at the base of the boulder and wedged the pry bar on top of it. Now that they were so close, her heart was beating fast, and her palms were slick with sweat as she gripped the bar. She'd been trying not to get her hopes up in case they failed, but she couldn't help it.

Please let this work. Please.

She glanced across the cavern at Ozben. His eyes

gleamed in the glow of her candles. "I'm all set over here," he said, sounding breathless in his excitement. "You ready?"

Lina swallowed and nodded. "Tell me if you get tired turning the crank, and I'll take over for you."

He sniffed and grinned at her. "I won't get tired. Just watch."

He started turning the crank. The thick wire connecting the boulder and the stalagmite pulled taut, and Lina pushed down on the pry bar with all her strength, trying to lever it away from the door.

Sweat broke out on her forehead as her muscles strained. Her hands slipped on the pry bar, and she had to wipe them on her pants, adjusting to get a better grip. The metallic *clink clink clink* of the crank turning, along with Ozben's breathing, were the only sounds in the chamber. Aethon, perhaps sensing that something momentous was happening, had retreated beneath the worktable, where he sat curled up in a ball, watching intently with his glowing orange eyes.

Minutes passed, and the muscles in Lina's arms began to ache. Her shoulders quivered, a telltale sign that she was losing strength. She wouldn't be able to hold down the pry bar much longer, and she hadn't felt any movement yet from the boulder.

Tears pricked the corners of her eyes. She couldn't fail again, not after all they'd gone through to get to this point. *Why won't you move?!* She screamed silently at the rock pile.

And then, just as her strength was about to give out, Lina felt the boulder shift. It was such a small movement that at first she thought she was imagining it, but there was no mistaking the rough scraping sound of the rock sliding across the cavern floor. Inch by agonizingly slow inch, they were moving it.

"It's working!" Lina called out to Ozben. "Keep turning the crank. We're moving it!"

"I've got it," Ozben said through gritted teeth. Lines of sweat ran down his face. He hunkered down and turned the crank with both hands.

This is it, Lina thought. *One more push, just a little longer.* She put her entire body's weight against the pry bar.

Suddenly, the bar slipped, and Lina lurched forward. She threw her hands up in front of her and slammed hard into the ground, skidding on her hands and knees. She sat choking down a cry of pain as the pry bar clanged against the ground beside her.

"Lina, what happened?" Ozben yelled across the chamber at her.

"Ow," Lina offered weakly. She shifted until she was sitting on her butt on the cavern floor so she could get a look at how bad the scrapes were. Her pants were ripped, and her knees and palms were raw and bleeding—she wouldn't be able to pick up the pry bar again until she'd bandaged them. "Um, Ozben?" she said. "Might need a little help here."

But Ozben had already abandoned the winch and was hurrying across the cavern toward her. He crouched down in front of her and turned her wrists gently to look at her palms. He winced. "You keep finding all these creative ways to hurt yourself," he observed.

"Look who's talking," Lina said, nodding at his hands. Two bright red blisters shone on each of his palms from turning the winch.

"It's nothing," Ozben said, but Lina could tell his hands hurt by the way he gently dropped them to his sides. "Looks like you just scraped the skin, but those cuts will need to be cleaned and bandaged up," he said. "You still have any of that medicine we used on your shoulders?"

Despite her pain, Lina flashed him a lopsided grin. "You know me—wouldn't be without it," she said. "But we can clean these up later—I just need a bandage. I felt the boulder move, Ozben," she said excitedly. "Just a little more prying and we're there." She caught him fighting a grin. "What?" she demanded. "What are you laughing at?"

"You," Ozben said, his shoulders shaking. "You didn't even see it, did you?"

"See what?" Lina said, annoyed. Then Ozben took her by the shoulders and turned her toward the *Merlin*.

Lina's mouth dropped open, and thoughts of her injuries flew out of her head. The only thing she could do was stare.

All four of the boulders, her nemeses, had shifted away from the airship's door. That last push with the combination of the pry bar and the hand winch must have done it. They'd been able to shift Lumpy just enough to dislodge the others and send them all tumbling into a heap a few feet away from the ship.

The way was finally clear. She could open the door.

"Lina? Hey, are you all right?"

Lina blinked and suddenly realized that Ozben was nudging her shoulder. She turned to look at him as the first tear spilled down her cheek. All the emotion of the past eight months—the frustration, the setbacks, the lonely nights spent digging in the chamber by herself—and now, the moment she'd been working toward had finally come.

That wasn't why she was crying, why her shoulders were shaking and her face was scrunched up like a lump of wet clay. She cried because Ozben was there to share the moment of triumph with her. There was so much that she wanted to say to him. She wanted to tell him how grateful she was, how overwhelmed that he'd helped a person he barely knew and kept her secret the whole time. She wanted to tell him how much she had needed a friend like him.

But the words and feelings got tangled up in her throat, and in the end, all she could say was "We did it!" She let out a whoop and threw her arms around Ozben as a laugh of pure joy welled up inside her.

Then Ozben was hugging her back and laughing with her, and when they'd calmed down enough that they were no longer screaming, Aethon ventured out from under the worktable and streaked across the chamber to climb in and out of their laps. Lina scooped him up and let his warmth wash over her like a tiny sun.

When her head finally stopped spinning, Lina got to her feet and half walked, half hobbled over to the ship to stand beneath the door. She started to reach her arms up to grasp the edge of the gangplank.

"Hey, what are you doing?" Ozben got up and scurried over to her. "We need to clean those cuts."

Lina gaped at him in disbelief. "And stop now?" she said, barely able to contain her excitement. "We need to open it."

"I'm pretty sure it'll still be here in ten minutes," Ozben pointed out. He raised his arms expansively to encompass the ship's bulk. "It's a little too big to run away, don't you think?"

Lina looked at the ship and then at her hands. She stifled a groan, but she knew Ozben was right. She'd waited this long, so she could probably stand the suspense for a few minutes more. Besides, her hands and knees were killing her, and she imagined Ozben's blisters hurt bad too.

"Let's go to the underground stream," she suggested. "It's back in the northwest corner of the chamber." She nodded at a darkened corner where the stalactites dipped low. "Grab one of the lanterns."

Ozben retrieved a lantern from the worktable, and Lina whispered to the lumatites for some additional light as they made their way across the cavern. Aethon decided to stay by the ship, either to stand guard or to give himself an impromptu bath. Lina couldn't help looking back three or four times to make sure that the ship was indeed staying right where they left it.

"The chamber goes back pretty far," Ozben said as they walked, their voices echoing in the cavern. Distantly, Lina heard the sound of flowing water from the underground stream.

"I don't come back here very much," she admitted. "The chamber gets smaller, and there's nothing to see besides the water."

"It's not so narrow," Ozben observed, holding the light above his head. "The *Merlin* could still get through here on its landing wheels."

"What are you talking about?" Lina asked, confused.

"It's just . . ." Ozben hesitated, and was lost in thought for a moment. When he spoke again, he seemed to be choosing his words carefully. "I've been exploring the cavern a bit the past few days, that's all."

"You have?" Lina was surprised to hear that. She hadn't noticed Ozben wandering off to explore, but the airship tended to absorb all her attention when she was in her workshop.

"I kept wondering what the people were thinking who brought the ship here," Ozben said. "You told me they rebuilt it in this chamber, but why would they do that unless they had a way to get it outside somehow so they could fly it? I mean, surely they intended to try to get the ship to fly, didn't they?"

Lina shrugged. "I guess so," she said. "Maybe they made a door, and it got buried by the same cave-in that buried the ship."

"That's what I thought too at first," Ozben said, "but then I started looking closer at the back walls—and I found something."

Holding up the lantern, he led her to a far corner of the cavern where a thick nest of stalagmites were arranged in front of the wall like a row of soldiers standing at attention. Shining the light beyond them, Ozben pointed with his other hand at the wall. "See that lump jutting out? It looks like stone, but it's not. It's metal."

Skeptical, Lina peered into the shadowy corner at the spot. It took her eyes a moment to separate the object from the surrounding rock, but when she did, she let out a sharp gasp, her breath fogging in the cold air.

Ozben was right. The lump jutting from the wall was made entirely of metal. In fact, it looked to be some kind of mechanism with a myriad of gears, cranks, and chains, but it had rusted so much, it was barely distinguishable from the rest of the cavern wall. And it had been hidden behind the row of stalagmites for who knew how many years.

"I can't believe it," she said, her voice hushed. "I never knew this was here."

"Like you said, you don't come back here much, and you'd never see this unless you were really looking for it," Ozben pointed out. He shone the light along the cavern wall. "I think the mechanism might have been used to open a door right around here. See how the stone is smooth, not rough and pitted like the rest of the wall? I think that part is man-made. And there are marks all along the floor that look like they were made from stone sliding across stone."

He was right again. Deep grooves in the stone floor ran in a straight line from one end of the chamber to the edge of their circle of light. Lina couldn't believe she'd never thought to look for anything like this before. "When did you find this?" she pressed him, excited by the discovery but confused—and just a little bit hurt—that Ozben hadn't told her about it immediately. It meant they'd found another piece of the puzzle that was the *Merlin*.

"Yesterday," Ozben said. He seemed to sense she was unhappy and added quickly, "But so much has happened in the past few days—the assassin, the flaming cat, us going into hiding—I didn't want to overwhelm you. I'm sorry I didn't tell you right away."

"I understand," Lina said, her hurt fading in the face of his concern. She knew Ozben had been worried about her, and she *had* been overwhelmed by the events of the past few days, but she was ready to turn all her attention to the *Merlin* now. "The mechanism looks broken," she said, glancing at the rusted contraption. "Or maybe just neglected. Either way, it'll need some work before we try to activate it."

"I could take a closer look at it later, see what it might take to fix it," Ozben offered.

For just a second, Lina thought she detected an odd note in Ozben's voice. She didn't know how to describe it, though, and so she thought she must be imagining things. She considered his idea but then shook her head. They were getting ahead of themselves. "First things first," she said. "Once we're inside the ship, we'll know soon enough if she'll ever fly again. Then maybe we can start thinking about fixing the door."

"Yeah, I guess you're right," Ozben said. He looked as if he wanted to say something else, but he fell quiet. Lina wondered whether he was feeling all right. Then she remembered the blisters on his hands. If they were hurting as much as the injuries on her hands were, the pain was probably distracting him. That must be it.

They left the mechanism and made their way back to the stream. Together they sat down at the edge. The stream was little more than a dark ribbon of water flowing through the back of the chamber, but it was clean and fresh, and when Lina dipped her hands in, she hissed at the numbing cold. It helped to put out the fire in her hands, though, and when she'd washed her wounds, she let Ozben apply medicine and bandage them as they sat beside the stream. Afterward, Lina treated the blisters on his hands.

"There," she said when she'd finished. "Hopefully we won't have to move any more boulders for a while." She picked up her leather wristband where the lumatites rested.

"Agreed. You know, you never told me about that project with the fireflies," Ozben said, studying the leather band. "You said your parents worked on it?"

Lina nodded. "My mom and dad were the ones who first discovered the lumatites," she said. "It's actually a funny story. A dozen of them had infested this scarlet fabric that a scrapper had scavenged from the meteor fields." She smiled at the memory. "Mom and Dad loved studying rare fabrics and tapestries. Stories told in cloth—that's what they liked to call them. When my mom saw the lumatites, she thought at first they were one of our native species, eating away at the cloth. Oh, she was furious." Lina giggled. "She told me how she had this big wooden ruler and she was dancing around with it, yelling. She couldn't decide whether she should swat the bugs, and risk smashing them all over the rare fabric, or let them keep eating it."

Ozben echoed her laugh. "She didn't squash them, though, right?"

"Oh no," Lina said. "When she looked closer, she realized that they weren't normal bugs and they weren't eating the fabric after all. That's when she knew she had something special, insects she'd never seen before, so then she *really* starts yelling, hollering for my dad and waving that ruler at him to help her get the bugs off the fabric."

"But you communicate with them, right?" Ozben said curiously. "I've seen you talking to them, and they *listen* to you. I've never heard of anyone communicating with bugs before."

"Mom and Dad used to say that it was more about recognizing what the species needed and developing a cooperative relationship," Lina said. "That's where they got the idea for the name of the bugs too. 'Lumatites' means 'illumination,' but it also encompasses the sarnun concept of *lumatia*—the connection with another."

Ozben snapped his fingers. "You're right—I know that word," he said. "I thought it was the sarnun word for 'love.' But it's not just that, is it—it means a . . . bond, doesn't it?"

"The recognition of a person who completes another's needs," Lina confirmed. She held up the leather band so Ozben could see the halpern stalks she'd woven into the leather for them to eat. "By studying the insects, Mom and Dad discovered that the lumatites needed the nutrients from these stalks to survive. But what they didn't know was that the lumatites were also studying Mom and Dad at the same time."

"Studying them?" Ozben echoed as he watched the lumatites. "What were they looking for?"

"Something that they could provide us in exchange for the halpern stalks," Lina said. "Somehow, they discovered we needed light. Probably by observing Mom and Dad stumbling around in the dark whenever their lanterns burned out."

"You're saying they spontaneously developed the ability to produce light from their butts just so they could help you see in the dark?" Ozben said, snorting. "You're serious?"

Lina scowled at him. "I think it's fascinating. Like you said, we've never observed an insect behaving in this way before or being able to evolve so quickly. The fact that they were reaching out to us, trying to communicate— it's like bridging a little of the gap between worlds. Mom and Dad were thrilled every day they worked on the project." Sadness rushed in on Lina unexpectedly, and her irritation spiked. Why had Ozben asked her about this in the first place if he was just going to make fun of her?

"I'm going back to the ship," she said. She stood up and moved off across the cavern. "We've wasted enough time here."

"Lina, wait." Ozben stepped in front of her, forcing her to stop. "I'm sorry. I shouldn't have joked about it."

"It doesn't matter," Lina said, trying to go around him, but he reached out and touched her shoulder.

"It does matter," Ozben insisted. "I didn't mean to insult your parents' work." He ducked his head, and he really did appear contrite. Then he looked up and met her eyes. "How did they die?" he asked.

The question shouldn't have caught her off guard the way it did, but Lina couldn't help the painful tightening in her chest, or the way Ozben's words brought the memory crashing down on her.

"They died of the crestara fever," Lina said quietly. "There was an outbreak here when I was nine. I got it too, but for some reason, I didn't have it as bad."

Sorrow creased Ozben's face. "I'm sorry. I remember the fever a little. It hit Ardra, but my parents said the outbreaks were worse farther south, especially in the archivists' strongholds."

"Because there were so many people in a confined space," Lina said, her thoughts far away as she remembered how Zara had explained it to her.

Zara.

Her teacher's name conjured a different memory, one she'd forgotten for a long time.

Until she discovered the memory jar.

"It has to be you, Zara." Her father was the one speaking, his voice muffled by weakness and the heavy oak door that separated nine-year-old Lina from her parents' sickroom.

Lina knew that if anyone passed by in the hall, they would make her go back to her bed. She scrunched herself into a tight ball against the door, her nightgown tucked around her legs, determined not to let anyone budge her. The door was locked, which Lina hated, but she knew it was to protect her from being exposed to the fever in the sickroom, even though she'd already had it and recovered. The archivists weren't taking any chances with the children.

But Lina had to hear her father's voice, to drink it in. Her mother had already slipped into a sleep from which no one would be able to wake her.

"You're the only one who can understand her," her father said, and Lina's tears made dark streaks down the wooden door. "She's going to need that understanding in order to thrive."

Lina was surprised to hear her father say that. She

knew Zara as well as she knew most of the archivists who worked in her parents' department, but she'd never thought the older woman was anything like her.

"Ethan, you know that I would do anything for you and Rachella," Zara replied. Lina recalled, with the crystal clarity of the memory jar, the way Zara's voice had trembled on her mother's name. They had been such close friends. "But are you sure this is what you want? I'm no good at this—being a mother . . ." Her voice trailed off, and for a long moment, there was only silence and the sound of Lina's breathing as she pressed her ear to the cold door as hard as she could to hear what was said next.

"I wouldn't trust anyone else," her father said, and Lina could imagine his eyes softening as he smiled at Zara. He used to do the same thing with her. Whenever Lina doubted herself, like the day he'd begun teaching her the alphabet and all the letters ran together in crazy loops and swirls in her mind. Or the day he'd taken her on her first trip to the library and told her that soon she'd be able to read every book on the shelves if she wanted to. All he'd had to do to get her over her fear was to pull out that smile of his. She was powerless against it.

As it turned out, Zara was too. Lina's parents died the next day, within hours of each other, and Zara agreed to become Lina's teacher and guardian.

But whereas Lina remembered every detail of that

night, from the roughness of the wooden door against her cheek to the cold seeping through her nightgown, at some point over the years, Zara had forgotten what her father had said and the importance of the promise she'd made.

Lina sighed and forced herself back to the present. Ozben was looking at her, concern etched in the crinkles of his forehead. "You looked like you were a million miles away," he said. "I'm sorry. I shouldn't have brought up bad memories."

"I'm all right," Lina said, but she didn't try to smile. It was still too close, the memory of sitting in front of that door. "It's just, Zara was supposed to be the one to take care of me because my mom and dad thought she understood me. I don't think that's true. I mean, at first, we got along great. She became my teacher, and she helped me, after they died."

The first few months had been the worst, but Zara was there for her through the nightmares and the lonely nights when she'd woken crying, curled up in misery on the bed. Back then, Zara had been more like a mother, gathering her up and rocking her back to sleep. They'd grown close, so when Zara began her studies, Lina had been excited to have her as a teacher as well. For the next two years, they worked side by side, and Lina gradually let go of the darkness of the past.

"What happened?" Ozben asked, drawing her from her thoughts. "What changed?"

"I don't know," Lina said. She looked around the cold, quiet cavern, listening to the drip of water. "One minute, we were best friends, and the next—it's as if she became a different person." Distant, distracted. "We had fewer and fewer lessons. She gave me work to do on my own. Whole days would go by, and I wouldn't see her. She'd just leave written instructions for what she wanted me to do. Eventually, she said her work on the council made her too busy to teach me, and she tried to assign me to another archivist." A rueful smile curved her lips. "It didn't go well. I started spending more time exploring and mapping the stronghold, searching for secret tunnels. And eavesdropping," she added, which made Ozben smile. She shrugged, wishing there were some kind of artifact that would allow her to bury the regrets of the past deep inside her, where they could never hurt again. "That brings us to where we are now."

They resumed walking, and soon the candles and lanterns illuminated the *Merlin* casting its shadow across the chamber before them. Aethon had fallen asleep under the ship's wing. Ozben was quiet, and Lina thought that meant they'd finished talking about Zara, so she was surprised when he spoke up again. "But Zara lets you explore Ortana as much as you want," he said. "And she let you hide me down here in your workshop. I mean, she must trust you, even if she doesn't always understand you, right?"

Lina considered his words. It was true she'd been

more amazed than anyone that Zara had let her carry out her plan for hiding Ozben. And Zara had been more lenient than any of the archivists about her explorations and eavesdropping. In fact, it was often those times when Lina thought her teacher was going to be most inflexible that she ended up surprising Lina.

"I guess you're right," she said, but the knowledge didn't take away any of her sadness. "I still wish we could go back to the way things used to be."

"I understand. Hey," Ozben said, nudging her in the ribs with his elbow. "Know what I think?"

"What?" Lina said, raising an eyebrow as that sly grin of his worked its way over his mouth. She realized he was using the grin to try to cheer her up, and it was working.

"I think it's time we open that ship," he said, nodding to the *Merlin*.

Familiar excitement swelled in Lina's chest, fighting off her sorrow. She grinned back at him. "Past time," she said.

⇒ ELEVEN ⇐

A s they stood before the *Merlin*, Ozben studied Lina, looking for signs of the deep sadness he'd seen in her eyes earlier when she talked about her parents. When she'd relived those painful memories, he had watched her mouth tighten and her eyes go steely, as if by sheer determination she could overcome every hurt and ache in her heart. She seemed focused on the ship now, which was a relief. He didn't like to see her sad, and he liked it even less when he was the cause of that sadness.

How strange was it that, when he first came to the stronghold, he'd thought it was going to be the dreariest place in Solace? He'd pictured a bunch of stuffy museum curators walking around telling him to be quiet and *Don't touch anything*. The last things he'd expected to find were wonders like Aethon or mysteries like the

Merlin. And he'd never thought there would be a person like Lina to show him all those amazing sights. Sharing his secret with her made him feel less alone in the world.

It made him wonder, not for the first time, why no one had ever made a best friend of Lina Winterbock. Maybe it was because she stayed hidden so much in her tunnels and secret caves. Or maybe it was simply that no one had made the effort to see just how special she was. One thing Ozben knew for certain: whomever Lina chose to let into her heart would be a very fortunate person, protected and cherished.

If things were different, he could stay here, be a part of Lina's world, and get to know the archivists better. Not as Fredrick the refugee but as himself. Maybe his parents would let him study at Ortana for a while once the war was over—as long as the archivists allowed it. He'd never been as good a fighter as his sister, and though he enjoyed his studies well enough, the idea of studying artifacts from other worlds and uncovering their secrets—that excited him in a way he'd never experienced before.

Now they stood on the cusp of another discovery. Ozben had been curious about the *Merlin* since Lina first showed it to him, because it was a way for him to get home to the Merrow Kingdom. That was still his goal, but right now, standing beside Lina as they prepared to enter the ship, he found his heart pounding with excitement and a hint of uncertainty. What would they find when they went inside? There was only one way to know.

"Well, how do you want to do this?" Ozben asked.

"If I'm right about the design, the top of the door will come down right about here and form the gang-plank," Lina said, pointing to a spot a few feet away on the ground. "You stand on one side of the door, and I'll get on the other; then, on the count of three, we'll pull it down."

"Got it," Ozben said, moving into position. Standing on tiptoe, he reached up and grasped the protruding edge of the gangplank while Lina did the same on her side. "One," he said.

Lina adjusted her grip. Her eyes were alight with excitement. "Two."

Just as they were prepared to shout *three*, from the depths of the ship came a hollow groaning sound and the ear-splitting creak of a mechanism long disused.

Then the gangplank began to descend.

On its own.

Ozben jumped back, scrambling to get out of the way. "Did you pull on the door first?" he cried.

"I thought *you* did," Lina said in a breathless voice. She was staring, transfixed, at the gangplank as it lowered to the cavern floor, revealing a set of metal stairs that ascended into the darkness of the ship. "When I fired up the steam engine a few weeks ago, I activated some sort of power source inside the ship," she said. "It must have triggered somehow when we touched the door."

A prickling sensation teased the hairs on Ozben's arms. He rubbed it away. "I guess so," he said. He didn't want to admit that the gangplank lowering by itself had unnerved him, especially when Lina didn't seem bothered at all. He told himself everything was fine. It wasn't as if they were going to find ghosts on the ship or anything. At least he hoped not.

"Come on," Lina said, stepping onto the stairs. "We'll find out in a minute what's powering the ship."

Ozben nodded and followed her onto the gangplank. He marveled at the fact that she didn't even hesitate as she climbed. She just called on the lumatites for brighter light, as if she wasn't the least bit afraid.

Ozben was right at Lina's back when they entered the darkness of the *Merlin*. They emerged inside a hallway whose walls Ozben could have almost touched if he stretched his arms out. The hallway ran the length of the ship. Along it, Ozben counted four metal doors, two on either side. At the back of the ship was another stairway leading up.

The air in the ship was drier than in the cave, but it smelled . . . well, like *nothing*, Ozben thought, surprised. He detected none of the musty smells he'd expected to find in a space that had been closed up for so long.

He was about to ask Lina whether she thought the lack of smells was weird when she pointed the lumatites toward a small cabin in front of them. "There," she said, and without another word, she headed straight for it.

"Hey, be careful," Ozben called, hurrying to catch up. By the time he got to her, she was standing in what looked like the ship's bridge.

But Lina wasn't listening. "Wow," she breathed. On the bridge, the lumatites revealed two chairs in front of a control panel with more knobs, switches, levers, and gauges than Ozben had ever seen in his life. He didn't know what any of the controls were for, but he knew enough to realize that all the systems appeared to be inactive.

Except one.

"Look at this," Lina said, taking a seat in one of the chairs and gesturing for Ozben to take the other. A faint humming sound issued from a gauge that had numbers on it from one to ten. The needle on the gauge hovered just below the number-two mark. "There's some power going to the ship, but it looks really weak, and I can't tell what its source is."

"How can you tell what any of it is?" Ozben asked.

"This might explain some of the loss in power," Lina said, pointing to a section of the control panel near the floor. A hole gaped in the console, the bare ends of dozens of tiny wires clinging to its sides. Black streaks stained the panel just above the hole, as if there had been a fire. "Looks like someone ripped a piece of the control panel out right here," she said. "I wonder why, though. I don't see any other damage."

"Maybe there's more damage somewhere else in the ship," Ozben suggested. He frowned. "Remember, Lina, we don't know where this ship came from or what's happened to it. We need to be careful how we handle it."

"One thing's for sure," Lina said, slowly shining the lumatites over the control panel. "This isn't a dirigible. Nothing looks like what I studied in my books. And this language—do you recognize it? It matches some markings I found on the outside of the ship."

Ozben ran his fingers beneath a series of strange symbols on the control panel. It could have been writing, he supposed, but none that he recognized. Again, he felt that prickling sensation along his arms, and it filled him with uneasiness. Everything about this ship was . . . well, the only word for it was "unnatural." It was beginning to frighten him. "No," Ozben said, shaking his head. "I've never seen anything like it before."

Lina looked at him, her face flushed and her eyes bright. "Ozben, this is big," she said. "This ship is incredible."

"But *what* is it?" he asked. He wanted to share Lina's excitement, but something didn't feel right. "How does it fly?"

"I don't know yet," Lina said, but she smiled at him, undeterred. "You're right. We need to search the rest of the ship." She stood up, though she seemed reluctant to leave the bridge.

"Come on." Ozben led the way back to the stairs and down the hall in the opposite direction. The sooner they finished exploring, the sooner they could get off the ship. "Wait." He stopped and looked to Lina. "Should we see what's behind these doors?" he asked. Ghosts, maybe? Not that he was worried about that. Well, maybe a little.

Lina didn't hesitate for even a moment. "Let's do it," she said, pulling him to the first door. They arranged themselves on either side of it. Ozben tensed as Lina turned the knob, eased it open, and shined the lumatites in, illuminating what looked like a tiny crew cabin. An upper and lower berth stood against the left wall, and a small metal chest of drawers with two shelves above it stood on the right wall. Only there were no mattresses in the berths. That was odd, Ozben thought, but maybe the ship was running on a skeleton crew and not all the rooms were needed.

"Well, no power source here, I guess," Ozben said, letting out a shaky sigh of relief that they hadn't encountered any ghosts.

They moved on to the next door and the one after that and found the same setup: a crew cabin with two berths—sparse and clean, no mattresses, and not even a hint of dust. The final cabin was slightly bigger than the others, which Ozben figured meant it was for the captain.

"Let's move on," Lina said. She walked to the end of the hallway, where there was a set of stairs leading up to a second level. She paused with her hand on the metal railing and turned back to look at Ozben. "What did you say?" she asked, shining the light in his face.

Ozben squinted and shaded his eyes. "I didn't say anything."

"Yes, you did," Lina said. "You whispered something."

Ozben shook his head vigorously. "It *wasn't* me." He looked over his shoulder, back the way they'd come, but there was no one there. He was beginning to think that rushing onto the ship had been a bad idea, but he couldn't bring himself to suggest to Lina that they leave right now. She would never agree, and worse, she might think he was a coward. His heart squeezed painfully at the thought.

Lina mumbled something, and Ozben turned back to her. "What'd you say?"

She scowled. "*I* didn't say anything." She shook her head impatiently. "Come on. It's probably just that little bit of power humming through the ship. It's making us hear things."

They started up the stairs, but Ozben glanced back

over his shoulder every once in a while. A strange feeling coursed through him. It reminded him of when he'd first ventured out into Ortana in disguise. He'd been sure people were watching him and whispering, that they were an instant away from discovering who he really was. Right now he felt the same—as if someone were examining him, peeling back all his layers until they could see right through him. He felt like an intruder inside the *Merlin*, trespassing where he didn't belong.

They reached the second level, which was laid out like the first level. The first set of doors on either side of the hall led to what looked like cargo areas, but both rooms were empty. Oppressive silence hung over everything, and Ozben's uneasiness grew. He started to fidget and hung back near the stairs while Lina shone the light ahead of them.

A few feet away, she paused and turned. "Did you find anything?" she asked. "Why are you lurking back there?"

"I'm not lurking," Ozben said, more sharply than he'd intended. "I just think something's wrong." He tried to put what he was feeling into words, but for some reason, they wouldn't come. His emotions rose up, scattering his thoughts, and he blurted out, "I feel like we shouldn't be here."

"A few minutes ago, you *wanted* to check out the rest of the ship." Lina lowered the light and walked back to where he stood. "You can wait outside if you want to. I'm going on."

"You're not going alone!" Ozben was about to say that he didn't need her to tell him to wait outside like a scared kid, but he bit back the words when he noticed Lina's face. She was pale and sweating. "What is it?" he asked, concerned. "What's wrong?"

"It's nothing—silly, really," Lina said. "I must have gotten overexcited. My h-heart . . ." Her voice trailed off, and she took a deep breath with her eyes closed as if to steady herself. "My heart is beating so fast, and I have this feeling like . . . like—"

"Like we should get out of here," Ozben finished for her. Nothing would have pleased him more. "I'm having it too," he said. "It's like the walls are pushing in on me, forcing me out."

"No." Lina shook her head. "I don't feel that. I feel . . . I don't know . . . terrified." But she said it as if she only half believed it. "That doesn't make any sense! I've been in much scarier places than this. This is nothing, yet—" She held up her hand, palm downward to the floor. It was trembling so badly that Ozben reached out and took it between both of his to try to comfort her.

"It's like we're both feeling things we shouldn't be," he said. "A few minutes ago, I didn't want to leave the ship, but now I can barely stand still." He loosed one of his hands and gripped the stair rail as the urge to turn and run threatened to overpower him. "Is it possible—could something on the ship be doing this?"

"I think it could be," Lina said, pressing a hand against her chest. "Maybe it's some sort of security system we've never seen before, maybe a gas that affects our bodies—something we can't detect."

"Well, if it is a security system, it's telling me in the strongest possible way that we need to get off the ship right now," Ozben said. "Maybe we should listen, at least until we know what we're up against."

"You're right," Lina said. "We should go." Her entire body was trembling now, making terror creep into Ozben as well.

He kept a tight grip on her hand as he turned to head back down the stairs. But when he tried to lead her, she resisted, tugging on him. "What is it?" he asked impatiently. "We have to go!"

"Ozben, I don't think I can make it down the stairs," Lina said in a choked voice. "I'm d-dizzy and I can't c-catch my breath—"

Her hand went limp in his, and then she dropped to her knees, slumping to the ground. Ozben was over her, shaking her shoulders in an instant. "Lina!" he shouted. "Lina, get up!" But it was no use. She was unconscious.

Terrified for her, Ozben forced himself to breathe, to

push aside the need to run. "It's going to be all right," he said as calmly as he could. "I've got you. We're getting out of here." He steadied himself and lifted Lina gently by the shoulders, leaning over until he could cradle her head against his chest. Then he hooked his other arm beneath her knees and lifted her. She was heavier than he'd expected, but the need to escape pulsed through him, keeping him steady as he maneuvered them down the stairs.

A loud metallic groaning sound filled Ozben's ears when he reached the main deck. He spun around, searching for a threat from upstairs. But there was nothing, not even a ghost. Then he realized that the sound was coming from the gangplank. It was lifting off the ground and closing, cutting off their escape.

"No!" Desperate, Ozben broke into a run, Lina's head jostling against his shoulder. It felt as if he were moving through sand. The candlelight from the cavern outside became a dim rectangle that got smaller and smaller. Ozben barreled down the narrow hallway, knocking his shin on the stair rail as he came around and dropped to his knees on top of the gangplank, trying to use his and Lina's weight to push it back down.

He'd sooner have been able to move one of Lina's boulders. The gangplank continued to rise under him until, with a screech, it clicked into place, and the small rectangle of light snuffed out.

Lina was very cold.

It wasn't as if this was a new sensation for her. She'd lived in the mountains all her life, and being underground day after day, she'd gotten used to her toes never being warm and her teeth chattering when she first threw the covers back in the morning.

But this was a different sort of chill, a mind-numbing, seeps-into-the-bones kind of cold. She tried to open her eyes, but her eyelids were stuck, frozen closed. Panic started in her stomach and worked its way up to her throat, but she couldn't scream either. Her mouth was so dry—as if she hadn't tasted a drop of water in days. She didn't know where she was or what was happening to her, which was enough to terrify her, but it wasn't the worst of what she felt.

The worst was the loneliness.

A horrible emptiness had taken Lina over, as if every wonderful memory and sensation had been carved out of her, leaving jagged edges. She remembered this hopelessness from the day her parents died. She'd never expected to feel it again, and somehow it was worse now. It was the certainty that nothing would ever get better, no matter how much she hoped for it, the feeling that no one knew or cared what happened to her in the world. As the emotions swamped her, Lina found she didn't want to open her eyes anymore, she just wanted to curl into a tight ball and try to sleep, to go to a place where she couldn't feel anything. It was the only way to get rid of the pain.

But Lina couldn't sleep. Something prodded her, a spark of warmth that jabbed into her ribs. She sucked in a breath. The jab wasn't painful, but she'd been so cold for so long that the sudden warmth was unfamiliar, intrusive. What was it?

Lina forced her eyelids open and uncurled her stiff limbs.

What she saw didn't make any sense.

She was standing in the doorway of the bridge, staring at the gangplank as two figures ascended it into the ship.

Then she was staring into her own face.

She was seeing herself and Ozben *entering* the *Merlin*.

It had to be a dream. She'd passed out and was reliving the moment when she and Ozben first came aboard the ship.

But why did she feel so strange? The loneliness that had cloaked her was temporarily pushed aside, replaced by fear and anger so strong that it made Lina dizzy. The feelings seemed to be directed at her and Ozben, as if shouting: *Not welcome! Intruders! Trouble!*

The feelings crowded Lina's heart, making it difficult for her to concentrate. *What's happening to me?* Her mind raced. *These aren't my emotions.* But if the feelings didn't belong to her, then who was in her head?

And was this really a dream?

Then an awareness started to creep into Lina's mind. She tried to look down at herself, to assure herself she was still Lina, with two hands, two feet, and all her other parts. But when she looked down, all she saw was the ship. She looked left and right, but there was only the ship's metal walls surrounding her. Everything that was familiar was the ship. The unfamiliar faces, the intruders, were Lina and Ozben, who were at that moment walking toward the bridge. They walked up to her and passed right through as if she were a phantom.

No, not a phantom. She wasn't a ghost.

She was the ship.

With that realization, Lina knew she wasn't dreaming, at least not in the usual way she did when she fell asleep in her bed. She remembered now: Ozben had wanted to leave the ship. She'd agreed, but her fear had overwhelmed her, and she'd passed out. The ship was doing something to her, making some kind of connection with her mind and heart. When she and Ozben had come aboard, the ship had been afraid. It had wanted them to leave, and somehow those emotions had seeped into the two of them. And what Lina was feeling now— the loneliness—that emotion was coming from the

Merlin too. But how could a machine communicate emotion? That was impossible. Unless . . .

Lina couldn't finish the thought. *No, it can't be. That's crazy.* And yet she saw no other explanation.

The *Merlin* was alive.

≽ TWELVE ≼

Lina closed her eyes to cut off the visions she was see-ing of herself and Ozben walking through the ship, and tried to stay calm as emotions that were hers and not hers waged a battle inside her. At this point, she didn't know who was more afraid: her or the ship that was now connected to her thoughts. Lina took a deep breath and tried to remember her training. Her parents and Zara used to say there came a time when every archivist was confronted with an artifact that was so far outside his or her understanding that it seemed impossible to figure out.

But Lina was certain none of them had ever encoun-tered anything like the *Merlin*. A sentient ship. There were no books to help her with this, no advisors. Even Ozben was lost to her right now. She was all alone, with only her instincts to guide her.

The Merlin *is all alone too,* she reminded herself.

"Well, at least we have something in common," she said. Hearing the sound of her own voice was soothing. It helped remind her that no matter what other emotions crowded into her head, she was still herself. Lina only.

"Lina only," she repeated, as if the words protected her. "But if I'm Lina, then who are you?" she asked, her eyes still closed, hoping that the ship would know she was addressing it. "Where did you come from?"

In response, words flowed wildly into her mind, but the language was one that Lina had never heard before. Accompanying the words were clickity-clacks, metallic whirring, and hissing like steam from a pipe. The cacophony swamped her—she wanted to press her fingers to her temples and drown out the nonsensical sounds. Thankfully, the storm passed after a moment, and the ship quieted.

"I don't know your language," Lina said, trying to stay calm. "I'm sorry." The ship seemed able to understand and respond to her, but if she couldn't understand the ship, that could be a huge obstacle. Yet she'd had no trouble interpreting how the ship was feeling. The fear, anger, and loneliness had come through loud and clear. "If you want to communicate, we can't do it with words," Lina said. "I have to know what you're feeling, so I guess I have to see through your eyes."

As soon as she said it, a stroke of white-hot pain slammed into Lina's head, blinding her. *No! No!* What was the ship doing to her? She didn't think she'd said anything to make it turn hostile.

But after a moment, the pain abated, and Lina cautiously opened her eyes.

If she was unprepared a few minutes ago to see her own face staring back at her on the ship, she was completely undone when she realized she was now suspended in midair, with the mountains sailing by thousands of feet below her.

"*Merlin!*" Lina cried, her stomach threatening a revolt. "I take it back! I don't want to see this! Oh, it's way too high, way too high!"

Panic flooded Lina, making it impossible to breathe as she stared at the rolling landscape. At any moment, she was going to fall. She was certain of it. She tried to close her eyes, but that made the feeling of weightlessness worse, so she forced them open, staring down and waiting to tumble to her death.

Minutes passed, and still Lina hung in the air, unmoving. Pushing through the wall of panic, she reminded herself that she wasn't actually hovering thousands of feet in the air. This was the ship. She was seeing through its eyes, just as she'd wanted. The landscape below her—it had to be a memory. The *Merlin* was trying to communicate with her by showing her its memories.

But did they ever *hurt*.

Above her, the sun shone on the snow's unbroken surface, creating a thousand tiny sparkles of light. The beauty of it, and the vast expanse of chiseled mountains stretching in all directions, was breathtaking. It made Lina pause and forget her panic for a moment as she drank in the view.

"Oh . . . wow," she whispered. "So this is what it's like to fly." To see the world as only a bird—or a living airship—could see it.

Gradually, her body relaxed, and Lina let herself be carried along with the vision. As she watched, a day passed by in a moment, and judging by the position of the sun, the ship was traveling east, making a steady course over the Hiterian Mountains. In the distance, she could see the bridges and the outline of the three archivist strongholds.

But if the ship was flying through the Hiterian Mountains, and the scrap towns were nowhere in sight, did that mean it hadn't been found in the scrap fields? The idea sent Lina's thoughts spinning in a dozen different directions, but they all led back to the same conclusion.

"You didn't come to Solace in a meteor storm, did you?" she asked excitedly. She dreaded the shot of pain when the ship tried to show her something, but she was dying to know. "Where did you come from?"

Sure enough, fresh agony crawled through Lina's

forehead, causing a whimper to escape her lips. In response to her cry of distress, a rush of emotion came from the ship: concern, and a question. Lina interpreted it loosely as *Are you all right?*

"I'm . . . f-fine," Lina said. "Keep going, please. Show me."

The scene sped up, only this time they were traveling in reverse. Days passed by in seconds as the ship headed west, hundreds of miles from the archivists' strongholds, over mountain peaks that scraped the sky and sheets of blue ice more beautiful than anything Lina had ever seen. They moved faster and faster, then suddenly the ship stopped and Lina's vision went dark.

"What is it?" Lina asked. "What's wrong?"

The ship didn't answer, but she sensed its uncertainty. The longer she stayed connected to it, the easier it was to separate the ship's emotions from her own. The *Merlin* was holding back, reluctant to show her what was beyond the mountains.

Beyond the mountains—a place no one in Solace had ever been.

"You came from the west," Lina said as the truth dawned on her, "from the uncharted lands of Solace."

Of course. Why hadn't she ever considered it before? She'd assumed that the ship's technology came from another world, but she'd never thought of the possibility that it might have come from an unknown part of

Solace. And why not? King Aron of the Dragonfly territories had wanted to build an airship that could explore past the Hiterian Mountains. It appeared that someone on the other side had beaten him to it.

"But why were you all alone?" Lina said. She could sense that too: the ship had come by itself. She remembered the pristine crew cabins. No pilot, no people—it was no wonder the ship had been lonely. Far from home, in an unknown country—it had to have been afraid. "How did you end up in the cave?" she asked. "What happened?"

The scene changed again, and the pain was scalding. Lina squeezed her eyes shut and drew in a shuddering breath as she waited for it to pass. Instinctively, she knew she couldn't take many more visions. They hurt too much. But she wanted to see, to understand what the ship had gone through to get here.

When she opened her eyes, she bit back a scream. The ship was losing altitude fast. She felt the *Merlin* straining, frantically trying to pull itself up, but it was no use. It had been aloft for too long. Lina sensed its confusion and despair. It hadn't expected the mountains to be so vast and for the journey to take so long. Its energy was waning.

Lina blinked, and suddenly she was seeing inside the ship to the bridge. But something was different this time. Where earlier she'd seen a gaping hole in the center console, there was now a sphere of golden light that was somehow connected to the wires and fastened into the control panel of the ship. It illuminated the bridge, leaving spots in Lina's vision.

"The *light!*" Lina gasped. "That was your power source, wasn't it?" Something had happened to it. Yet she remembered that one of the gauges on the bridge had still been functioning, and she'd felt vibrations in the ship's wings after she'd briefly activated the steam engine. Where had *that* power come from since the light was gone? It must have been part of a reserve supply that was all but depleted now.

But Lina sensed confusion and resistance from the ship, as if she'd used the wrong word or a word that wasn't strong enough to describe the light. What was a stronger word than "power?" Lina wondered. Her thoughts raced as she tried to come up with the answer. The light filled the bridge and expanded, curling around Lina like an embrace. Her heart warmed at its touch.

And then Lina knew. Her heart. Of course. The ship was alive. Its power source was much more than something mechanical. The golden light was its heart.

But as she watched, that light sputtered and dimmed. Seconds later, a great roar filled her ears, and this time Lina did scream as she and the ship plummeted to the ground.

* * *

When Lina screamed, Ozben's heart leapt into his throat. He'd watched for the last half hour as she had twitched and gasped as if she were in the throes of a nightmare. For a while, he hadn't wanted to touch her in case she was injured, but when she had whimpered, he'd given in and tried shaking her shoulders, calling her name over and over to try to wake her up. Nothing had worked.

Now all he could do was hold on to her as her scream died away and she grew calm again. Her breathing was still labored, and sweat stood out on her forehead, but she lay quietly. He carefully wiped the sweat away with his sleeve. Was it his imagination, or did she have a fever? If only he could get her out of the ship. But even if he could, he'd never get her back through the narrow passages up to the medical wing while she was unconscious, not without the risk of hurting her more.

"Lina, whatever's happening to you, you have to snap out of it," Ozben pleaded. He took her hand. It was icy cold, yet she was sweating. She definitely had a fever. He'd thought something on the ship was affecting her, but if that was true, why wasn't it still affecting him as well?

He searched for the emotions that had been swirling in him earlier, the fear that was so intense it had almost driven him to run off the ship and leave Lina behind. But there was nothing. He was afraid, yes, for Lina's safety and his own, but it wasn't the same as he'd felt before. If this was all part of some security system within the ship, it seemed it was only targeting Lina now.

"Why are you doing this?" Ozben said aloud. Maybe there was someone hidden in one of the cabins, secretly controlling the ship's security system. "We didn't mean any harm," he continued, his voice rising into panic. "You're hurting her!" His shout echoed off the walls.

He watched Lina twitch and squirm for a few more minutes, but then he couldn't take it any longer. They were getting out of there, even if he had to bash the door open.

He started to gather Lina up in his arms, when suddenly she jerked, her whole body convulsing as her eyes flew open and fixed blankly on his.

"Lina!" he cried, relieved. When she still looked at him as if he were a stranger, he added tentatively, "Do you know who I am?"

"Oz . . . ben?" She blinked several times, and then seemed to come back to herself. Carefully, she sat up and looked around. "How long was I unconscious?"

"A while," Ozben said. "I was so worried. You were twitching and breathing so hard, like you were caught in a nightmare but you wouldn't wake up."

Lina looked at him and abruptly she laughed. "Something like that," she said.

And then she told him what had happened.

When she finished, Ozben sat back against the wall,

staring at the ship around him as if seeing it for the first time. "Lina, are you sure?" he asked. "I mean, a *living* ship? It sounds crazy."

"I know," Lina said, "but no one's ever been to the uncharted lands. Who knows what it's like there, what the people are like? For all we know, there could be organic technology all over the place. Maybe they use it as readily as we use steam engines!" Her eyes were bright with excitement and the vestiges of her fever.

"You said the ship crashed in the mountains," Ozben said. "But how did it end up here, then, in the stronghold?"

Lina's excitement dimmed. "The ship showed me an image in its memory of three men and two women. I think they were archivists. They spoke our language, and they wore work aprons as we do, but their clothing underneath was a different style—older. They must have found the ship a long time ago."

"But how?" Ozben asked. "The mountains are enormous. It'd be like looking for a needle in twenty haystacks."

"One of the men saw the ship in the sky just before it crashed," Lina said, "and he brought the others to help him salvage it." She shuddered. "I heard bits of their conversations. The ship recorded them. The five of them decided not to tell the rest of the archivists what they'd found. They wanted to keep the discovery to themselves.

So they scouted the area and found this cave. They were the ones who built the door mechanism you found."

"But what happened to the archivists after they brought the ship here?" Ozben asked.

"They studied it," Lina said. "The *Merlin*'s heart was exhausted after the long journey over the mountains, and that's what caused the ship to crash. As a result, the heart was damaged, so the archivists removed it to fix it. The ship didn't try to stop them, because it thought the archivists intended to return it." Lina's face creased with sadness. "By the time it realized that the archivists were only interested in keeping the power source for themselves, it was too late. And then the cave-in happened."

A sick feeling churned in Ozben's stomach. "What happened to the archivists?"

"They all died," Lina said quietly. "The cave-in buried them, and the ship was left alone without its heart. It's been here ever since."

They sat in silence while Ozben tried to digest everything Lina had told him. As amazed and awed as he was by the idea of the living ship, he couldn't get past the fact that they were still stuck inside it. And Lina looked pale and weak, as if she'd had all the energy drained out of her. The ship had done that to her. In his mind, that meant the *Merlin* was dangerous and not to be trusted.

"What happens now?" he asked, and he wondered

as he said it if he was talking to Lina or to the *Merlin*. "What does the ship want?"

"It doesn't want to hurt us," Lina said, as if reading his mind. She put her hand against the ship's hull. "It was just scared when we came aboard, and I can understand why. The last time people were inside the *Merlin*, they took its heart." Her voice wavered. "The ship wants it back. It asked for our help."

"But you said its power source is gone," Ozben said, "buried in the cave-in."

Lina shook her head. "No, it wasn't." Something about her expression made the hairs on Ozben's arms stand up.

"What?" he asked.

"I know where the power source is," Lina said. "I didn't recognize it in the vision until after the crash, when it had dimmed to just a single flame burning inside a metal sphere."

A flame inside a sphere—why was that familiar? Then it hit Ozben like a bolt of lightning, and he gasped. "The Special Collections wing!" he cried. "The Sun Sphere! It's in the museum!"

"And we need to get it back." Lina stood up, taking a second to steady herself, and then walked over to the gangplank. "We need to leave now, please," she said, addressing her request to the empty air.

A low groan hummed through the ship, and slowly

the gangplank lowered to the ground. Ozben gaped at it. "Yeah, I don't know if I can get used to the idea that the ship's *alive*," he said, then turned his attention to Lina. "And you were . . . connected to it? How does that work?"

Lina shrugged. "I don't know that either. I wanted to ask more questions, but all of a sudden, the visions stopped, and I woke up. I don't know what happened."

"It could've realized it was hurting you," Ozben said. But he wondered if the ship had listened when he'd said to leave Lina alone. The idea reassured him. Maybe the *Merlin* wasn't as dangerous as he'd first thought. And if it was intelligent, that could work to their advantage.

Maybe if they helped the ship get back its heart, it would help him in return by flying him home. The *Merlin* was still the best way to get there. His family needed him more than ever, especially now that Ozben knew assassins were still after him. They would likely still be after his family too.

He stood and followed Lina down the gangplank, grateful to get back out into the cavern. Aethon was asleep beneath Lina's worktable. He hadn't even noticed they were gone. "Listen, we need a plan," Ozben said.

"You're right," Lina agreed. "We have to get hold of that sphere." She tapped her chin as she spoke. "But sneaking the Sun Sphere out, especially after I already grabbed it once, is going to be tricky. I'm sure they've added more security to the Special Collections wing now that they've seen how easy it is to steal from there. We'll have to risk it, though. The archivists stole the *Merlin*'s heart. The least we can do is steal it back."

"And if we can return the power source to the ship, the *Merlin* could theoretically fly again," Ozben said. "I mean, it must want to go home, right?" He looked up excitedly and added, "And it could fly me home too!"

As soon as he said it, Ozben regretted the slip. He'd been so eager—he hadn't meant to blurt his plan out like that, but it was too late. Lina had heard him loud and clear. She'd been walking over to her worktable, but she stopped and swung around to face him. "What did you say?"

No point in hiding his intentions now. "I want the *Merlin* to take me home," he said firmly. "Back to the Merrow Kingdom."

Lina looked at him as if he'd asked to go to the moon. "But you can't leave. Your parents sent you here to protect you," she said.

"It obviously hasn't done much good," Ozben said. "The assassin found me here anyway. And the longer I stay, the more people I'll put in danger. I need to go home, where I can help protect my family."

"But you never mentioned anything about going home before," Lina said. She sounded hurt, and it tore at Ozben's heart. "I thought you were starting to like being here. I know it's not your home, but it isn't so bad, is it?"

"No," Ozben said quickly. "Well, yes, but . . . Oh, Lina, don't look at me like that." He was saying everything wrong. "Ortana is a nice place, but it's *your* home, not mine. If someone took you away, wouldn't you do everything you could to get back?"

"Of course, but it's not like that. You talk as if you were brought here against your will."

"I was," Ozben said flatly. She needed to know the truth, no matter how much it hurt. "I never wanted to come here, and now I have a way to get home."

Slowly, Lina's expression shifted from wounded to suspicious. "You've been planning this all along, haven't you?" she said. "Since I first showed you the ship, you wanted to use it to get back home."

Ozben opened his mouth to deny it—he knew that if he confessed, it would make her angry and even more hurt. But when he looked in her eyes, he knew he couldn't lie to his friend. "Yes, it's what I've wanted from the beginning."

He braced himself for her to shout at him, or to cry, or both, but to his surprise, Lina did neither of those things. She nodded once, a sharp jerk of her head, turned around, and ran from the cavern.

"Lina, wait!" Ozben cried, but she didn't even slow down. He took off after her, grabbing one of the lanterns from her worktable. Aethon watched them sleepily from his place on the ground.

Ozben considered himself a fast runner, but Lina was

faster and more agile navigating in the cramped tunnels than he was. The lantern swung wildly as he careened around the stalagmites and stalactites, trying to close the distance between them. "Lina!" he called out again, hoping she'd listen to reason. "I'm sorry! I didn't mean to hurt your feelings—ouch!" He cut the last corner too tight and banged his shoulder against the unforgiving stone wall. All he could see of her now was the bobbing lights of the lumatites on her wrist.

He reached the last tunnel, the one Lina called the Hourglass, just as she was about to squeeze through the narrowest gap.

"Stop following me!" she yelled at him. "You have to stay hidden, you idiot."

"Then stop running and talk to me!" he yelled back. "If you leave the tunnel, I swear I'll follow you, assassin or not."

"You're impossible!" But Lina relented. She stepped away from the Hourglass and turned to face him. Her shoulders were rigid, her fists clenched, and the expression on her face made Ozben wish he hadn't tried quite so hard to catch up with her. She looked as if she wanted to strangle him or maybe hurl him off the top of a mountain. Or both. Probably both, he guessed.

"Why did you run off like that?" he said, still out of breath.

"Because," Lina said through clenched teeth, "I was

afraid if I stuck around, I'd end up hitting you. I ran off so I wouldn't do that."

"Oh," Ozben said, and cringed at the murderous look she threw him. He should have given her a minute or two to calm down, but surely she wasn't angry enough to take a swing at him, was she?

Ozben steeled himself and reached out, laying a hand on her shoulder. "You'd better just let me have it," he suggested, though he could hardly believe what he was saying. "I can take it." And then he closed his eyes and hoped he really could.

≈ THIRTEEN ≈

Lina took Ozben's advice. She didn't hit him, but she did pretty well with words. "So all this time, you were using me!" she yelled, and as she did, fury blossomed inside her, and she did nothing to stop it. Fury was best, because if she let herself feel the hurt that lurked in the shadows around her heart, it would cripple her. She didn't want to think about how he'd never been interested in her friendship, just what he could get out of her. "You planned to steal the ship and fly it home—as if you could! As if there weren't a hundred different things wrong with that plan!" Fists clenched at her sides, she took a step closer to him, and Ozben took a step back, his hands raised.

"I didn't want to *steal* the *Merlin*," Ozben said, avoiding her gaze. "I hoped that when I explained everything, you'd go along with my plan—holes and all," he said sheepishly.

"Then you're an idiot," Lina said, her voice quavering on the word "idiot." "Nobody is taking my ship."

"Wait a minute. *Your* ship?" Ozben crossed his arms. "That's an interesting way of putting it. Because I was inside the *Merlin* with you, and even though I wasn't connected to its mind, I can tell you that ship doesn't belong to anybody, and it never will. It needs your help, Lina. You can't just keep the *Merlin* hidden away because you want it all for yourself."

"Are you really lecturing me about taking what isn't mine?" Lina said, incredulous. "You . . . you . . . ship thief!"

"Fine!" Ozben yelled. He turned and kicked the wall. "You're right, I'm no better than you, but I don't know what else to do! I want to get back to my family. They need me."

"No, they don't need you!" Lina cried. She could feel her cheeks turning red in anger and frustration. "They need you to be safe, and if you go home now, you'll just cause more trouble for them! That's why they got rid of you!" As soon as the words were out of her mouth, she instantly regretted them. But she couldn't take back what she'd said, and so she had to endure the stricken expression that passed over Ozben's face. It was a knife in her heart.

He looked into her eyes, and his sadness was visible. "You don't understand," he said. "It's not about me. My grandfather says that everyone has to be strong to protect the family legacy." He hesitated, and his shoulders slumped, misery dragging him down. "Remember the night you showed me the memory jar? Well, my memory was of Grandfather telling me I didn't measure up to that legacy, that I was the least important member of the family. I have to go back and prove him wrong. If I don't at least try . . . if I just sit here, doing nothing, and something happens to them . . ." He trailed off, as if he couldn't bear to think about his family in danger.

"Oh, Ozben." Lina reached for him, wanting to offer comfort, but he stepped back, batting her hand away.

"Don't!" he snapped. "I don't want you to feel sorry for me! That's the last thing I want."

"I don't feel sorry for you!" Lina crossed her arms over her stomach. "Your grandfather's wrong, Ozben. So wrong."

"He's the king," Ozben said, as if that trumped everything.

"That doesn't make him any less a stupid, cruel person," Lina said. "I'm glad you're nothing like him. And so what if you don't fit into his *legacy*," she said, as if the word was something sour in her mouth. "Did you ever think that maybe you're supposed to be here instead? That you fit in *my* world?"

"Do I really, Lina?" Ozben said. "Or are you just saying that because I can fit in this crack or that crevice? So I could help you dig out your airship?" Anger and hurt filled his voice. "That's all you wanted me for, right? I was the perfect partner—safe, someone you could manage. You knew I wouldn't tell anyone your secret because you knew mine. You never really trusted me."

Lina was so shocked by the accusation that at first she couldn't speak. How could Ozben think she didn't trust him? He was the only person she'd let into her workshop. She'd shared the *Merlin* with him. Wasn't that proof enough of her faith in him? "Ozben . . . no, you're . . ."

But Lina couldn't finish. It hurt to admit it, but maybe Ozben was right. *Would* she have let Ozben in if he didn't also have a secret that he was protecting? No, she would never have risked revealing her workshop.

Or risked opening her heart.

Ashamed, she gave him a jerky nod. "You're right. I didn't trust you," she said, scrubbing tears from her cheeks. "But why should I trust people? Every time I try, they mess it up, or they leave!"

"You don't give people a chance," Ozben said. "You're too busy hiding from them—or eavesdropping on them," he added.

His words cut like knives, and Lina couldn't stand it. Ozben didn't understand anything. She'd given Zara a chance, and her teacher had pulled away from her. "You're not being fair!" she snapped. "I don't hide! I go where I want to, I see and hear everything."

"But it's not the same. You're not really a part of things, are you?" Ozben challenged. He thumped his fist against the side of the tunnel. "There's still a wall between you and the rest of the world. Admit it, you're hiding."

"You sound just like Zara!" Lina said angrily. "I'm not hiding!"

But Ozben wouldn't back down either. "Yes, you are, and you know it."

They stared at each other, faces flushed with anger. Lina felt as if a great weight were pressing down on her chest. She didn't want Ozben to be right about any of it. She wanted to scream at him that there was no way he could understand what she'd been through, the disappointments and loss. At least he had a family; she didn't.

Then again, she'd never had a family member who made her feel that she was worthless. She'd never experienced that kind of cruelty. But Ozben obviously cared very much for the rest of his family. Lina had seen the frustration and sadness in his eyes when he talked about getting home to them. He must have been going crazy these last few weeks, worrying about them, not knowing if they were all right. Yet he'd stayed cheerful and brave, never complaining, and he'd helped her accomplish the thing she wanted most in the world: to free the *Merlin*.

But he'd done more than that. He'd become her best friend. Lina knew it, because no one else, save maybe Zara, had ever been able to see her heart so clearly.

Lina let out a sigh and felt some of her fury fading, replaced by weariness and sorrow. "You're right," she admitted. Her voice dropped. "I *am* hiding." Because she was scared, and the walls were the only thing keeping her heart safe. She hated to admit it, but it was true.

Ozben's face softened. "I'm sorry. I shouldn't have said all those things. Look, it's true I didn't want to come here, but I never thought I'd meet someone like you. You're amazing and weird, and you talk about these incredible artifacts that sound like magic to me. I want to follow you everywhere, even down deep dark tunnels where there might be legions of poscil rats—I've never seen one, but after hearing you describe them, I never want to.

"But I'd follow you into the dark, because you're not afraid of anything and because when we come out the other side, you're there to show me a dozen more incredible things. I want to go to the Special Collections wing with you every month and finish my story. You know— the one about the girl and the shipwreck. It's like a whole other world here, and you made me feel as if I belonged to it. How could I have known any of that would happen?"

He smiled at her tentatively as he spoke, and as much as Lina wanted to be angry at him, his words and the hopeful expression he wore warmed her heart.

"I didn't just want you to help me with the ship," she said, stepping forward to take his hand. "It might have started that way, but it didn't take long for me to realize that you're the only one who understands me. You told me the night we met that you wanted to find a way to make yourself important." She swallowed a lump in her throat. "I've never had anyone be as important a friend to me as you are. That's why I don't want you to go. I want you to stay here with me."

Ozben squeezed her hand. Lina thought he was going to say something, but then he tugged her toward him and wrapped his arms around her shoulders. Lina hugged him back, and when they pulled apart, Ozben wiped his eyes quickly.

"So what do we do now?" he asked. "Where do we go from here?"

But before Lina could reply, a scream echoed through the quiet tunnel. A voice cried out, "Help! Somebody—" and then it cut off.

Ozben's eyes got as round as saucers. "What was that?"

A chill passed through Lina. "It came from outside the tunnel." She was sure of it. "It must have been the guard—the one Zara has watching the secret entrance."

"The assassin!" Ozben cried. "We have to help the guard!"

Without thinking, Lina turned and forced her way through the narrow Hourglass passage, tearing her clothing even more as she went. She thrust the curtain of deepa ivy back, scattering leaves everywhere, and tumbled out onto the ground. Ozben came out right behind her.

The guard lay sprawled at the end of the hallway, in front of the gates to the museum. It was late, and the gates were closed but not yet locked for the night. The padlock hung open on the latch, as if the guard was just about to lock it when he was attacked. But there was no sign of any intruder.

Ozben ran down the hall, straight to the guard, and Lina was right at his heels. They both dropped to their knees beside the man, and Ozben leaned down to inspect him more closely.

"Is he alive?" Lina asked anxiously.

"Yes, but it looks as if he got hit in the back of the head pretty hard," Ozben said. "We need to get him to the medical wing." He looked up at Lina, and his gaze strayed over her shoulder in the direction of the Heart of the Mountain.

Then his eyes widened. "Lina!"

Lina started to turn to see what he was looking at when a loud hissing sound filled her ears. At the same instant, Ozben barreled into her, driving them both to the ground with a force that knocked the breath out of her. She ended up on her back, tangled with Ozben in almost the same way as when they'd first met.

"What are you doing?" Lina gasped. She raised a

hand to try to push Ozben off her and became aware of a sharp stinging pain in her left arm. Ozben shifted so he wasn't crushing her, and that was when Lina saw that her sleeve was torn and blood seeped from a deep gash on her arm.

Ozben saw the wound and sucked in a breath. "Sorry, I wasn't fast enough."

Lina hissed in pain as she pulled part of her torn sleeve over the wound and pressed down to staunch the bleeding. Then, out of the corner of her eye, she glimpsed what Ozben had saved her from.

Protruding from the wall near where they'd just been crouching was a crossbow bolt. A drop of bright blood stained its shaft. Her blood. Realizing this, Lina forgot about her wound. She rolled onto her stomach, pushing Ozben off her so she could get to her feet. She glanced around to see where the shot had come from.

Then she saw it. At the end of the passage, just inside the Heart of the Mountain, a shadow crouching in the sculpture garden, not far from the stone servoya tree where Lina had hidden the first night she'd met Ozben. The shadow stood up, stepping forward so she could see him. He was tall and slender, and he wore black from head to toe.

Ozben's assassin.

Lina's heart stuttered as she realized the deadly danger they were in. Somehow, the assassin had figured out where they were hiding. He'd used the guard's cries to lure them out. And they'd done exactly what he'd wanted them to.

As Lina stared, paralyzed by fear, her arm throbbing, the assassin cast aside his empty crossbow and drew a thin, wicked-looking knife from a sheath on his belt. And then he charged directly at them.

That broke the paralysis. "Ozben, run!" Lina screamed. She grabbed his arm and steered him toward the museum gates. There was no time to squeeze back through to the workshop—the assassin would catch up to them before they got past the ivy curtain. She wrenched open the gates and shoved him in front of her; then, hands shaking, she pulled the gates shut, fumbling to fasten the padlock in place on the latch from the other side of the gate. The assassin closed the distance between them without a sound. Panic gripped Lina's chest. She'd never seen anyone move like that. Her fingers shook as she tried to fit the padlock into place.

"Lina, hurry!" Ozben cried. Finally, Lina slammed the lock into place and clicked it closed. They turned and took off running just as the man hit the gates, swiping his knife at them through the bars.

"You're not getting away from me this time, little prince." The man's raspy voice echoed in the dark gallery, raising the hairs on the back of Lina's neck. She risked a glance over her shoulder to see the assassin climbing the gates. He would be over the top in a matter of seconds.

"Faster!" Lina yelled. "This way!" She grabbed Ozben's arm and steered him left into a long gallery lined with stone pedestals. On top of them was a series of illuminated manuscripts, their colors shining even in the dim glow of the lumatites. Lina flew past them and out a door on the far side of the room.

Next is the map room, Lina thought, conjuring an image in her head of the layout of the museum. Ancient and modern maps of Solace hung on the walls side by side with scavenged pieces of torn and faded paper illustrating unknown lands from dozens of different worlds. She paused, calculating their next move.

"Three doors out of this room—stairs to the left, straight on gets us into the art galleries, and to the right is . . . to the right is . . . Oh goddess, what else is on this level!" Panic left Lina's mind empty. She couldn't think.

Footsteps pounded behind them. The assassin was inside the museum. "Lina, we have to go!" Ozben cried, pulling her in the direction of the closest door.

Still trying to get her bearings, Lina let Ozben drag her into the next gallery. Landscape paintings covered the walls, and in the middle of the floor were several large sculptures of human figures in various poses. Lina pointed to a sculpture of a woman reclining on a divan. "Quick, hide back there," she whispered. It was easy to get lost in the galleries if you didn't know your way around, especially at night, when the lights were dim and the shadows thick. Lina hoped that would give her and Ozben an advantage.

Together they huddled behind the reclining statue, trying to stay silent, but even their breathing sounded loud in the quiet gallery. Lina found herself staring at the statue's bronze plaque, which told the name of the sculpture: *The Sleeping Beauty.*

Lina glanced up at the statue's serene marble face. The woman's eyes were closed, her cheek resting against her stone pillow. *That's the problem—everyone's asleep.* They couldn't hide forever; they had to get help, but most people would be asleep by now, even Nirean and the other chamelins. The museum had human guards, but they usually patrolled only at the beginning and end of the night. The strongholds were so well protected just by being in the mountains that most people didn't worry about break-ins.

Lina bit her lip in frustration. The pain in her arm and the fear of discovery were making it hard to come up with any kind of coherent plan. She touched her sleeve to see if the bleeding had stopped. The fabric was wet, but she didn't think the bleeding was getting worse. Oh, but it stung, so much that Lina broke out in a cold sweat.

Ozben touched her shoulder, and Lina glanced at him. Saw the concern etched in his face. He didn't speak, but he nodded at her wound. She offered him a weak smile, as if to say, *I'll live.*

Then she heard the footsteps.

Lina stiffened, and Ozben's grip on her shoulder tightened. They pressed as close together as possible, making themselves into a tight ball behind the statue. The footsteps were faint and sounded as if they were coming from two galleries away—too close for Lina's comfort.

"Where are you, little prince?" The assassin's voice was a singsong echo through the galleries. "Come out. Come out. It must be frightening, hiding in the dark," he taunted. Then the voice got louder, as did the footsteps. Lina tried to keep her body from trembling. The assassin was probably in the map room now, right next to their gallery.

Please go another way. Please take one of the other doors. Don't come in here, Lina silently pleaded as she held her breath.

Then, as if the universe had heard her, the footsteps receded. The assassin was moving through one of the other doors. Lina's heart pounded with fear and hope. If they were very lucky, the assassin would think they'd gone upstairs to the next floor. Once he was far enough away, they could backtrack through the museum and the Heart of the Mountain to get to Nirean or Zara.

The assassin's voice rang out again in the stillness. "Do you really think you can hide from me, little boy?"

he asked. "Do you think you can get away"—he paused—
"when your parents couldn't?"

Lina felt a tremor go through Ozben's whole body.
A soft cry like a wounded animal escaped from his
throat. Lina reacted without thinking, wrapping one
arm around his shoulders and clamping her other hand
over his mouth to silence him. He struggled in her grip,
his eyes wild.

"Ozben, no!" she hissed into his ear. "He's lying. It's
a trick." She prayed it was, at least.

Twisting in her grip, Ozben grazed her wounded arm
with his hand, and the pain made her light-headed. She
couldn't help it. She jerked her arm back, releasing him.

Ozben sprang up from behind the statue, his eyes
blazing. "I'll kill you!" he screamed.

For an instant, there was only silence as the echoes
of Ozben's voice died away, but then Lina heard a sound
that chilled the blood in her veins.

Laughter. A rumbling, mocking sound. The assassin
was laughing at them.

And then he was running, his boots clicking on the
marble floor, closer and closer.

Lina jumped up, grabbed Ozben by the arm, and tried
to pull him through the doorway behind them. Only he
wouldn't budge. "Ozben, come on!" she screamed.

"I'll kill him," Ozben repeated, and with a shudder,
Lina realized she believed him. If he could manage it,

Ozben would kill the assassin. And probably get killed in the process.

"Ozben, he's got a knife," Lina said, trying to reason with him. "We don't stand a chance, not like this. We have to find another way. Do you hear me?"

The assassin's shadow appeared in the doorway. He saw them in the corner and broke into a run, his knife flashing in the dim light.

"Ozben!" Lina screamed, and she didn't know whether it was her voice or the glimpse of the assassin's knife that pulled Ozben out of his rage, but he let her haul him out the door, and they took off running down a hallway between galleries.

The assassin was right on their heels now. They couldn't hide.

At the end of the hall was another set of galleries. They ran straight through the first two; in the third room, Lina veered them to the left and into a small resting room with three stone benches, a few chairs, and several portraits of humans and sarnuns hanging on the wall. She skidded to a stop, turned, and slammed the door to the previous gallery shut. There was no lock, and they had only a few seconds to block the door before the assassin burst through it.

"Quick, help me move that," Lina said, pointing to one of the big chairs. She and Ozben each grabbed an arm of the chair and lifted it, half carrying, half dragging it over to the door. "Wedge it under the knob," she directed, "as tightly as you can." Together, they managed to shove the back of the chair snugly beneath the doorknob.

"That should buy us a little more time," Ozben said. "Let's keep moving." There were two doors leading out of the room to the left and right. Ozben turned and headed for the door on the right.

"No, wait!" Lina pulled him up short, turning them toward the door on their left. "We want the stairs. We need to go up!"

"Whatever you say, just hurry!"

Lina heard the fury underlying the urgency in Ozben's voice. She didn't know how long she could keep him from turning and confronting the assassin. She had to do something fast.

She pulled him out the door and across a short hallway to a flight of stairs going up and down. She steered them up, and as she climbed, her mind raced with their options. They could activate the fire bell. She remembered there was one at the top of the stairs. Setting it off would bring the museum's night watchmen running, but they weren't armed, and there was a good chance the assassin would catch Ozben before the watchmen managed to summon the chamelins for help.

No, what they needed was to get the chamelins to come to them. Lina knew of only one way to do that, and it involved going up, to the top floor of the museum. After that . . . Lina's stomach did a little flip as a plan started to come together in her mind. She couldn't believe she was even considering it, but it looked as if they had no other choice.

"Ozben," Lina said, the breath burning in her chest as they crested the third-floor landing, "are you afraid of heights?"

"No, I'm not afraid," he said, but then he shot her a sidelong glance. "Wait, how high do you mean?"

"High," Lina said.

They hit the fourth floor and continued up, but their pace was slower now. Lina's legs ached, and there was a fire burning in her chest. Soon it would be unbearable. But they couldn't afford to stop and rest.

Next to her, Ozben was panting, his face covered in sweat. Lina started to encourage him when she caught her foot on the next riser and tripped. Her shin hit the stair hard, but she managed to grab the railing with her right hand to steady herself. She bit back a cry as pain flooded her leg.

"Are you all right?" Ozben asked, cupping her elbow to pull her to her feet.

"I think so," Lina said. She was lying. Her shin throbbed when she put her weight on it, and her arm ached, but she kept going, gritting her teeth against the pain.

Finally, after another grueling flight of stairs, they reached the museum's top floor. Ozben started to plunge ahead, but Lina grabbed his arm, forcing him to stop. "Let me think a minute."

"Love to, but we don't have a minute," Ozben said, "unless you want to fight that guy here." His tone told Lina that was exactly what he wanted to do. He glanced over the railing to the stairwell below. Lina didn't have to look. She could hear the assassin's boots pounding on the stairs. He'd broken through the barricaded door and was catching up. He was relentless.

"I just . . . I have to remember whether the ventilation shaft is in this gallery or the one to the east—or maybe the west." Lina tried to get her bearings even as she sucked in a lungful of air. "Why can't I . . . Ozben, I can't remember!" she shrieked, giving in to the panic that clawed at her.

"Yes, you can," Ozben said, gripping her shoulders. "You know Ortana better than anyone. You can do this."

"You're right. You're right." Lina blocked out the sound of the assassin's footsteps and forced herself to concentrate on her mental map. The top floor of the museum was the steam-power galleries—she'd spent a good portion of time there when she was researching the *Merlin*'s engines. Then there was the nautical wing, with its sextants, its star charts, and the hulls of wooden sailing ships recovered from the scrap fields. Whenever she walked through there, she heard a soft, constant ticking sound because it was right next door to—

"The clock room!" Lina cried, and suddenly everything fell into place. She knew where they needed to go. She grabbed Ozben's arm, and they took off running again.

When they entered the expansive chamber, sure enough, the sound of ticking filled the air. Clocks of every shape and size covered the walls or sat on pedestals in the center of the room. Most had twelve numbers on their faces, but some had only seven, and a few had seventeen. One of the largest clocks hung on the back wall, designed in a peculiar style that made it appear as if the clock were melting.

"Back there," Lina said, pointing to a far corner of the room where, attached to the wall, sat an old iron grate about a foot and a half off the floor. Next to it was an old grandfather clock, its pendulum hypnotically swinging back and forth. "Watch the doors while I get the grate open," she told Ozben.

With Ozben standing lookout, Lina went down on her knees in front of the grate. She reached into her apron and pulled out her screwdriver. Holding the smooth grip in both hands, she forced herself to take three deep breaths.

"Stay calm, be steady," she murmured to herself. "You can do this. Fast as lightning." Blocking everything else out, she fitted the screwdriver to the first screw and went to work. Seconds later, the last screw fell onto the floor, and Lina yanked the grate off the wall and tossed it aside. "Let's go!" she called to Ozben.

"Where does this shaft lead?" Ozben asked, his voice echoing all around Lina as she crawled headfirst through the opening.

You don't want to know, Lina thought. "Just stay close," she said, dodging the question. "It's not too far."

Ozben crawled into the shaft behind her. "We should have stayed to fight him," he said, anger punctuating each word. "He killed my parents."

"No, he didn't," Lina insisted. She couldn't be certain, of course, but the assassin's words rang false to her. "If he had killed your parents, word of their deaths would have reached us long before the assassin got here. Think, Ozben. He was just trying to lure you out of hiding."

Ozben didn't answer, and for a minute, they crawled on in silence. Then Lina heard a banging sound coming from the bottom of the shaft, and her heartbeat quickened. The assassin had found the grate. He was crawling up the shaft after them. She'd half hoped he would be too big to fit, but then she remembered how slender he was.

It doesn't matter, she told herself, trying to stay calm. *We have a good head start. We'll make it to the end of the shaft before him.*

And then the danger would get even worse.

Great job staying calm, Lina.

The shaft angled upward slightly. Lina raised her hand and called on the lumatites for more light. When she could see better, she crawled faster. Ozben was right behind her, his breath coming in short gasps.

"I'm sorry, Lina," he murmured. The anger in his voice was gone. "You're right. If it weren't for me, we'd have gotten away back there in the gallery. On top of that, you got hurt because of me."

"What, this? It's nothing—a kitten scratch." Lina wiggled her arm and then hissed as a wave of pain broke over her. "Okay, maybe a really mean kitten."

"No matter what, I won't let the assassin get to you," Ozben said. "If it comes to that, I'll let him have his kill."

"No, you won't. Sacrificing yourself is *not* part of the plan," Lina said. She wasn't about to lose her only friend to an assassin. She tried to keep her tone light, but her voice quivered as she rambled on. "I know exactly what the plan is, and maybe if you're lucky, I'll let you in on it in a few minutes, but sacrifice is so far outside the plan that I can't believe you brought it up. Don't you trust me to get us out of this? Have I ever steered us wrong—" She stopped and thought about that for a second. "You know what, never mind. But I *will* get us out of this."

Ozben's soft chuckle filled the shaft. "I know you will. I trust you."

Lina's heart warmed, and hope overcame some of her fear.

As they traversed the shaft the air got steadily colder. Lina was soon shivering, her breath making little clouds in front of her face. She heard Ozben curse softly when he put his hands against the frigid metal of the shaft.

"Pull your sleeves over your hands," she advised him.

"Why is it so cold all of a sudden?" Ozben asked, his voice hushed.

"Because we're almost to the end of the shaft," Lina said. "After thirty feet or so, it empties to the outside."

"Outside?" Ozben said. His voice had gone up an octave. "But won't that put us—"

"On a three-foot ledge on the side of a mountain, several thousand feet in the air," Lina said. "Or maybe a two-foot ledge."

"And *why* are we doing that?" Ozben asked. "So the assassin can more easily shove us off the mountain to our deaths?"

"Not at all," Lina said. "He'll barely fit on the ledge."

"He's a *trained assassin*, Lina," Ozben said in exasperation. "Don't you think he's probably had extensive training in killing and ledge-walking? Unlike us!"

"Of course that's possible," Lina said, matching his exasperated tone, "but I prefer to think positively! It will put some distance between us on our way up to the aeries."

"The aeries?" Ozben's voice was even higher.

"You said you trusted me, remember?" Lina pointed out.

Ozben had no comment for that, but Lina's plan was good. She knew it was. All they had to do was get close enough to the aeries to signal one of the chamelins. The top level of the chamelins' living quarters was open to the sky, and in their shape-shifted forms, they had keen night vision. Someone would see them and come to help.

By now, Lina could hear the wind whistling in frigid little gusts down the ventilation shaft. Twenty feet ahead of her loomed a wide, dark hole. They were almost there. "Brace yourself," she said. "When we come out, the ledge will be icy. Find sturdy handholds before you try to move, or you might slip, and don't look down."

"Don't worry," Ozben said. "Whatever happens, just keep moving."

Lina listened to the distant thumps of the assassin crawling through the shaft behind them. It was too much to hope for that he'd get stuck in the narrow space.

A gust of frigid air hit her in the face as she reached the end of the shaft. Taking a deep breath, Lina poked her head out into the open. Oh, she would give anything for a scarf to wrap around her face right now. When she'd recovered from the icy blast, the first thing she noticed was the stars. Thousands of them glittered in the blue-black expanse, an immeasurably beautiful canvas. Below them, moonlight shone on the snow-covered mountains. And though she'd warned Ozben against it, Lina looked down. The world fell away into a dark, bottomless pit, and her stomach flipped over.

"Lina, I'm right behind you," Ozben said. The sound of his voice was a comfort. "Is the ledge there?"

"Yes," she said, forcing herself to concentrate on the narrow rock shelf that extended to the left and right in front of the shaft. It had been carved there by hundreds of years of chamelin claws. They landed on the ledges to clear snow and ice from the shaft openings that lined the mountainside and provided ventilation for the stronghold.

Lina eased out onto the icy shelf and turned sideways so she could hug the mountain as much as possible while she crawled. Once she'd left the security of the shaft, fear rose up inside her again, stronger than ever. Taking in the sight of the bottomless pit on her right and the sheer rock wall on her left, Lina thought it was entirely possible that this could turn out to be the worst idea she'd ever come up with. No matter what, it would be the most memorable.

Unless they fell, of course.

Lina bit back a hysterical laugh and started to inch forward as the wind howled in her ears.

FOURTEEN

Ozben waited until Lina was safely on the ledge before he crawled out behind her. The wind hit him full force, and for a moment, all he could do was crouch there at the opening and try to suck in a breath of air. If he fell, it would probably be because all his limbs went numb from the cold.

But he knew he had no choice but to face the icy night. It was either forward or back into the arms of the assassin and his knife. Ozben risked one last glance back at the dark shape of their pursuer moving steadily toward him.

"Come on, Ozben," Lina called, her voice muffled by the wind.

Ozben swallowed, steeled himself, and followed Lina out onto the narrow ledge. In his opinion, she'd exaggerated its size by a wide margin. And between the snow, ice, and loose rock, finding a proper handhold would take a miracle.

Ozben pressed his body against the side of the mountain to help him keep his balance. Ahead, the light of the lumatites bobbed on Lina's wrist. Ozben focused on the light, not daring to look down at the abyss on his other side.

"How far away are the aeries?" he asked, shouting to be heard above the wind.

"Too far for us to crawl all the way there," Lina shouted back. "But we just have to get around the side of the mountain a little ways so we're within sight of them. Then I'll try to signal them with the lumatites. They'll see the light and come to investigate."

"But how can you be sure we'll be able to get close enough to them from here?" Ozben asked. The mountain was huge, and they were like two tiny insects crawling on it.

"Because I've been out on these ledges when I was first mapping Ortana's tunnels," Lina said. "I needed to see which ventilation shafts emptied to the outside."

Of course she's been out here before, Ozben thought. And for no other reason than she'd needed to see where all the ventilation shafts went. Ozben knew he shouldn't have been surprised, and despite the danger coming up behind them, he couldn't help shaking his head and grinning at Lina in pure admiration.

"You're crazy," he called to her. "Completely insane. You know that, right?"

Lina glanced back at him, her frizzy hair whipping around her face. She matched his grin. "It's a good kind of crazy, though, isn't it?"

"The best," Ozben said.

Lina's expression turned serious. "Stay close," she said. "When we see the aeries, I'll signal with the light."

Ozben nodded. He was about to ask what would happen if none of the chamelins were outside to see the lumatites, when a voice rang out in the darkness.

"Well, aren't you a brave one, little prince!"

Ozben looked over his shoulder and choked back a cry of shock and fear. The assassin had reached the end of the ventilation shaft, but Ozben hadn't put as much distance between himself and the opening as he'd thought. Holding on to the inside of the shaft, the assassin reached out and seized Ozben's ankle.

"Got you!"

Ozben yelped and instinctively dropped flat to his stomach, wrapping his right arm around the rock shelf and digging his left hand into a crevice in the side of the mountain. The assassin yanked on his ankle, dragging him backward across the icy stones.

"Ozben, hold on!" Lina cried. She was trying to turn around to help him, but there wasn't enough room on the ledge.

"Keep going!" Ozben shouted at her. Before Lina could react, the man yanked him back another few inches and leaned out to make a grab for his other ankle. Desperate to get loose, Ozben kicked out with his foot, clipping the assassin on the chin. The man grunted in pain and let go of Ozben's ankle. Off balance from the blow, the assassin grabbed the edge of the ledge to try to steady himself and slipped. For an instant, he scrambled to find a handhold, falling half out of the ventilation shaft. His heart in his throat, Ozben thought the assassin might fall out of the tunnel and down the mountainside, but the man caught himself at the last second by grabbing the lip of the shaft.

Ozben wasn't about to wait around to help. He surged forward, crawling fast and recklessly around the side of the mountain. Ahead of him, Lina was just as careless, and more than once they slipped and had to fall to their bellies on the ledge to keep from plunging off the mountain. Ozben trembled with cold and fear, but he kept moving. They had to put as much distance between them and the assassin as possible.

He risked a glance over his shoulder and saw that the assassin had recovered from his near-fall and was edging out onto the rock ledge.

But he was standing, not crawling.

"I knew he was a trained ledge-walker," Ozben yelled to Lina. Sometimes he hated being right.

But Lina didn't hear him. She continued to crawl for several more feet until finally she stopped. "There!" Lina shouted above the wind. "We're here, Ozben—look!"

He craned his neck to see over Lina's shoulder and glimpsed what appeared to be a large dome carved out of the tip of one of the mountain peaks about a hundred yards above where they were. Six open archways were visible around the dome, evenly spaced and large enough for a chamelin's height and bulk. Golden light glowed from within the structure, like a lighthouse in the middle of a dark sea. Seeing it gave Ozben a surge of hope. *Please, let the chamelins be watching.*

As he looked on, Lina said something to the lumatites that Ozben couldn't hear, then lifted her arm above her head. The fireflies took off, leaving the sanctuary of the leather band on her wrist to hover several feet in the air above Lina's head. Ozben stared in fascination. He'd never seen the insects leave Lina's wristband. Their twinkling lights were tiny but bright, cutting through the vast darkness.

"Come on," Ozben murmured, shooting a glance over his shoulder. His heart skipped a beat. The assassin was only twenty feet away. Though he moved slowly, Ozben calculated they had a minute at most before he caught them.

"Come on!" Ozben repeated, his voice rising in desperation. "We need help over here!" He squinted into the darkness, straining to see any sign of movement from within the dome above. But there was nothing.

They weren't going to make it. Ozben shot another quick glance over his shoulder and came to a decision. No way was he going to let the assassin get Lina too.

Slowly, Ozben began shimmying backward on the ledge. He would close the distance between himself and the assassin, creating a buffer to protect Lina.

At least, that was his intention. Until he felt Lina's hand snag his wrist and clamp down in a grip that was like cold iron.

"What do you think you're doing?" she yelled at him. She'd managed to turn around and was staring at him, her face red and chapped from the wind, her eyes two angry brown dots.

"Let go, Lina," he said, using his most commanding tone. He didn't dare try to pull free, or he risked knocking her off the ledge. "The chamelins aren't coming. We're out of time."

"They'll come!" she insisted. "Trust me, Ozben." Her gaze was pleading.

"I've always trusted you, Lina," he said. His chest tightened. "But I can't let you get hurt." He glanced down at the abyss below them, vowing that if the assassin pushed him off the ledge, Ozben would make sure he took the man with him. It was the only way to protect Lina.

Then, as he stared down at his fate, he realized there was something else out there besides empty air and the infinite dark.

A winged shadow glided through the night. Ozben would never have seen it if it hadn't flown over a patch of moonlit snow. The shape—a melding of a lizard and a bat—was unmistakable.

It was a chamelin, and not just any chamelin.

"Nirean," Ozben gasped, and all the hope he thought he'd lost suddenly blazed inside him. "We're going to make it!" he cried. He looked up at Lina. "We're going to—"

"Ozben, watch out!" Lina screamed, and before Ozben realized what was happening, she jerked hard on his arm.

With a cry of shock stuck in his throat, Ozben fell, plunging headfirst off the ledge.

FIFTEEN

When Lina saw Ozben grinning and shouting that they were going to make it, hope stirred inside her. Then she looked over Ozben's shoulder, and it vanished. The assassin was no longer moving carefully on the ledge. He was running toward them, his knife in hand, murder gleaming in his eyes.

"Ozben, watch out!" she screamed, and before she had time to consider what she was doing, Lina jerked on her friend's arm.

Ozben's eyes went wide as he lost his balance, and then he was toppling off the ledge. The assassin slashed the air with his knife, missing Ozben's neck by a hairs-breadth. Lina held on to her friend, stopping his fall, but Ozben's weight wrenched her arm and dragged her halfway off the ledge. She flailed with her other hand against the mountain, trying to find something to stop them both from falling over the edge. Her fingers dug into a small crevice, clutching it with all her strength.

Lina looked up, and the assassin overbalanced. He scrambled to grab the icy rocks, but his feet slipped out from under him, and he sailed over Lina, catching the rock ledge at the last moment. Lina watched his knife spin away into the darkness.

"Lina!" Ozben cried. He was trying to get his footing on the side of the mountain, but the surface was too sheer. "Let me go, or we'll both fall!"

"We're not . . . arguing about this . . . again," Lina said, straining with every muscle in her body to keep hold of him. She knew she was fighting a losing battle. She wasn't strong enough, not against the cold and the pain in her injured arm.

"Lina, it's all right," Ozben said, and—she couldn't believe it—he actually smiled at her. While he was dangling by one arm, thousands of feet above the ground.

And he thought *she* was the crazy one.

Then Lina saw it: the source of Ozben's hope. A shadow flew toward them, beating its wings against the wind, and when Lina saw who it was, tears of relief and joy filled her eyes.

Nirean landed on the ledge in front of her, her claws digging into the rock. She plucked Lina and Ozben up, one in each arm, as if they weighed nothing. Then, with one massive beat of her leathery wings, she launched herself off the mountain in the direction of the aeries. Lina looked down at the dizzying view of the assassin below her. He strained to hoist himself back onto the ledge, but he was slipping.

And then he fell.

Lina's heart stood still in her chest, and a chill went through her. The assassin was falling to his death. But . . . could it be? Another shape materialized out of the blackness below. There was a second chamelin. Wings flapping, he caught the assassin midfall and bore him away. In only a few moments, Lina lost sight of them completely.

She turned to Ozben to ask if he was all right, but her vision blurred and her head started to spin. She looked down and noticed that she was trembling, cold and shock seeping into her body. All around her, the lumatites hovered, one by one returning to her wristband. Lina tried to hold her arm steady to help them. Their silvery lights wavered and danced in her vision. Lina closed her eyes and let her head drop onto Nirean's shoulder, trying to clear the dizziness.

"Are they all right? Get them up here quick!" a human voice called from somewhere above. It almost sounded like Zara, but why would she be in the aeries? Lina tried to open her eyes but found she didn't have the strength. She was slipping into a deep kind of blackness, and now that she and Ozben were safe, she was more than willing to let it take her.

≈ SIXTEEN ≈

The first thing Lina became aware of when she awoke was that she was warm—wool-socks-and-a-thick-quilt-in-front-of-a-fire kind of warm. And when she opened her eyes to look around, she realized that her imagination wasn't far off. She was lying in a large four-poster bed beneath a blue and white patchwork quilt. To her left, a fire roared in the fireplace, giving off waves of delicious heat. Lina closed her eyes and soaked it in. During her and Ozben's journey on the mountain, she'd become convinced she'd never be warm again.

She had her eyes closed for only a few moments when she remembered Ozben, and they flew open. Was he safe? What had happened to the assassin? She remembered Nirean saving them, and another chamelin had rescued the assassin. But where were they all now?

And come to think of it, where was she? Lina didn't

recognize this room. It was small but cozy, with a tapestry of a colorful garden hanging on the back wall. On the other side of the fireplace, there was a small table and three chairs. A tea tray with a china pot and two cups sat on the table next to a thick hardbound book.

Carefully, Lina sat up, and as she did so, the quilt slipped off her shoulders, and she looked down at herself. Someone had bandaged her arm and dressed her in a thick cotton nightgown. She lifted the blanket to get a look at her feet. Yep, she even had on the wool socks.

She was about to climb out of bed to search for her clothes when the door on the far side of the room opened and Zara poked her head in. When she saw Lina, a bright smile crossed her face.

"I'm glad to see you're awake," she said, stepping into the room and shutting the door behind her. "You were asleep for over twelve hours."

"That long?" Lina threw the covers back and started to get out of bed.

"Not so fast," Zara said, holding up a hand. "I want you to stay put for a few minutes while I check you out." She took one of the chairs from the table and brought it over beside the bed. Sitting down, she put her hand against Lina's forehead. "You're a little warm," she said.

"It's the fire," Lina said. Zara's hand was cool on her flushed skin. "Is Ozben all right?" she asked.

"He's fine." Zara sighed and folded her hands in her

lap. Lina noticed there were dark circles of sleeplessness under her teacher's eyes. "When I saw you two hanging limp in Nirean's arms . . ." Zara shook her head. "You scared me to death."

So it was Zara's voice that Lina had heard just before she lost consciousness. "I thought we were going to fall off the mountain," she said, shuddering at the memory of clinging to the ledge and trying to hold on to Ozben. Lina's arms were stiff and sore.

"Nirean got to you just in time," Zara agreed. "Both of you were nearly frozen. Ozben woke up a couple hours ago, but then he was less banged up than you are."

Lina thought that seemed like good news. So why was there such sadness in Zara's eyes? "What is it?" she demanded. "What's wrong?"

"I'm afraid Ozben's had another shock," Zara said. "We received a message from the palace in Ardra. His grandfather, King Easmon, is dead. He succumbed to his illness."

Lina's heart sank. Poor Ozben. She wished she could have been with her friend when he got the news. "Where is he now?" she asked. "Can I see him?"

"He's in his room. Nirean's with him," Zara said. "You can see each other shortly." She frowned. "He's also been asking to speak to the assassin."

Lina wasn't surprised to hear that. "The man told him that he'd killed Ozben's parents," she explained. "I said it was a trick." Dread coiled in her stomach. "He *was* lying, wasn't he?"

Zara nodded. "Yes, it was a lie. I contacted the palace in Ardra an hour ago to assure the royal family that Ozben is safe."

"You contacted the palace an hour ago?" Lina said, confused. "How is that possible?" It would take a messenger several days to reach the palace under the best conditions, but with the winter storms in the mountains, it would likely take over a week.

Her teacher smiled enigmatically. "We have ways. We're experimenting with a new technology that's been in development for some time, a form of long-distance communication that uses wires."

"Wires?" Lina was intrigued. "Can I see it?"

"Maybe when you're recovered," Zara said. Her brow furrowed, and she looked at Lina intently. "Are you really all right?" she asked. "Ozben told me everything that happened—"

"Everything?" Lina interrupted. Did that mean he'd told Zara about the *Merlin?*.

Zara raised an eyebrow. "Everything about your run-in with the assassin," she said. "We found your guard unconscious by the museum gates. He's going to be all right."

Lina was grateful for that, but as soon as she could, she needed to go back down to her workshop to check on Aethon and the *Merlin*. Knowing the cat, he'd probably slept through all the excitement, but what about the ship? What was it thinking right now?

Lina's chest tightened. If she and Ozben had died, Aethon would have had to fend for himself, and Zara would never have known about Lina's secret, the wondrous airship. Worst of all, though, the *Merlin* would have been alone again, lost, without ever knowing why Lina had abandoned it. She'd made so many mistakes, she wasn't sure how she would go about untangling all of them.

But she could at least start here with Zara.

"There's something I want to tell you," Lina said slowly. "But it might take a while to explain, so if there's something you need to do, or . . ." She trailed off uncertainly.

"Wait," Zara said.

The woman stood up, and a wave of disappointment hit Lina hard. Zara was going to leave again, and Lina didn't know if she'd have the courage to tell her teacher everything later. "Don't go!" she blurted without thinking.

"I'm not going far," Zara said, shooting Lina a look of surprise. The teacher walked to the table, picked up the tea tray, and carried it back over to the bed. Placing it beside Lina, she sat back down in her chair. "Do you want to pour the tea, or should I?" she asked.

Relieved, Lina relaxed back onto the bed and nodded for Zara to pour her a cup. Steam rose from the pot, and the scent of chamomile tickled her nose. It was her favorite tea. Zara added one small lump of sugar, just the size Lina liked, and handed her the cup.

"Thank you," Lina said, taking a sip.

"You're welcome." Zara made herself a cup and sat back in her chair. "Whenever you're ready," she said. "Take your time."

Warmth spread through Lina's chest that had nothing to do with the tea or the cozy fire. She snuggled in against her bed pillows with the teacup warming her hands and told Zara everything.

But she started her story *before* the beginning, before she'd discovered the *Merlin*. She told Zara about her nine-year-old self, sitting outside the door of her parents' sickroom, how she'd hated being locked out but that she'd overheard her father ask Zara to be her teacher. She told her how much Zara's broken promise had hurt.

"I had no idea you were out there," Zara said, leaning forward to take Lina's hand.

Lina gave her a watery smile. "I've been hiding and listening for a long time," she said.

And then she told Zara about her explorations of Ortana. She described her maps of all the ventilation shafts and the secret tunnels she'd discovered over the years and how they had carried her to every part of the stronghold that was off-limits or forgotten. As she spoke she waited for Zara to get angry with her or to tell her she'd been wasting her studies, but when she sneaked a glance at her teacher over the rim of her teacup, she saw that Zara's expression was thoughtful, interested.

"You know," Zara said, toying with a strand of gray hair, "I can think of several archivists in the architectural department who would give anything to get a look at your maps," she said. "They could help when conducting repairs or tests of the stability of certain caverns. And I'm sure our maps of the ventilation systems are out-of-date. You could update them and make Archivist Heffmin very happy."

"Really?" Lina put down her cup as she considered this. She'd never thought about the possibility that her maps would be valued by the archivists. "I always thought that if I revealed the location of the secret tunnels, they'd be sealed off."

"You're not a small child anymore, Lina," Zara said. "Back then, we were worried you'd get lost or stuck in the tunnels and we'd never be able to find you."

Lina had to admit it was a fair point, considering the Hourglass passage to her workshop. "I never got lost," she said, and tried to push back the bundle of nerves gathering in her stomach, "but I did find something that was."

And then she told Zara about the *Merlin*, leaving

nothing out. As she spoke she expected her anxiety to get worse, but instead it felt like a weight lifted from her shoulders. She hadn't realized until now how much she'd wanted to share her discovery with Zara, to ask her teacher's advice about a being that Lina couldn't begin to comprehend and that in some ways frightened her.

By the time Lina finished her tale, Zara was sitting in stunned silence. Her teacup slipped from her grasp, but she caught it in a clumsy juggle before it shattered on the stone floor. With shaking hands, she set it back on the tea tray and stared at Lina.

"I can't believe it," she said. "I mean, I believe everything you said, but it's the most extraordinary thing I've ever heard. A sentient ship from the uncharted lands. We've never had an inkling of what's behind the Hiterian Mountains. There could be a whole species of organic technology. Goddess, it boggles the mind." Then her expression darkened. "And the archivists who found it kept it a secret from everyone, kept it for themselves. How could they have acted so irresponsibly?"

Lina's cheeks grew hot. She had done the same thing. She was no better than those archivists. "Maybe they were afraid someone would take the ship from them. They were only thinking of themselves—like I was."

Zara shook her head. "You're not like them, Lina."

"Yes, I am." Lina wouldn't meet Zara's gaze. "At first, I wanted the ship for myself too."

Zara reached out and lifted Lina's chin with her finger so Lina's eyes had to meet her teacher's. "But how do you feel now?"

Lina remembered the ship's loneliness, its longing for home. "I want to help it," she said, then shook her head. "No, I *have* to help it." How could she explain what she felt? "For a long time, I thought you'd abandoned me, and I was angry," she said, and winced at the sadness and guilt that passed over her teacher's face. "But I didn't understand," she rushed on. "I thought I knew what it meant to feel alone, but I was wrong. The *Merlin* was abandoned. For years, it was in a dark cave, cut off from light, sound, and every living thing. I'd never felt real loneliness and despair until I connected to the ship." Remembering it brought tears to Lina's eyes. "But the worst part, the part I don't understand, is that someone had to have sent the ship over the mountains. Whether they're human or something else, if they can feel as the *Merlin* can, why didn't they come after it?" She looked at Zara imploringly, needing some kind of explanation for the cruelty. "Why did they abandon it?"

"I don't know," Zara said. "Maybe they lost contact with the ship and thought it had stopped functioning and died in the crash. Another possibility is that they did send another ship, but it couldn't find the *Merlin*, because it was buried so deep in the mountain. We'll probably never know."

"All it wants is to go home," Lina said. "I have to try to fix it so it can."

Zara smiled. "Spoken like a true archivist," she said. "You said that its power source is missing. How are you going to replace it?"

"It's not missing," Lina said. "I know exactly where it is." And she told Zara about the Sun Sphere in the Special Collections wing. "I don't know how it ended up there, but—" She stopped speaking when she realized Zara had gone pale. "Are you all right?" Lina asked, leaning over the side of the bed to touch her teacher's shoulder.

"I—I'm fine," Zara said. "It's just . . . I mean, I never knew . . ." Her voice trailed off. There was a faraway look in her eyes, as if she were lost in some memory. "I can't believe it," she murmured.

Lina had a flash of inspiration. "You know, don't you? You know how the sphere got into the museum."

Zara blinked and refocused on Lina. She laughed weakly. "I know exactly how it got there," she said, "because I put it there."

"*You* found it?" Now it was Lina's turn to be stunned. Her mouth fell open, and she threw the quilt back to sit on the edge of the bed. "But how—? Where—? What—?" In her excitement, she couldn't form proper sentences.

"I—my, this is a lot to take in," Zara said. Like Lina, she fidgeted in her chair. "Let's see, it was probably thirty years ago. There'd been another cave-in below the museum in one of the big storage chambers. I was trying to find an opening to get to the blocked-off cavern. I hoped I could salvage some of the artifacts that were lost. I didn't get very far, because there was too much debris and the tunnels were still unstable, but while I was searching, shifting aside rocks and trying to see through the dust, I saw this light shining through the cracks in a rock pile. I thought maybe it was a lantern lost by one of the archivists who'd come down to search the rubble, but when I dug it out of the rock pile, I knew it was special. I spent a long time studying it before I gave up and put it in Special Collections."

It is special, Lina thought. *It's the heart of the* Merlin. *And Zara was the one to find it.* "I didn't know you used to explore those tunnels," she said.

Unexpectedly, Zara grinned. "Who do you think drew all those old maps of the ventilation systems?" Her smile faded. "Your parents were right about us, Lina. We're very much alike. We're explorers, but sometimes we get so wrapped up in our own worlds that we don't see what's going on around us. And we make mistakes."

"What do you mean?" Lina asked, confused.

Sorrow deepened the lines in Zara's face. "I have a daughter, Lina. Her name is Julia." She closed her eyes for a moment, as if gathering her strength. "You asked me the reason why I stopped teaching you. Julia is the reason."

Lina was stunned. She'd never known Zara had a child. Neither her teacher nor the other archivists had ever mentioned the girl. "Where is she?" Lina asked. "Does she live here in Ortana?"

"No," Zara said, "but let me explain. You need to understand. I had just been elected to the council when Julia turned sixteen. She was so excited for me at first, but later, when I started to spend all my time either going to meetings or studying artifacts, we got into arguments. Big ones. Her father had passed away a few years before, so it was just the two of us, and that made things hard enough. Then, after a while, the arguments stopped, and I thought everything was fine. We drifted apart so gradually, I didn't notice it at first. But when she came to me one day and told me that she was leaving Ortana, that she didn't want to be an archivist, it was like someone had dumped a bucket of cold water over my head. She said she didn't want to spend her life in a hole in the ground while the rest of the world went on without her. So she left, and she hasn't been back here since. We sometimes exchange letters, but even those have gotten fewer and fewer over the years."

"I'm so sorry," Lina murmured. She couldn't imagine what Zara must have felt, losing her daughter like that, not knowing where she was or what she was doing.

"Don't be," Zara said. "It was my fault for being so absorbed in my work that I couldn't see what was happening right in front of me. And what did I learn from it? Nothing. I told your parents I'd take care of you, Lina, and I meant it. I had such good intentions when I first started teaching you."

"But," Lina asked in a small voice, "why did you stop?"

"Because I got scared," Zara said. "I was scared of you."

Lina blinked. "Me?"

"Yes, you. You were a bright, curious, caring young girl—just like Julia, though I didn't think about the similarities back then. Those first two years I taught you, I was also helping you through your grief over your parents' deaths. I didn't have time to worry about my own heart, because I was focused on healing yours." She hesitated, her eyes full of memories. "And then, after you had healed, I realized that I loved you like a daughter." Tears sprang to Zara's eyes, and Lina's heart stuttered in her chest. "I was happy, but I was also terrified that I would mess everything up again, and I couldn't stand the pain of losing another child. So I pulled away. I told myself it was the best thing for both of us, even though I knew I was wrong. I thought I would get you an incredible teacher, someone who would see all the potential in you that I did, and you'd be happy. But you wouldn't let go of me." Zara wiped her eyes. "I was going to make you, but I just couldn't. You were so stubborn, so determined. And now, when I find out all that you've been through with the *Merlin,* and you didn't confide in me—"

"I'm sorry," Lina said, tears spilling down her cheeks. "I should have told you."

Zara waved it away. "We both should have trusted each other more. And I hate that it took almost losing you to make me realize how many mistakes I've made." She squeezed Lina's hand. "I'm sorry for breaking my promise," she said. "If there was a way we could start over after all this, I would gladly take it."

Lina jumped off the bed and threw her arms around Zara's neck. "I want to," she said. "I want another chance to have you as my teacher." She pulled back and looked at Zara. "But I have to take care of the *Merlin* first. Will you help me do that?"

Zara swiped a tear from Lina's cheek with her thumb. "I'll help you however I can," she said. "For what it's worth, I think you were right to keep the ship a secret between you and Ozben. Those archivists who found the ship are proof that not all of us have the best intentions."

"You think if we told the archivists, they wouldn't let the ship go home?" Lina asked.

"I hate to think that, but it's possible," Zara said. "Maybe we're not ready yet to have contact with people and technology from the uncharted lands. We already have enough problems fighting each other over resources. Introducing a living ship, one that either the

Merrow Kingdom or the Dragonfly territories could use as a weapon in the war, would be disastrous. No, I think the best thing to do is get the ship's heart back to it and let it go without anyone being the wiser."

Lina nodded. "I want to do it today," she said.

"You need to rest today," Zara said. "You're taking on a huge responsibility, one you'll need all your strength for."

Lina wanted to argue, but she knew Zara was right. "By the way," she said, looking around the room, "where are we?"

"This is my chamber," Zara said. Her mouth quirked in a smile. "I never showed it to you because I didn't want to find dralfa moss growing here one day."

Lina rolled her eyes, but she grinned. "You let *one* experiment go awry, and nobody trusts you again."

They both laughed, but Lina caught her breath when the door to Zara's chamber burst open and Ozben rushed in. He wore his usual bandaged-up disguise, but he ripped it off and threw it on the floor the moment he was safely inside.

Zara shot the boy a stern glance. "A knock would have been polite, Ozben," she said.

Lina's heart lifted when she saw her friend, but she could tell immediately that something wasn't right. Ozben was breathing heavily, as if he'd been running for miles, and his eyes were wide and panicked. When he saw her, relief replaced the panic in his eyes but only for an instant.

Before he could speak, another figure stepped through the door. It was Nirean in her human form.

"Please excuse our intrusion, Zara," she said grimly, "but we have news that couldn't wait." Her expression softened when she glanced at Lina. "I'm happy to see you're up and around," she said.

Lina nodded her thanks but barely heard the chamelin. Her attention was still on Ozben. "What's happened?" she asked.

"The assassin offered a full confession in exchange for leniency in his sentence," Nirean said.

"A confession?" Lina scoffed. "He was caught trying to push us off a mountain. He doesn't need to confess."

"We were wrong, Lina," Ozben said, speaking for the first time. His voice was hoarse, as if he'd been shouting. "The Dragonfly territories didn't hire the assassins to kill me and my family." He hesitated, and his face screwed up in an expression of misery that made Lina's heart ache. "My grandfather hired him."

⇚ SEVENTEEN ⇛

Astunned silence fell over the room. Ozben took in Lina and Zara's shocked faces and Nirean's solemn frown, but it was as if everything were happening from a distance—as if he were far away, treading water in a deep, dark lake, trying not to drown.

When Nirean had told him his grandfather's plan, he'd shouted at her over and over. It just couldn't be true—she had to be lying. He'd called her names that made him ashamed, which he'd need to apologize for. But now all he could do was stand there as Nirean took up the story for the second time, filling Lina and Zara in on everything the assassin had confessed. Ozben listened, hoping that maybe this time the story would be different, that his grandfather wouldn't be guilty of treason and conspiracy to commit murder.

After they'd taken him into custody, the chamelins

had searched the assassin and found a hidden pocket in his clothing that contained a handful of black sapphires. The discovery was what first triggered the suspicion that King Easmon might have hired the assassin, as the king had the only known collection of the rare gems. When confronted with this evidence, the assassin confessed to having a contact within Ortana, an archivist who had arranged to smuggle him into the stronghold and given him information on Ozben's whereabouts. Zara went pale with shock and fury at the revelation, for the only people who knew that Ozben was hiding in Ortana were the council members and a handful of chamelin guards, like Nirean, who'd been assigned to protect him. But only someone on the council would have had the authority to get the assassin into the stronghold past its security. In exchange for leniency, the assassin had named the archivist: Councilwoman Vargis.

Once she learned the identity of the assassin's contact, Nirean had gone with a group of guards to take the councilwoman into custody and conduct a search of her office. There, in a hidden compartment in Vargis's desk, they'd discovered several incriminating documents, letters signed by King Easmon and bearing his personal seal. The documents named a large sum of coin for Vargis's cooperation in the plan. With Vargis and the assassin now in custody and the king implicated in the plot, they both seemed eager to spill their secrets in exchange for mercy. Between the documents and their testimonies, they outlined an elaborate plot that began with Ozben's death and ended with the Merrow Kingdom winning the Iron War in one decisive battle.

It started with Ozben's father. King Easmon had been appalled that his son wanted to pursue peace talks with the Dragonfly territories. Ozben remembered their late-night arguments on the subject, but he'd never imagined how badly his grandfather wanted to *win* the war, to crush the Dragonfly territories and make them submit to his rule. No matter how much Ozben's father disagreed with this intention, while Easmon was king, his word was final.

But then Easmon fell ill. Ozben had known that his grandfather was sick, but he hadn't known that the king was dying. Easmon kept that information secret from everyone except his personal physician. He didn't want the Dragonfly territories to find out and take advantage of his weakness. But he also had to make sure his legacy—the Iron War—would be won, even after his death. As soon as he died, he knew that his son would try to make peace with King Aron. He couldn't let that happen.

He hired the assassins to storm the palace, but their intent was not to kill the entire royal family, as everyone believed. Their only target was Ozben.

When Ozben thought about it, it made perfect, if

morbid, sense. Ozben's father and mother were great military strategists, and his sister was a fine and honorable soldier and the heir to the throne. They were vital to the kingdom. Ozben was the extra heir, the expendable prince.

If Ozben was assassinated and it came out that the Dragonfly territories was responsible, Easmon believed that his son would be consumed by grief and rage and give up any notion of pursuing peace. Then Easmon could die knowing that his legacy was assured. Thankfully, that part of his plan had been foiled.

Except that King Easmon's plot didn't end there.

Just before his death, he dispatched a message to the commander of the troops mustering in the west near the archivists' border. In it were orders for the army to attack Kalmora, the largest city in the area, and burn it to the ground. The army was then instructed to sweep a path of destruction through the western portion of the Dragonfly territories all the way to the iron mines, wiping out the cities in their wake. It was a bold but risky strategy. Easmon had been sending thousands of his troops west, leaving his other armies vulnerable, but if he succeeded in his push, he would cripple the Dragonfly territories and cut off their access to the iron mines. Yet if King Aron managed to hold out against the attacking force, Easmon would lose half his army. Whoever won the battle would win the Iron War.

When Nirean had finished telling Lina and Zara the story, the room again fell silent, but not for long.

Zara spoke first. "Do either the assassin or Vargis know when the attack will start?" she asked.

"As soon as the troops are in place—a day, maybe two if we're very lucky," Nirean said.

Zara nodded. Worry was etched in every line of her features, but she kept her tone matter-of-fact. "Is your sister still in command of the Merrow armies?"

"Yes," Ozben said, finding his voice at last, "but Elinore doesn't know about the attack. Grandfather knew she would never carry out orders like that—she's a soldier, but she doesn't burn cities or kill innocent people—so he'd been keeping her away from the army gathered in the west, even though it's the larger force."

"He's right," Nirean said. "King Easmon's kept her back from the front lines, overseeing their outposts under the pretense that she's too important to lose. The orders for the attack were dispatched to Commander Cartwell. He's the one who's really in command in the west."

"I heard his name when I eavesdropped on the council meeting," Lina spoke up. She looked at Zara. "I also heard he's a cruel man."

"He is," Ozben said grimly. "He's exactly the type of person Grandfather would choose for this attack."

"But if King Easmon is dead, then Commander Cartwell has to follow the new king's orders, doesn't he?" Lina asked. "Ozben's father just needs to get a message to Cartwell to stop the battle."

"There isn't time," Nirean said. "It would take several days for the fastest courier to reach the army with the king's message. The battle will begin long before that. King Easmon planned well in his final days," she said, anger thick in her voice.

His grandfather *had* planned things well but not flawlessly, Ozben thought, as an idea suddenly occurred to him. He should have realized it sooner, but he'd been too upset. "We don't have to get a message from Father to the front lines," he said excitedly. "All we have to do is get my sister to retract the order." He turned to Lina. "Nirean's scouts told her they saw Elinore moving between some of the smaller outposts a few days ago, trying to boost morale, so she must be close enough to where the troops are mustering to get there in time." Ozben looked to Zara for confirmation. "She's the supreme commander of all Merrow's armies, even if she doesn't fight on the front lines. Only Father's and Mother's word overrides hers. She can stop the battle before it starts."

Zara looked away, exchanging a quick glance with Nirean. Ozben saw the look that passed between them, and a fresh wave of fear crashed over him. "What is it?" he said. "Elinore *is* nearby, right?"

"She was," Nirean said, "but there's a problem."

"How many more problems can there be!" Lina exclaimed, throwing up her hands. "Where is Ozben's sister?"

"The winter storms," Zara said. "In the last twelve hours, they've gotten much worse. About five miles west of where the Merrow armies are mustering is a place called Hawthorn Pass. It's a narrow, snow-filled valley that begins in the Merrow Kingdom and ends in the archivist nation. Up until now, refugees from the Merrow Kingdom have been using it to get to our strongholds. But the storms have cut off the pass, trapping a couple dozen refugees. Princess Elinore was at an outpost about two miles away when the storms hit. Word reached her about the refugees trapped in the pass, so she took a small group of soldiers to try to free them."

"But why would she go on a mission like that herself?" Lina asked. "Like you said, she's too valuable to lose."

Ozben sighed in exasperation. "Actually, that sounds just like something Elinore would do," he said. "If she couldn't be on the front lines fighting with her soldiers, she'd be doing everything she could to protect her people, even if it meant risking herself for a group of refugees."

Zara nodded. "This all took place yesterday, and we've had no word from Nirean's scouts about where the princess is now," she said. "We think she might have gotten trapped in the pass with the refugees."

"The storm is showing no signs of letting up anytime soon," Nirean said. "I've had every chamelin I can spare trying to fly into Hawthorn Pass, but after a certain point, there's a complete whiteout. We can't see to get to the refugees, and we risk more people getting lost."

"So what do we do?" Lina demanded. "We can't just sit and wait for the storm to pass. The battle will have started, and there won't be any stopping it."

Thousands of people were going to die, Ozben realized, maybe tens of thousands. And all because his grandfather had been a cruel, power-hungry old man. The war would end, one way or another, but the price of victory would be horrible.

Zara looked pale and grave, her head bowed in deep thought. She paced the chamber, then looked up at Nirean. "I have to call an emergency council session," she said. "Nirean, come with me. We don't have much time, but there has to be something we can do to break through the storm." Zara followed the chamelin to the door, and then turned and looked meaningfully at Lina and Ozben. "The two of you stay here for now." She raised a hand when Ozben started to protest. "We'll be back soon, but in the meantime, rest and get your strength back. You hear me?" she said, addressing Lina specifically. "Remember what we talked about and what you decided to do."

Lina didn't answer her teacher. She just nodded and gripped the folds of her nightdress. Ozben was shocked that she didn't argue or get angry about being left out. What was she thinking? Was she planning something?

When Zara and Nirean left, closing the door behind them, he turned to her. "I need to know what they're planning," he said. "We'll listen in on the meeting, just like you did, and then—"

But Lina cut him off. "We don't need to," she said. "The meeting won't help. There's no way for the chamelins to get through the storm into Hawthorn Pass, and I think Zara knows it."

Ozben clenched his fists in frustration. "There has to be a way!"

"There is," Lina said quietly. "I think Zara was thinking the same thing. That's why she left us alone here." She looked at Ozben, her expression serious. "We can ask the *Merlin* for help."

"Lina, are you sure?" Ozben asked.

No, she wasn't sure at all. Lina thought of the obstacles that lay between them and getting the ship into Hawthorn Pass. They had to reconnect its power source and hope that all those years spent lying dormant had recharged it, fix the door mechanism at the back of the cavern to get the ship outside, and then somehow fly it to Hawthorn Pass to rescue the refugees and Ozben's sister, all in the space of a day. And that wasn't even the hardest part.

"I have to think," she said. She shivered and walked over to stand in front of the fire. She stared into the flames, going over the events of the past few days. "This is all happening so fast."

"Tell me about it," Ozben said. He came to stand beside her at the fire.

Lina was comforted to have her friend with her. Ozben's whole world had been shaken, but he stood beside her calmly, trusting her to come up with a plan. Lina's heart warmed, but she was so conflicted.

She'd sworn to help the *Merlin*, no matter what.

"We have to get the *Merlin* outside the mountain," Lina said. "The ship is so lonely. It just wants to go home. But if we take it to Hawthorn Pass, the ship will be seen. How can we ask it to risk getting itself captured again?"

"I know we don't have any right to ask," Ozben said, "but this is so much bigger than us now. The refugees could die in that storm, and all those soldiers—there are thousands of them waiting to start the fight of the century. Whatever we do—or don't do—in the next twenty-four hours could decide the outcome of the war. The one thing I know for sure is that my sister is the only one who can stop the battle that's coming."

"And if she can stop this one battle, your father might be able to stop the war," Lina said. Her mind raced with the possibilities. She'd told Ozben there were a hundred different ways his plan for flying the ship to the Merrow Kingdom could go wrong. By her calculation, there were closer to a thousand things that could wreck this plan. But they had to try. There was no other way. "It has to be the ship's choice," she said. "We can't force it to help us."

"Agreed," Ozben said. "If it wants to go home, we have to let it."

"Let's go, then," Lina said. "We don't have time to waste."

"Wait," Ozben said, laying a hand on her shoulder. "I don't like that look in your eyes."

Lina bit her lip. A big part of her worried that their plan would fail before it began. "You said the ship and I understand each other, but what if we're too much alike? How can we get it to trust us when it's been used before?"

Ozben hesitated, seeming to think it over. "I think it's already trusted us a little bit. It reached out to you and told you its story. It let you feel how lonely it is and asked for your help. And remember when you told me about the cave-in and how the ship's wings deployed over your head? That wasn't an accident. It knows you, Lina. You're its best hope."

And it's our best hope, Lina thought. But would their connection be enough to convince the ship that they could save each other?

Slowly, she shook her head. "No, it's not enough," she said. "You're right. The *Merlin* let me see its memories so I could understand what it was going through.

That's why you have to connect to the ship too," she told Ozben. "You have to let it see what we're trying to protect."

"I don't think I'm the one for that," Ozben said doubtfully. "If my father was here, he'd be perfect."

"That's not true!" Lina blurted out, and Ozben looked at her in surprise. But she had to make him understand. "You say that you're not a soldier like Elinore or a great strategist like your parents, but so what? I'll tell you one thing: you're the bravest person I've ever met. You want to protect people. That's what a leader does, right? He puts himself between danger and the people he cares about. Without even blinking, you put yourself between me and a knife-wielding assassin, because that's just who you are." Her voice caught. "I love Ortana, but it's not the whole of Solace. The *Merlin* came over the mountains because it wanted to explore, to see what else was out there in the world. Ozben, you have to show it who we are."

Ozben was quiet. He stared at the fire for a long time, the flames reflecting in his eyes. When he finally turned to face her, he looked scared but determined. "I'll try," he said, and he leaned over and wrapped Lina in a tight hug. "Thanks for saying that."

Lina returned the hug, and when she pulled back, she smiled at him. Then her expression turned serious. "We need to get going," she said.

Ozben nodded. "I think I have a plan, or at least a place to start. We should split up. You go to the Special Collections wing and get the *Merlin*'s power source. In the meantime, I'll go back to the workshop, check on Aethon and the ship, and work on opening that door."

"Sounds like a solid plan to me," Lina said.

She just hoped they would be able to make it in time.

It turned out to be easier than Lina had thought to get the *Merlin*'s heart from the museum. Word had spread quickly through Ortana about the refugees trapped in the pass and the approaching battle, and most of the archivists had gathered in the council building to listen to the emergency session. While the council debated what was best to be done, Lina sneaked into the empty museum and removed the Sun Sphere from its alcove on the stairway.

As she made her way back to her workshop Lina thought about the energy contained within the sphere. She'd always thought it was a simple, inextinguishable flame, but now she knew it was so much more than that. It was an energy source of unknowable power. Lina carried it as if it were a sphere of delicate glass, but still her hands trembled.

She exited the museum and closed the gates behind her, cradling the sphere in one hand. When the gates were secure, she turned and almost jumped out of her skin. Simon stood in front of her, blocking her path.

"Simon!" she squeaked. "Wow, you can move like a cat when you want to. That's a good talent to have, sneaking—helpful in catching people doing nefarious things." There was no point in trying to hide the Sun Sphere. He'd already seen it. Her best bet now was to not look too guilty. "I'm glad you're here, actually," she said, trying to twist her expression into something that would indicate that Simon wasn't the *last* person in Ortana she'd wanted to encounter. "Councilwoman Zara asked me to retrieve this from Special Collections to take it to her office, and—"

"Don't even bother," he said, cutting her off, a scowl pinching his already unpleasant features. "Winterbock, has anyone ever told you that you're about the worst liar in the history of the world?"

Lina sighed. She did *not* have time for this. "Oh, come on, there must be a few people out there that are worse than me," she said. "All right, you want the truth—fine. Simon, the truth is, this sphere is actually the energy source for an ancient airship from the uncharted lands. It's hidden in a secret cavern deep in this very stronghold, and I'm going there now to restore the ship's power, fly it to Hawthorn Pass in the hopes of rescuing the refugees and ending the Iron War, and then let the ship go back to where it came from." She held up the sphere in one hand and rested her other hand on her hip. "Satisfied?"

Simon's scowl deepened. "If you're going to lie, keep

things simple. The more elaborate you get, the less people will believe you."

"Good advice," Lina said dryly. "I have to go now." She started to walk around him.

He stepped in front of her, blocking her path. "You're not going anywhere with that. It could be as dangerous as the flaming cat," he sneered. "You already caused enough trouble during that mess."

Lina gritted her teeth in anger. After their confrontation over Aethon and Simon's near-apology, she had thought the senior apprentice might actually have it in him to be reasonable. Obviously, she'd been wrong. "All right, I get it!" Lina practically yelled. "You hate me. Your teacher hates me. Yes, *he* has his reasons for being angry. I did grow purple fungus all over his favorite room. That was a bad idea. I eavesdropped on a private council meeting. That was worse." She narrowed her eyes at Simon. "What I don't get is *your* reason for hating me so much. What did I ever do to you?"

The question seemed to catch him off guard. He even took a step back, ducking his head so he wasn't looking her in the eye. "It doesn't matter," he mumbled. "Just put the sphere back, and I won't tell Councilman Tolwin you took it."

Now it was Lina who was caught off guard. Simon should have relished turning her in for a crime like this. "I can't do that, Simon," she said more calmly. "I really do need the sphere. It's important."

Simon's face reddened. "Why, so you can take it to your secret hiding place back there?" he asked angrily, pointing down the passage toward the curtain of deepa ivy. "Don't bother lying about that either," he said when Lina's mouth fell open in shock. "I've seen you coming and going from there. You didn't know I was watching, but I was." He sounded proud.

Lina couldn't believe it. She had always thought she was so careful to keep her workshop hidden. And that it was Simon who had found it was the worst of all possible circumstances. Yet he obviously hadn't told Tolwin about it, or the councilman would have had the tunnel sealed up long ago. What was going on in Simon's head?

"If you knew where I was all this time, why didn't you turn me in?" Lina asked suspiciously. "You had to have known it would make me miserable, so why didn't you take advantage of that?"

"I said it doesn't matter!" Simon snapped. He was more angry and flustered than ever. "Just give me the sphere and get out of here." Simon took a step forward as if to snatch it from her, but Lina jumped out of his reach and put the sphere behind her back, mindful of its tiny flame.

"Tell me why," she insisted. "Were you saving it for the right moment? One day when you were bored, you'd say, 'Oh, I know, I'll go ruin Lina's life today. That'll be hilarious.' Is that what you were waiting for?"

"You don't know anything!" Simon shouted, so loud

that Lina looked around anxiously to make sure no one had overheard him. His face was beet red to the tips of his ears, and he still wouldn't look her in the eye. "I never hated you, you idiot. I wanted to go with you to your hiding place!"

Lina's mouth worked, but at first, no words came out. She was too stunned. "You mean you wanted . . . to follow me?" she asked at last.

"I wanted to see where you went all the time," Simon said, more subdued now. "I tried to go after you a couple of times, but I couldn't fit through the tunnel."

The Hourglass. Of course. At fifteen, Simon already had the broad shoulders and thick chest of some adults twice his age. He would never fit through the passage.

"It wasn't just that, though," Simon went on, his voice tight. "You're always getting away with things. Zara never piles work on you, never shouts at you in front of people, like Tolwin does with me when I mess up. And she never threatens to tell your parents when you're not 'performing adequately.'"

"Zara shouts at me plenty in private," Lina said. "We argue all the time." And though she didn't say it, she would have given anything for her parents to be alive to scold her about not performing adequately.

Simon shook his head. "But you still get to do what-ever you want to. You have the perfect life."

"The perfect life?" Lina repeated. "How can you

think that I—" But then she stopped. Simon's miserable expression, his slumped shoulders, made her hesitate. She'd never considered things from Simon's perspective, what it must be like to have Tolwin for a teacher. Lina and Zara had their share of problems, but Zara had always been kind to her. Lina tried to remember a time when she'd seen Tolwin show kindness to anyone. She'd thought that uncaring nature made the two of them a perfect match, but now she was starting to think she was wrong. Before, when Simon had told her he'd never intended to hurt Aethon, maybe he'd wanted her to realize that he could be different from Tolwin. Maybe Simon was just as miserable as she would be under Tolwin's tutelage. It was no excuse for making Lina's life hard in return, but in that moment, she felt a pang of sympathy for Simon that she'd never felt before. It also gave her an idea.

"Listen, Simon," she said. "I'm sorry that you can't go down to my workshop, but if you let me go now and don't say anything to Tolwin, and if everything goes the way I hope in the next few hours, I'll be able to show you what I've been working on down there all this time."

He snorted. "Right. Because you've got a functioning airship squirreled away in your workshop? I'm not stupid, Lina."

"Just give me a few hours to prove it to you. That's all I'm asking," Lina said. She grinned at him. "Come on,

Simon, doesn't a little part of you want to be involved in a secret, high-risk plan that'll have disastrous consequences if it fails? Everyone needs to do that at least once in his life."

Simon shook his head. "You're crazy," he said, and Lina's hope faded. He wasn't going to let her pass. Well, it had been a long shot.

And then, miraculously, Simon stepped out of her way. "Fine, go ahead," he said, gesturing down the tunnel impatiently. "But don't expect me to cover for you when you get caught."

"Thanks, Simon!" Delighted, Lina took off. "Watch the skies," she called over her shoulder. "You might see something amazing."

Hopefully, it wouldn't be her and Ozben crashing into the side of a mountain.

EIGHTEEN

"**Y**ou were gone a long time. What kept you?"

Ozben was sitting on the floor playing with Aethon when Lina ran into the cavern. He jumped to his feet when he saw her, and Aethon ran over to twine his warm body around her legs. The workshop seemed even more frigid than usual, and the cat's heat was a welcome presence. Lina reached down and scratched him under the chin.

"I ran into Simon on my way here, but he's not going to turn me in for stealing the sphere," she assured him. Actually, she had a weird feeling that things might be better between them from now on. "Did you have any luck with the door mechanism?"

"See for yourself," Ozben said, grinning. He took her hand and led her around the *Merlin* toward the back of the cavern, but Lina was able to see almost at once that he'd been successful.

It looked as if a large slice of the wall had peeled back like a sliding door, to reveal a snowy landscape beyond. Small drifts were beginning to form in the doorway. Lina shivered and buttoned up her coat. That explained the extra chill in the air. She glanced down at Aethon to make sure he wasn't going to make a run for it, but the cat pressed against her, meowing and bumping her knee with his head. He didn't seem the least bit interested in going outside. In fact, when she took a step closer to the door, he let out a little hiss of displeasure and shrank back, refusing to follow her. Maybe carnelian cats, with their love of heat, hated the snow.

"The machinery was rusty, but it still worked," Ozben said, drawing her attention back to the door mechanism. "The cave-ins must have partially blocked the door, though, because I couldn't get it to open more than three quarters of the way, but I'm pretty sure it's big enough for the ship to fit through."

"That's great news," Lina said, giving him a quick hug. Then she knelt and let Aethon lick her hand. "Sorry I ran off earlier," she told him. "I have to leave again for a little while, but I'll be back soon. Look after the place while I'm gone, all right?" She kissed his wrinkled head, and Aethon curled up on the floor, a tiny ball of heat in the cold cavern.

Ozben watched the cat with a troubled expression. "I hate to be the one to bring this up, but what if we don't?" His voice dropped. "What if we don't come back?"

Lina didn't want to think about that, but Ozben was right. "Zara knows Aethon is down here. If the worst happens, or even if we're hurt and can't get back here right away, she'll coax him out, or have one of the other apprentices come and get him."

Ozben nodded. "But are you sure you want people to know about your workshop? It's your secret place."

Lina shrugged. "If I'm dead, it won't matter, and if I'm not . . . well, in a few hours, most of my secrets are going to be revealed anyway," she said. "I think it's for the best." She looked up at the *Merlin*. "We've all been in hiding too long."

Holding the sphere in her hands, she walked over to the ship. Ozben stayed beside her, and with every step Lina took, she felt a change in the air. It became denser, with crackles and bursts of emotion—anticipation, hope, fear—all emanating from the ship.

Before they reached it, the gangplank began to lower on its own, inviting them in. Lina walked up into the dark ship and was prepared to call on the lumatites for light when she noticed that the sphere in her hands was changing. The light grew brighter, filling the room with a yellow radiance that made orange spots pop in front of her eyes. She expected the light to burn her fingers, but it gave off no heat, only the steady, dazzling glow.

"Wow," Ozben said, his voice hushed. "They're reacting to each other, aren't they?"

"Its heart has been missing for so long," Lina said.

A lump rose in her throat. How had the ship survived all these years without being whole? It would have taken unimaginable strength.

By the time they reached the bridge, it was too bright for Lina to look directly at the sphere's light. She sat down in the pilot's chair and waited while Ozben sat in the other seat. She squinted, shielding her eyes as she held the sphere over the empty, burned-out spot in the center console. "Put your hands over mine," Lina told him. "We'll do it together. Remember what I told you about your memories?"

"I remember," Ozben said. He put his hands over hers, and Lina felt the trembling in his fingers.

"It'll be all right," she said, trying to soothe him. "Ready? Close your eyes."

Lina held her breath, and they gently lowered the sphere into place.

She didn't see what happened next, but she felt it. The loose wires on the sides of the console sprang to life like the feelers on a sarnun's head. They glided over her fingers, weaving themselves around the bands of the sphere, tightening, securing it into place as if it had never been gone. Lina and Ozben jerked their hands back so their fingers wouldn't get tangled in the wiring. Lina tried to open her eyes, but the light filled the small space, blinding her, and suddenly, she was overwhelmed by a rush of emotion so intense it made her heart flutter in her chest. Beside her, she heard Ozben cry out in alarm.

"Don't worry," she tried to say, but the words stuck in her throat. Tears rolled down her cheeks as she identified the emotions racing through her.

Hope.

Excitement.

Joy.

Gratitude.

They bombarded Lina, but she forced herself to focus, to push back against the tide and assert her own thoughts. Time was running out. She needed to communicate with the ship. With her eyes squeezed shut tightly, Lina opened her mind to the *Merlin*, letting her thoughts and emotions blend with it. She hoped that Ozben was doing the same.

And that they wouldn't lose themselves in the process.

Ozben was terrified.

He'd never felt anything as strongly as he felt the *Merlin*'s emotions. Wave after wave, they crashed into him, and he was drowning.

It reminded him of the time he'd gone swimming in the ocean, years ago, when he visited Noveen on a diplomatic trip with his father. The current had been so strong. The waves had swept him up and slammed him down on the sand. He'd sucked in a breath of foamy water that left him coughing and gasping until his father pounded him on the back. After that, he hadn't wanted to go back in the ocean until his father showed him the secret.

"You have to swim out past the breakers," he'd told Ozben. "There's calmer water just a few more feet from the shore. But you have to let go of the land to get to it."

Ozben didn't want to let go. He didn't want to lose his mind or be overcome by the ship. He thought he heard Lina calling to him from a distance, but he couldn't make out what she was saying.

You have to do this, he told himself. He had to open his mind and memories—but where to begin? How could he sum up everything his family and his kingdom meant to him and communicate that to the *Merlin*? Would it even understand?

It had to. Its emotions were so strong—so human— that it had to understand.

He started with the memory of his father taking him swimming in the ocean, how they'd floated in the calmer waters offshore. Ozben's fear had disappeared, because he knew his father would be there if anything happened. From that memory, he sent his mind spinning away to that day in the garden, the swordfight with his sister that the memory jar had shown him in such vivid detail.

He recalled how he'd wanted to protect his sister, to be brave, but he'd been cowed by his grandfather, who it turned out had never really cared about any of his family. He'd only cared about strength and power and how he could use them to get what he wanted.

He'll destroy everything if we don't stop him. Ozben imagined Easmon's army charging into battle, sweeping through the city of Kalmora and burning everything in its path. And the only person who could stop it was Elinore. But she was lost somewhere in Hawthorn Pass, alone in the middle of a storm where Ozben couldn't reach her.

I want to protect her. Was she safe? Was she thinking about Ozben, wondering if he was all right? She wouldn't believe it when he told her about his and Lina's escape from the assassin. She'd demand to hear every detail, from their run through the museum to the dangerous trek on the ledge. Ozben hoped that at the end of the story she'd be proud of him. He wanted to tell her all about Ortana too, and finding Lina. Oh, she would love Lina. Five minutes after they met, they'd be like sisters.

Somewhere in the storm of memories, Ozben felt moisture on his cheeks. He hardly ever cried, except in front of his mother and now Lina. He missed his family so much. He felt as if he were standing at the edge of a cliff, teetering back and forth, trying not to fall.

So close to losing everything.

"I know I don't have the right to ask you to care about any of this," Ozben whispered, needing to speak the words aloud. He hoped the ship could understand him. "You came to this part of the world to explore, and look how we welcomed you. You don't have any reason to trust us, but I swear we're more than what you've seen. We can be selfish, cruel, and heartless to one another, but we can also love." That was a legacy to fight for. Did the ship know what love was? Could it recognize that emotion shining from the memories Ozben offered it? "There are so many things here worth saving," he said, "but we can't do it alone. We need help."

He waited, tense and adrift, for some kind of acknowledgment from the ship, but there was only silence. The emotional storm receded, replaced by a void that Ozben couldn't penetrate. He couldn't tell if this was a good sign. Was the ship considering his request? Did it want to listen?

As he waited Ozben slowly became aware of himself again. His legs sank into the padded chair he was sitting on, and the chill of the air touched his face. He opened his eyes and saw that the blinding light of the sphere had subsided to a dull glow nested in the console.

If nothing else, the *Merlin*'s heart was back where it belonged. Lina deserved most of the credit for that, but Ozben was proud to have played his part. He looked across at her. She opened her eyes and gazed at him, her mouth pinched tight in concern.

"I didn't get an answer," she said. "Did you?"

He shook his head. "I didn't feel anything. What do you think it means?"

Tears shone in Lina's eyes. "Maybe it means no," she said. She stood up and wiped her eyes. "Come on. We'd better leave. You've opened the door, and now that the ship has power, it should be able to take off on its own."

Ozben stood up and trudged after Lina. The weight of hopelessness settled on his shoulders and spread like a fog in his mind. What would they do now? What would become of the war? What about his family?

The questions piled on top of each other, then suddenly Lina stopped short and Ozben ran into her from behind. "What's wrong?" he asked.

And then he caught his breath.

The gangplank was rising, sealing the ship with them still inside. At first, Ozben didn't dare to hope, but then a feeling washed over him like a breath of cool, crisp air. It reminded him of the way he felt when his mother came up behind him and put her arm around his shoulders. He always felt safe and reassured, as if no matter how bad things got, everything would turn out all right in the end.

That was the *Merlin*'s answer. It was going to help them.

"Thank you," Ozben said, reaching out a trembling hand to touch the ship's hull. Words could never express all that he felt, but he had to say them. "Thank you."

Lina and Ozben hurried back to the bridge and strapped themselves into the pilot and copilot seats. The Sun Sphere made a low humming sound that grew louder as the *Merlin* powered up, and Lina's heart pounded that much harder in response.

"What should we do?" Ozben asked her, his hands hovering helplessly over the control panel. The needles on the various gauges were moving, but Lina didn't have the first clue how to read them. She assumed that the ship could control all its systems on its own, and as for the steam engines in back—Lina didn't think those were even running. As far as she could tell, the steam engines were meant as a backup system in case the ship's primary power source failed, probably something that would be used only when the ship had a crew on board to operate them.

"I think for now we sit back and let the ship do the flying," Lina said. "It came over the mountains on its own with no pilot. If it needs us to do something, I think it'll let us know."

"But how do we show it where to go?" Ozben asked. "There are no windows up here."

He gestured at the wall in front of them and, as if in response to his request, the metal shimmered like the sun on the surface of a lake. Lina's mouth fell open as the effect faded to reveal a pane of glass. Through it, she could see into the cavern. Unable to resist, Lina shrugged out of her seat harness and pressed both hands against the glass.

"Amazing," she said, turning to grin at Ozben. "It's real glass, or at least it is now."

Ozben's eyes were wide. "What kind of metal can do that—change to glass whenever it wants to?"

"Organic metal," Lina said. "The ship must be some kind of shape-shifter, like the chamelins."

A low rumble went through the ship. Lina felt the vibration in her legs, and suddenly the ship began to move. Teetering on her feet, she fell back into her chair and strapped herself in. "Hold on," she said as a thrill of excitement and fear rushed through her.

She wasn't sure whether the wheels of the ship's landing gear would still be functional after having the boulders wedged around it from the cave-in. But aside from a few wobbles and groans, the ship was moving, backing steadily toward the rear of the cavern, where Ozben had uncovered the exit.

A flash of light out of the corner of her eye drew Lina's attention to the center console. The Sun Sphere's light was pulsing.

"What do you think it means?" Ozben asked, but Lina had no idea.

Then a tingling sensation crawled over the back of

her neck, as if someone were standing behind her. The ship's presence seemed to grow around her. On instinct, Lina closed her eyes and opened her mind. When she did, the ship gave her what felt like a mental nudge toward the console.

Lina opened her eyes. "It's the *Merlin*," she said. "I think it wants me to touch the Sun Sphere."

"Maybe it needs you to guide it," Ozben said. "Can you picture in your head how to get to Hawthorn Pass?"

"I think so," Lina said. She'd been there once or twice when the apprentices were sent on field assignments to study the environment around Ortana. They'd covered geology and the seasonal weather patterns of the mountain climate.

Cautiously, Lina leaned over the console and put out her hand. The Sun Sphere radiated warmth but not enough to burn. She dipped her hand into the bright light and let her fingers rest on the metal bands encasing the sphere.

An image of the mountains immediately surrounding Ortana filled Lina's mind. She recognized them. They were from the ship's memories of the time before it had crashed. The *Merlin* was trying to figure out where it was and where it had to go. As best she could, Lina added her own images to the mix, calling up every memory she had of trekking through the mountains with the other apprentices. When she came to Hawthorn Pass, with its steep walls and snow-covered valley, she lingered on the image. She thought of the storm that was hitting the pass, imagining fierce winds and blinding snow. She was trying to get across what they were in for. Would the ship be able to navigate through those conditions?

Lina felt Ozben tugging on her arm. Her link to the ship faded, and she opened her eyes.

"Sorry, but I think you're going to want to see this," he said.

Lina looked out the window and realized with a jolt that they were outside the mountain. Curtains of snow already blanketed the window, but as Lina watched, the delicate flakes melted and ran down the glass in dozens of thin rivers. It was as if the ship was giving off its own heat waves. The rumbling within the ship had grown louder, filling her ears, and that's when Lina realized they were hovering in the air.

Ozben was right. She wouldn't have missed this for the world.

Lina fumbled at her harness straps again, intending to get up out of her seat and press her face against the glass for a better view, but Ozben reached across the space between them to stop her hands.

"I wouldn't do that right now," he advised. "We don't know how fast the ship can go. One minute you might be staring out the window, and the next you could end up as a Lina-sized pancake splattered against the glass."

Lina couldn't help giggling at the image his words conjured. She knew he was right, but still, she itched to get up and watch the ship's ascent. So far, they were rising straight up the mountainside, propelled by the updrafts beneath the ship's wings or by the Sun Sphere or by both. The rocky outcrops and snow-filled crevices rushed by as the *Merlin* picked up speed, and a burst of exhilaration washed over Lina. It seemed to emanate from both her and the ship—a surge of freedom and the thrill of uncertainty accompanying it.

We've come out of hiding.

They were venturing forth into the world, and none of them knew what would happen next. Lina was used to being in situations she could control, to having the safety of tunnel walls around her, but now she had to put her faith and trust in the *Merlin*. Her heart pounded in her chest, and when she looked over at Ozben, she saw his eyes wide with excitement as he gazed out the window.

And then they cleared the mountaintop, and the whole of Ortana spread out below them.

Lina looked down and gasped. She'd never seen the stronghold from above like this, and at that moment, she envied the chamelins their wings and keen vision. Through the blowing snow, she glimpsed the lights of the domed aeries shining in the darkness. Below it were the turrets of stone and glass she'd described to Ozben, along with the crescent-shaped balcony where the archivists brought their telescopes out on cold nights to look at the sky over Gazer's Gorge. Those astronomers would have loved the view out the *Merlin*'s window.

"Goddess, that's amazing," Ozben breathed. As the ship rose higher in the air, the strongholds of Geligaunt and Ironstar came into view. Immense stone bridges stretched from each of the strongholds to span the gorge, with lanterns hung on tall iron posts lighting the way across.

"I've never seen the bridges like this," Lina murmured, gazing down at the glittering paths. They were moving forward now, soaring over the strongholds, and Lina wondered whether any of the archivists were looking up and seeing the airship. How would they react? With awe? Fear? Lina shook her head. She would worry about that after they returned from Hawthorn Pass.

The snow fell harder as they flew away from the stronghold, heading north. Wind buffeted the ship, making Lina glad she'd heeded Ozben's advice to stay strapped into her seat. Clouds obscured the moonlight, and after a few minutes, Lina couldn't see anything out the window but snow and darkness.

"This isn't good," Ozben said. "How does the ship know where we're going if we can't see a foot in front of the window?"

"I don't know," Lina said, feeling helpless. She'd

shown the ship an image in her mind of the path to Hawthorn Pass, but that had been in daylight on a clear afternoon. How did it know where to go now? And even if they reached the pass, they'd have to descend into a steep ravine without crashing into the canyon wall, then somehow find the refugees and Ozben's sister in the middle of the storm.

"There must be something we're missing," Ozben said. "The ship could be using a form of navigation we're not familiar with, the same way it communicates by emotions instead of words. Maybe it has other senses that are telling it where to go."

"I hope so," Lina said. But even if that was the case, how would they find the refugees? Did the ship have a way of sensing them too?

They flew on into the darkness, leaving Gazer's Gorge and the strongholds behind. The deeper they traveled into the mountains, the worse visibility became. As time passed, Lina's anxiety grew.

Suddenly, a spike of wariness surged through her, an emotion that Lina immediately recognized as not her own.

"Did you feel that?" Ozben asked, and Lina nodded. On the heels of the warning, an image flashed through her mind, a group of large winged shadows fighting through the storm and the wind buffeting them against rock walls.

"It's the chamelins," Lina said. "The ship is sensing

them. They're trying to get into the pass." She flinched as she saw a chamelin slam into the side of the mountain, his wings twisting around his body. He dropped onto a ledge and rolled, his claws digging for purchase on the rocks. They were fighting a losing battle. "The storm's too much for them," Lina said. "They'll never get through."

The wind had intensified, battering the ship from side to side. For the first time since they'd put it back in the console, the Sun Sphere flickered, its power wavering as the ship tried to push forward into the storm.

"Maybe there's a way we can bring the chamelins on board," Ozben said. "I think I remember seeing an access hatch on the upper level. It only opens from the inside. We could bring the chamelins in through there and—" But he stopped, making a noise of frustration. "The snow's so thick, they won't even know we're out here with them."

"Maybe we can fix that," Lina said, scanning the control panel. She wished she could read what each button and knob did. She needed the ship to guide her. "We want to rescue the chamelins and bring them on board," she said, raising her voice to address the *Merlin* directly. "But they can't see us in the dark." A gust of wind struck the ship, throwing Lina against the back of her seat. The Sun Sphere flickered again, and Lina knew the ship must be hurting too, yet it continued on—for them.

She hated just sitting here doing nothing while the

ship took on all the burden of the rescue mission. The *Merlin* was meant to have a crew, or at the very least a pilot—someone to share the workload. There had to be something she and Ozben could do to help.

"You don't have to do this alone," Lina said to the *Merlin*. "Show me how to help fly the ship."

Ozben's head whipped around in surprise. "I'm sorry—did you just say you want to *fly* the ship now?"

"Why not?" Lina asked. Her excitement built as the idea took root in her mind. "I mean, I don't expect to become a fabulous pilot overnight, but we need a crew to help the ship. Think about it. It's doing everything right now—routing power, compensating for the storm, navigation, and probably a hundred other little things we're not aware of."

"All right, I'll give you that, but what about me?" Ozben asked, raising an eyebrow. "What am I going to be doing while you get to be *the first human to pilot an airship from the uncharted lands*? Not that I'm jealous or anything," he added quickly.

"Oh, don't worry," Lina said, shooting him a mischievous grin. "You get to go topside to rescue the chamelins. How did you put it? 'The least important prince of the Merrow Kingdom' gets to save the day by getting on top of an airship in the middle of the worst blizzard in history."

Ozben considered that for a second, and then he

smiled. "Yep, that's pretty good," he said. His expression quickly turned serious. "But won't an air rescue be risky?"

Lina bit her lip. "Yes and no." The ship shuddered, jostling them in their seats. "Feel that?" she said. "The wind is already batting the ship around as if it's a toy. If we land now, we might not be able to land again to pick up all the refugees. I don't know what the limits of its power source are."

"You're right," Ozben said. "I'll make sure the chamelins get on board safely, but whatever happens, be careful, Lina."

"You too," she said, reaching over to squeeze his hand.

Carefully, Ozben unhooked his harness. He put a hand against the wall, bracing himself, as he made his way to the stairs at the rear of the ship. Lina watched him go for a moment, her stomach churning with worry. She'd tried to be light-hearted about it, but she knew that what they were about to do would be dangerous. If the ship couldn't hold steady, Ozben could fall, or if she didn't steer the *Merlin* correctly, they might crash into the side of a mountain.

Lina forced those doubts and fears aside. "All right," she said, her hand hovering over the Sun Sphere. "If this is a bad idea, you'd better let me know now." She waited for a flicker of emotion from the ship, but she didn't feel anything. Lina wondered if that meant the *Merlin* was as uncertain about this as she was.

Only one way to find out.

Lina closed her eyes, put her hand on the sphere, and reached out to the *Merlin*. Images flew through her mind, mostly of the control panel and the corresponding functions of the ship. At first, Lina couldn't grasp them at all. They were too far beyond anything she'd studied in her books. Then, gradually, she realized that the ship was showing her two main controls. The first was how to steer the ship while compensating for the wind, and the second . . .

Lina opened her eyes and smiled. She reached for a dial on the control panel. "I hope the chamelins are ready for this," she said to the ship.

Ozben found the hatch. A ladder bolted to the floor led to the small recessed square of metal in the roof of the ship. The chamelins would barely fit through it in their winged forms, but this was their best option.

He climbed up the ladder and had his hand on the latch when Lina shouted up to him from the bridge. "Ozben!" she called. "I'm going to signal the chamelins, let them know we're here. Brace yourself!"

Brace himself? What did that mean? "All right!" he shouted back, then unfastened the bolt on the hatch and pushed it up. A blast of wind and wet snow hit him in the face, blinding him. Ozben scrubbed his coat sleeve over his eyes and blinked several times to clear his vision. Hooking his left arm over the top rung of the ladder, he pushed the hatch all the way open, and it slammed against the roof of the ship.

Swirling snow, darkness, and frigid air greeted Ozben as he poked his head out the hatch. The wind howled in his ears and burned against his face. For a second, he felt as if he was back on that mountain ledge with the assassin chasing him. He couldn't see in any direction, and there was no sign of the chamelins. Ozben didn't know how Lina was going to signal them, unless there was some way she could use the lumatites again. Though even their glow would be a paltry thing in this storm.

At that moment, Ozben's world exploded in light.

He teetered on his unsteady perch and grabbed onto the top rung with his right hand. Balancing carefully, he looked around for the source of the brilliant light and was shocked.

It was the entire ship.

The *Merlin*'s metal skin had turned a dazzling gold that lit up the sky like a thousand candles. They'd become a beacon in the night.

When Ozben's eyes had somewhat adjusted to the dazzling light, he glimpsed five shapes not too far from the ship. They fought the wind, making a slow but steady path toward him. Bracing himself with his feet, Ozben waved his arms in the air, beckoning the chamelins to the hatch. A few minutes later, the first of them landed on the roof of the ship, claws digging little furrows into the metal. Ozben winced, hoping that the damage didn't hurt the *Merlin*. Could the ship feel pain the way humans did? He had no idea, and no time to consider it now as he reached out and grabbed the chamelin by the arm to try to steady him as he climbed to the hatch.

Behind Ozben, another chamelin landed on the ship with a loud bang. He scrambled across the slick metal surface and grabbed the edge of the hatch just as Ozben started to climb down the ladder to help the first of the chamelins inside.

When they were safely in the ship and out of the storm, the chamelin flapped the snow from his wings and stared at Ozben in bewildered recognition. Ozben didn't blame him. As the chamelin shifted back to his human form, his wet wings drawing into his shrinking body, Ozben wondered which of the thousand questions the chamelin surely had would get out of his mouth first.

He was surprised when the chamelin simply bowed his head to Ozben and said, "Thank you for the rescue." He was out of breath, shivering as he adjusted his dripping robe to his human form. "You got here just in time."

Ozben flushed, suddenly embarrassed. "Oh, you're welcome," he said. He was saved from saying anything else as, one by one, the rest of the chamelins descended the ladder and shape-shifted to their human forms.

"Everything all right up there?" Lina called from below.

"We're all here," Ozben answered. He glanced at the chamelin who had thanked him. "Were there only five of you?"

"Yes." The chamelin nodded. "I'm Malror," he said, holding out his hand.

"Ozben," Ozben said, shaking it.

Malror's lips quirked in a wry smile. "I know who you are, Prince Ozben." He took in his surroundings and let out a low whistle. "I never knew the archivists had an airship," he said. "With this, we may actually make it into the pass."

"That's the plan," Ozben said. He decided not to mention the fact that the archivists didn't actually know about the airship.

"Where is the rest of the crew?" one of the other chamelins asked.

"We just have a pilot," Ozben said, fidgeting. He realized that he should have been better prepared for the questions the chamelins would ask. "We needed to make as much room for the refugees as we could."

"I see." Malror nodded, but Ozben could tell by his expression that he sensed there was more going on.

"Ozben!" Lina shouted. "Little help here, please!"

"On my way!" Ozben heard the controlled panic in her voice and sprinted for the stairs. "You might want to hold on to something," he called back over his shoulder to the chamelins. He didn't mention that the pilot was an apprentice, not an archivist, and that she wasn't actually a pilot. Why burden them with details?

When he got to the bridge, Lina was sweating, one hand with a white-knuckled grip on the steering controls in front of her and the other flying over the panel, adjusting dials and checking gauges. Ozben was impressed— and a little frightened.

"How did you learn how to do all that in the last few minutes?" he asked.

"The *Merlin*'s guiding me," Lina said, distracted by all she was doing. "We're coming up on the pass," she said. "I'm trying to hold the ship steady while it descends, but this wind is horrible." She muttered something Ozben didn't catch and thumped one of the gauges with her knuckle.

"What can I do?" Ozben asked, strapping himself into the seat beside her.

"Keep an eye out for the refugees," Lina said. "We don't want to land until we're within sight of them."

"Will do." Ozben leaned forward, straining to see out the window. The ship was still glowing like a star. Even if the refugees had taken shelter somewhere among the rocks, surely they would notice the beacon shining above them.

He glanced over at the Sun Sphere, and a wave of foreboding went through him. The power source's glow was noticeably dimmer than it had been when they'd started their journey.

"Umm, Lina," he said. He didn't want to distract her, but they had the beginnings of a serious problem.

"I saw it," Lina said tersely. "I can feel it too. The ship is bleeding power. It needs time to recharge."

"Can it recharge while we're on the ground?" Ozben asked.

"I hope so," Lina said. Suddenly she jerked the controls to the left. "There's a break in the wind. We're going down. Hold on!"

The ship groaned as Lina pointed the nose downward and fought to keep the controls steady. Ozben's stomach churned at the sudden weightlessness as the ship dropped, then dropped again. *Oh, please don't let me throw up now.*

"Argh! This isn't going to be gentle!" Lina yelled, jerking the controls again.

"Yeah, I kinda guessed that," Ozben said weakly. Then a faint light broke through the darkness beyond the window. Nothing more than a brief glimmer, and it was gone before he could call Lina's attention to it.

His nausea forgotten, Ozben leaned forward, straining against his harness to see out the window. "Come on," he muttered. "I know you're out there somewhere, Elinore. Give me a signal—something!"

As if his sister had heard him, flickering lights started appearing on the ground below them. They were never visible for more than a second or two before vanishing, but it was enough to convince Ozben.

"I see them!" he cried excitedly, pointing to the specks of light. "I think they're trying to use signal lanterns, but they can't keep them lit. They're right below us!"

"Goddess, I hope they get out of the way," Lina said, her voice strained.

Rock walls rushed past them, so close that Ozben gulped. He imagined the ship's wings scraping along the rocks or snapping off completely. Ozben kept his gaze on the flickering lights and tried to push those thoughts out of his mind.

Almost there. Just a little bit more.

The ground came up fast. The ship's landing gear had barely deployed before they touched down and dragged through deep snowdrifts. Ozben rocked back against his seat and lost sight of the lights.

"Hold on! Hold on!" Lina screamed, and Ozben didn't know whether she was talking to him, the chamelins, or the *Merlin*. They were still moving, sliding along the ground, but now the snow was helping them. The heavy drifts slowed the ship down, and eventually they ground to a stop with a rock wall rising steeply to their left out the window.

When they were no longer moving, Lina began turning dials and pulling levers to power down the ship. The Sun Sphere's light faded to a single flame. It looked as it had that first time Ozben had seen it in the museum.

Next to him, Lina sat back in her chair and closed her eyes. She crossed her arms over her chest, holding herself, and Ozben realized she was trembling.

"Hey, easy now," he said. He shrugged out of his harness and leaned over to pull her into a hug. "You did it. You were amazing. Hey, you hear me? We made it."

Lina nodded, but she didn't speak, just leaned her head against Ozben's shoulder. He could feel her heart pounding. After a minute, she lifted her head and gave him a tremulous smile. "I'm not a very good pilot," she said.

He snorted. "Best I've ever seen." He nodded out the window. "Come on. We're not out of this yet. The refugees are outside, and I want you to meet my sister."

≋ NINETEEN ≋

Lina followed Ozben down the gangplank with the chamelins in tow. The wind bit through her heavy coat. She also wore a thick scarf, mittens, and heavy boots. Ozben was similarly attired. They'd armed themselves as best they could against the freezing temperatures in the pass.

The ship's light had diminished to a dull glow, but there was still enough of it to see the dozens of shapes moving in the darkness in front of the ship. Lanterns flickered here and there, fighting to stay lit against the wind and damp snow swirling in the air.

As they approached the crowd of refugees, a woman separated from a group and came forward. Long, straight black hair poked out from beneath her hooded cloak, and a thick wool scarf covered most of her face, but even through the snow, Lina recognized the blue-

and-yellow military uniform, the Merrow Kingdom's colors.

The woman held up her lantern and uttered a wordless cry of disbelief. She broke into a run, battling through the snowdrifts until she reached them.

"Ozben Cornelius Merrow," she said in a tone somewhere between exasperation and relief. "What in the wide world are you doing out here, and what . . ." She trailed off and just stared at the *Merlin*, her mouth hanging open and her lantern dangling from her hand. "*What is that?*"

Ozben couldn't control the smile that spread across his face. He struggled against the wind up to his sister and threw his arms around her, hugging her tightly and jostling the lantern. "Missed you," he said, and then he murmured something in a low voice that Lina couldn't hear, but beneath her hood, his sister's eyes softened, and she whispered something back to him.

They broke apart, and Ozben turned to Lina. "Elinore, this is my friend Lina Winterbock. She flew the ship here."

"Well, not exactly," Lina said. "That is . . ." She faltered as Elinore eyed her curiously. She realized she couldn't just blurt out that the ship was alive. Smiling weakly, Lina held out her hand. "I've heard so much about you," she said.

As the girls shook hands, Ozben looked over the

crowd of refugees. "Listen, Elinore, I promise I'll explain everything later, but right now we're in big trouble."

"More trouble than this blasted storm?" Elinore said, shivering as she wrapped her cloak more tightly around herself.

"Believe it or not, we've got something that tops a blizzard," Lina said. "Your brother will fill you in." She turned to Ozben. "I'm going to check on the ship and see if we'll be able to take off. The storm's not getting any better. We need to get the refugees on board as quickly as possible."

"We'll take care of that," Malror said, walking up to them. The other chamelins were already moving through the crowd of refugees, gathering everyone and checking them over for injuries. For the most part, they seemed all right, but here and there, Lina saw makeshift stretchers, their occupants swaddled in thick blankets. A couple of these were children. The others stuck close together to share warmth, and many of them stared at the airship in wonder, pointing and murmuring. All told, there were a couple dozen of them, and five Merrow soldiers that had accompanied Elinore into the pass. The *Merlin* was designed to carry passengers and crew, but not very many. Even if they used every cabin and storage area, the ship was going to be full for the journey home. Lina just hoped they had the power to take off with so many people aboard.

She tromped through the heavy snowdrifts and climbed back up the gangplank. Hurrying to the bridge, she sat down in the pilot's seat and, pulling her mittens off, let her hand hover over the Sun Sphere. Its light had begun to brighten again since they'd landed, but she didn't know if it was regenerating power fast enough.

"Are you all right?" Lina asked softly. "I'm so sorry. I know the trip was hard on you."

In response to her words, she felt a brush of affection from the *Merlin* and then a wave of determination.

"You're right. We can't give up now," Lina said. "We've already come so far. Ozben found his sister. She's lovely. Well, what I could see of her under the cloak was lovely." Lina let her hand rest absently on the steering controls. "Don't tell anyone, but I envy her. I would have liked to have a little brother like Ozben. I'm sure she missed him a lot when he was gone." Her voice dropped to a whisper, and her chest ached.

The affection humming from the ship grew stronger, enveloping Lina like a warm blanket. She smiled and sat back in her seat, watching the Sun Sphere brighten. Her smile turned wistful. "I'll bet you have people waiting for you at home too."

The *Merlin*'s affection wavered, sliding into uncertainty. Lina realized that she was getting better at recognizing the changes in the ship's emotions. "Don't worry," she said, trying her best to be soothing. "They're all waiting for you. I know it. Your family—dozens, hundreds of airships, or whatever your uncles and cousins might look like—they're all searching the sky, waiting for you to come home."

I'll make sure you get there, Lina thought as hope ignited within the *Merlin*. Somehow, she would get them all home safely.

A few minutes later, Lina heard voices coming up the gangplank. She stood and ran to help the chamelins guide the refugees through the ship. It was a tight fit, just as she'd feared. Ozben and his sister came last, and Elinore's face, when she pushed back her cloak hood, was ashen. Obviously, Ozben had told her about King Easmon's plot.

"Are we ready to take off?" Ozben asked as the gangplank rose and sealed behind them.

"I wish we could stay here another half hour or so," Lina said. "The ship's still resting."

"Resting?" Elinore asked, raising an eyebrow. "That's a funny way of putting it." She paused a moment, then added, "As you said, the storm's not letting up. We don't have time to waste."

Lina exchanged a nervous glance with Ozben. Elinore didn't know what they were dealing with here, but they hadn't discussed whether to tell her the truth or not. Would she believe them if they told her about the ship?

Ozben seemed to understand what Lina was thinking. He turned to Elinore and put a hand on her arm. "You don't understand," he said quietly, so the others wouldn't hear. "This isn't an ordinary ship."

"I assumed as much," Elinore said, crossing her arms. "Is there something else I should know, Ozben?"

But before Ozben could reply, Elinore's eyes widened, and she put a hand against her chest as if she was in pain.

"Elinore?" Ozben said worriedly, clutching her arm. "What's wrong?"

Lina suspected she knew, but she waited for Elinore to say it.

"I—I'm all right," Elinore said, rubbing her chest absently. "For a second I thought I felt something, except . . . except it wasn't coming from me. But . . . that's crazy."

"Not on this ship," Lina said.

Elinore looked from Ozben to Lina, confused. "What do you mean?"

"The *Merlin*—that's its name—is more than just a ship," Ozben said. "It's alive."

Elinore frowned at her brother. "Surely you don't expect me to believe—"

Her words cut off as she gasped and clutched her chest again. She staggered, and Ozben and Lina had to steady her, one at each arm.

"Take a breath," Ozben said. "The strangeness will pass in a minute. It's a little overwhelming at first."

Elinore leaned on them for support. "Ozben, this is . . . I mean . . . where did you . . . how did you . . ."

"Wow, you know you're onto something impressive when my sister's at a loss for words." Ozben grinned, but his smile vanished quickly. "You can't tell the others, Elinore."

"If the ship doesn't take off, it won't be for lack of trying," Lina said. "But it's dangerous. The ship's power source—its heart—is drained."

"I—I understand," Elinore said unsteadily. "This is all just a little bit much to take."

"I know the feeling," Ozben said. "But we'll do our best to get back in the air."

"And then I can get to my soldiers—order them to stand down," Elinore said. A look of determination came over her face. "Can I do anything to help you two up here?" she asked, nodding to the bridge.

Lina shook her head. "The best thing you can do is look after the refugees and hold on tight," she said. "It's going to be a bumpy takeoff."

Elinore nodded, reached over to ruffle Ozben's hair—he swatted her hands away, but he was grinning—and headed for the stairs at the back of the ship.

Lina followed Ozben to the bridge and strapped herself into the pilot's seat. She shot a nervous glance at the

Sun Sphere. Still not at full power. "This is going to be difficult," she said.

"Well, so far everything else has been, so why not this too?" Ozben said, adjusting his harness.

Lina took a steadying breath and reached out to the ship with her thoughts. *We're ready when you are.*

In response, a low rumble shuddered through the ship as its systems powered up, and Lina put her hands on the steering controls to hold the ship steady. The vibrations ran up her arms and made her whole body tremble. She imagined the ship readying itself, drawing in energy as if it were preparing to spread its wings and fly like the chamelins. But the *Merlin* was so much heavier than a chamelin, and there were a lot more people on board now.

With a loud groan that echoed in Lina's ears, the ship lifted off the ground, hovering about five feet in the air. The needles on the gauges flipped to the right as far as they could go, and the whole ship seemed to be straining. Wind gusted down, dropping them a couple of feet, like a hand pressing them back toward the earth.

Lina gripped the controls until her hands ached. She didn't know if she was helping any, but she knew the *Merlin* was in pain. She could feel it—not the pain itself but fear emanated from the ship.

"You can do it," Ozben urged. Lina looked over at him, but he wasn't addressing her. His attention was fixed on the flickering light of the Sun Sphere. "We're all with you," he said. "We believe in you."

Lina closed her eyes and thought back to the night in her workshop when a cave-in had almost buried her, and the time when she'd chased the fiery carnelian cat toward a library full of paper. She thought of her and Ozben crawling on the rock ledge on the side of a mountain. All those times she'd been fighting for something. She'd been afraid but had pressed on as best she could.

Think of home, she thought to the *Merlin,* putting all the love and hope she could into the emotion. That's what they fought for—Ozben, the refugees, the ship—they were all fighting to get home.

We have to end it. End this war, so we can all go home again.

The ship surged upward, pushing back against the wind to rise ten feet, and then ten more. Up and up they climbed, and the rock walls of the pass flew by on either side of them. Lina held on to the controls as her heart beat wildly with hope.

"That's it," Ozben murmured. "Higher. Higher. You're doing it!" he cried. "You're almost there!"

And then, with a burst of speed, they cleared the pass and were airborne again, with the mountains scrolling by beneath them. Ozben and Lina let out a loud whoop, which echoed throughout the ship.

Lina steered the ship around and let it settle into a

course back toward Ortana. Then her hands slid off the controls, and she sank back in her seat and closed her eyes for a moment.

Thank you. She sent the thought to the ship with a burst of love that was too great to be contained.

They were going home.

TWENTY

Once they were clear of the pass, the swirling snow finally began to abate. Lina held the ship steady while the chamelins opened the top hatch. She watched through the window as most of them flew out into the night, back toward the stronghold to let the archivists know to prepare to receive the refugees, some of whom were wounded or suffering from frostbite. Two other chamelins stood just outside the bridge, waiting to fly Elinore to the front lines so she could rescind Commander Cartwell's orders to attack.

"Do you think you'll make it in time?" Ozben asked anxiously. He stood at the door to the bridge, watching as his sister fastened her cloak and pulled on her gloves.

"I'll make it," Elinore said. "I have to."

From her seat on the bridge, Lina heard the weariness in Elinore's voice. She'd been fighting for a long time, Lina realized, and was more than ready for the war to end.

One of the chamelins came down the stairs from the upper deck, still in human form. "We're ready to leave when you are, Your Highness," he said.

"Excellent." Elinore turned to Ozben and pulled him close for a quick hug. She said something in his ear that Lina didn't hear, but she saw Ozben nod in response. They broke apart, and Elinore met her eyes. "I know you'll look out for him," she said, smiling. "Thank you for everything."

Lina nodded. "Be safe."

If only Elinore could have stayed with them longer, Lina thought. She knew how much Ozben had missed his sister, and Lina would have liked the chance to get to know her better.

Elinore turned and quickly followed the chamelin down the passage and up the stairs to the upper deck. A few minutes later, Lina caught a glimpse of two chamelins flying away from the ship, one holding Elinore tightly. It wouldn't be a comfortable journey, Lina thought, but she believed the chamelins would get Elinore to the front lines in time. The mission to Hawthorn Pass had been a success, and Lina couldn't have been more grateful.

Yet now that they'd rescued the refugees, Lina had time to worry about what lay ahead. The chamelins would of course tell the archivists who—and what—it was that had saved them. Zara would surely try to explain things, but Lina still had no idea what kind of reception to expect when they landed.

And she didn't have long to wait. As Lina gazed out the front window, the strongholds appeared in the distance. Lina took hold of the controls once more and began to descend.

Ozben stepped onto the bridge and sat down beside her. "I'm going to try to have the ship land on the bridge outside Ortana," she told him "We'll get the refugees out, then take off again as quickly as we can."

"Wait, you mean we're going with the ship?" Ozben said, surprise in his voice. "But its next stop is the other side of the Hiterian Mountains—to the uncharted lands."

"Don't worry," Lina said, her lips quirking in a smile. "I'm not planning on stowing away. But I want to make sure the *Merlin* gets on its way safely." She'd been thinking for a while about the best place to go. "We'll fly it to the other side of Gazer's Gorge and send it off from there."

What she didn't say to Ozben was that she also wanted a chance to say goodbye. Lina bit her lip as tears welled up in her eyes. She blinked them back and concentrated on the ship's descent. The wide stone bridge that spanned Gazer's Gorge grew larger in the window as they approached. So focused was she on keeping the ship steady, Lina didn't immediately notice the dozens of figures standing on the bridge, pointing at the sky. As they got closer, she saw more of them pouring out of Ortana's front gates. Her stomach flipped over, and Lina shot Ozben an anxious glance. "Looks like we're going to have a reception," she said.

"Hopefully it's a warm one," Ozben said.

The ship hovered over the bridge for a moment before settling onto its landing wheels. Lina checked the Sun Sphere and was relieved to see its light holding steady.

They had done it. Lina took a moment to savor the relief and joy that washed over her. She leaned over and hugged Ozben.

"Great job," he murmured in her ear.

"You too," Lina said.

They stood, and Lina grasped Ozben's hand as they left the controls behind and headed for the gangplank. The ship, sensing their desire to leave, slowly opened. A freezing wind swept in, stealing Lina's breath. As the gangplank lowered, loud voices echoed from just outside the ship.

"It's opening. Get ready!"

"Clear a path! Out of the way!"

Lina and Ozben descended the stairs, and the crowd surged toward them through the snow. There were dozens of archivists, apprentices, and even refugees. She looked around for Zara but didn't see her.

"What if someone recognizes me?" Ozben murmured

apprehensively. He'd pulled his hat down low over his brows and wrapped his scarf tightly around his face so that only his eyes and nose were exposed.

"Let's hope they're too distracted by the ship," Lina whispered back. She didn't think anyone would be expecting a prince of the Merrow Kingdom to step off the ship.

Luckily, the chamelins were there also, some in human form and some not. They kept the crowd a safe distance away from the gangplank as the first of the refugees emerged from the ship.

"I said clear a path!" Malror bellowed, dividing the crowd. As he did, a team of archivists from the medical wing pushed through with stretchers and blankets.

That's when Lina caught a glimpse of Zara. She and Tolwin led the other council members through the crowd. Lina tried to push down the nerves fluttering madly in her stomach.

"I suppose a 'Welcome back' is in order," said Councilman Davort. His voice was unsteady, and his gaze was locked on the ship. He cleared his throat before speaking again. "When the chamelins told us how you'd rescued the refugees, I could hardly believe they weren't making up fanciful stories. But then Zara"—he turned to Lina's teacher with a raised eyebrow—"claimed it was all true. It sounds as if you have a marvelous story to tell."

"I'd like to hear it too," said a voice that Lina recognized.

She looked over Zara's shoulder and saw Simon working his way to the front of the crowd. Nirean wasn't far behind him. He came right up to Lina, shaking his head, an actual smile on his face instead of his usual sour expression.

"You were telling the truth," Simon said when he reached her. "I didn't believe you, but you really were telling the truth about everything."

"I told you I'd show you what I've been working on," Lina said, smiling.

"You mean to tell me you knew about this?" Councilman Tolwin's voice was sharp. He wove his way to Simon in the press of people and put a hand on the boy's shoulder. "You neglected to mention it to me."

Simon didn't flinch under Tolwin's hand, which surprised Lina. He nodded at his teacher, not denying the accusation. Then he turned back to Lina. "Thanks for showing me," he said to her.

"You're welcome," Lina replied.

"All right, that's enough of this foolishness," Tolwin said, refusing to be ignored. Lina felt a stab of irritation at the man even as she braced herself for his wrath. "We should get the rest of the refugees back inside," he said. "Simon, take charge of the apprentices. Council members, I volunteer my services to lead the team of archivists from the technology division while they search and secure the ship."

Lina and Ozben stepped forward to block the

gangplank. "You can't do that," Lina said firmly. She'd been afraid this moment was coming. She didn't know what to say to the archivists; she just knew that, no matter what, she couldn't let them take the *Merlin*. "We did what we had to do and rescued the refugees. Now it's time for the ship to go."

"Go?" Tolwin repeated. The other council members and archivists murmured among themselves, but no one else spoke. "Of course it's not going anywhere. We have to get the ship inside and seal it off from the public until we know more about what it is and where it came from."

"I told you where it came from, Tolwin," Zara spoke up. She offered Lina a brief, encouraging smile. "It originated from the uncharted lands, and it's going back there."

"How?" Tolwin scoffed. "Flown there by children? The ship came from the lower tunnels. It's the property of the archivists of Ortana, and it should be processed and studied just like any other artifact from the meteor fields."

"Yes," one of the other council members added. "We have not discussed this issue in a formal council session. Now that the refugees are safe, we can consider the best course of action with regard to the ship."

"No!" Lina burst out with more force than she'd intended. "You're not having a *meeting* about this! The *Merlin* isn't yours to take apart and study!"

"*Merlin?*" Tolwin repeated. "What kind of an absurd name is that?"

"It's my name for the ship," Lina snapped, "but only because I don't know its real name. It can't speak, but it can *feel*, because it has a soul. I know you probably won't believe that, and a few weeks ago, I wouldn't have believed it either, but it's true. The ship is alive, and it doesn't belong to anyone. I'm going to make sure it gets home, no matter what the rest of you say."

Silence fell in the wake of her outburst. Beside her, Ozben smiled and nudged her with his elbow.

Lina knew she should feel proud of standing up to everyone and protecting the *Merlin*, but she was too nervous. Would the archivists believe her? Would they really let the ship leave?

"This is ridiculous!" Tolwin said, sniffing derisively. "The girl is obviously making up stories." He turned to Nirean. "Escort the children inside so we can proceed. We've wasted enough time standing out here in the cold. We can wage a debate in the council room once the ship is secure."

Lina took a step back up the gangplank, and Ozben followed, staying by her side. "We're not going," he said.

"You don't have a choice." Tolwin's face had turned an angry red. "I said escort the children inside, Nirean!"

But the chamelin didn't move, and neither did anyone else.

"What are you saying, Lina?" Councilwoman Jasanna asked, stepping forward. "How do you know the ship is a living thing?"

"The same way a memory jar lets you remember important things you've lost, or how the same book can tell a different story to each person," Ozben offered. "You don't know how or why those things exist, right? You just accept that they do, and that they're amazing."

"But this is more than just an artifact that fell from another world," Lina said. "It's not lost. The *Merlin* has a home to go back to in the uncharted lands. The archivists who found it were wrong to keep its heart, and you're wrong to try to keep the ship here."

"You don't understand," Tolwin said. He seemed calmer now, but his steel-gray eyes passed over the ship in a way that Lina didn't like at all. "The value of a ship like this, especially if it comes from the uncharted lands, is immeasurable."

"So you would take it prisoner against its will, Tolwin?" Zara asked. "Is that the way of the archivists now?"

"Don't be naïve, Zara," Tolwin said. "This girl may have you wrapped around her little finger, but the rest of us aren't blind to her childish games."

Lina decided she'd had enough of being insulted. "I'm not lying!" she said angrily, and suddenly, an idea flashed into her mind. Before she could consider the consequences, she said, "You want me to prove to you that the ship is alive, Tolwin? Fine. Come and stand with us on the gangplank. I'll show you."

A murmur of uncertainty went through the watching crowd. Ozben nudged Lina again. "Are you sure that's a good idea?" he asked.

"Not at all," Lina murmured back. It was true she didn't want Tolwin coming anywhere near the ship, but she had to do *something* to convince the council that she was telling the truth, and now seemed like the time for drastic measures. "What are you waiting for, Councilman Tolwin?" she pressed. "You said you didn't want to keep standing out here in the cold, so come on. Prove me a liar."

Lina watched Tolwin's face carefully as she spoke. If she went too far, he'd just dismiss her as a child again. But he had to be curious about the ship. If she knew Tolwin at all, his love for technology would overcome his pride.

She was right. Eyes pinned on Lina, Tolwin walked briskly to the ship's gangplank. He stopped briefly before he continued up the walkway to Lina and Ozben and crossed his arms over his chest. "Go ahead," he invited. "Show me proof of your living ship."

Lina took a deep breath and closed her eyes. *It's up to you now.* She sent the thought to the ship. *Let him feel what you made me feel the first time we met.*

She exhaled, and a moment passed in tense silence.

A fierce gust of wind howled across the bridge, making Lina shiver. She opened her eyes and gazed over the faces in the crowd, their cheeks and noses red from the cold. Nirean and Zara both nodded their encouragement. They were with her. Simon met her eyes, but Lina couldn't tell what he was thinking. The rest of the crowd was watching Tolwin and the ship. It was as if everyone on the bridge was holding their breath in expectation of what would happen next. The moment was agonizing.

What if the ship didn't connect with Tolwin? The thought filled Lina with dread. Or what if Tolwin wasn't receptive to the ship's emotions for some reason? As mean as he could be sometimes, surely Tolwin wasn't heartless. Was he?

And then it happened.

Tolwin drew in a quick breath, and his hand clenched into a fist. Then he closed his eyes and became utterly still. Lina tried to take a step toward him, but Ozben stopped her.

"Wait," he whispered, his breath fogging the air. "Let him feel it."

Lina's heart pounded. What *was* Tolwin feeling? What was he thinking?

Suddenly, Tolwin let out a cry and, trembling, fell to his knees. His cry broke the spell on the crowd, which surged forward even as Lina and Ozben crouched on either side of the man to see if he was all right. In an instant, there were people everywhere, pushing to get closer to the three of them. Lina tried to scramble farther up the gangplank and narrowly missed getting her hand trampled by a group of refugees.

"What is it, Tolwin?" Councilman Davort cried from the press of bodies. "Is it true?" His question was echoed by at least a dozen others, voices overlapping in a noisy cacophony.

"Everyone get back! Give them room!" Nirean bellowed, stepping in to shield Lina and Ozben with her body. "Stop pushing!"

Then, as if things couldn't get any worse, Tolwin's breathless voice joined the shouts. "It's true," he croaked. "The ship . . . it . . . it's sentient. . . . We must secure it!"

Oh no. No, no, no. Panic welled in Lina's chest. This wasn't what was supposed to happen. Tolwin was supposed to back off once he felt the ship's emotions. But it appeared she'd accomplished just the opposite. Tolwin was climbing to his feet, shakily. Determination blazed in his eyes.

"He won't quit until he gets on the ship!" Ozben shouted at Lina.

"I know," Lina cried. She looked at her friend, desperate for an idea, as the crowd pushed in. Step by step, she and Ozben were being pushed back up the gangplank. She wasn't sure whether the people were trying to get to Tolwin or to the ship itself, but either way, in another few seconds, the ship was going to be filled with people.

"Out of the way!" Zara's voice cut through the crowd, and she and Nirean were suddenly in front of them, pulling the refugees and archivists back from the gangplank. But before Lina could separate herself from the people, Tolwin was looming over her. He grabbed her shoulder and shoved her hard. Lina screamed as she lost her balance and started to topple backward.

An arm reached out and grabbed her, yanking her back to her feet. Lina didn't see who it was that had saved her at first, but then Simon's forest-green tunic materialized in front of her. He reached around her and grabbed Tolwin by the shoulder, hauling him backward with a strength Lina hadn't known the boy had. He didn't stop until he'd drawn Tolwin off the gangplank entirely, where he held him in place by the arm. Tolwin might have been able to break free if he hadn't just been hit with the blast of the ship's emotions, but as it was, he struggled weakly in his apprentice's grip.

"Thank you," Lina said, hoping Simon could hear her over the noise of the crowd.

"You'd better get out of here," Simon called back. He nodded to the ship. "Take it somewhere safe."

"He's right," Ozben said. "Lina, we need to go now."

"Everyone calm yourselves!" Councilman Davort's voice boomed over the crowd. "We will have order here! Stand back from the children now, all of you!"

Lina shot a glance at Zara, who was corralling the refugees. Her teacher nodded. "Go," she mouthed. "Be careful."

Lina knew it was their chance. She scrambled up the gangplank, Ozben on her heels. "Close the door," she called to the ship, but the gangplank was already lifting. A couple of the archivists tried to grab the edge and pull it back down, but Nirean descended on them, yanking them away. And with a clang, the ship sealed and the noise outside cut off.

Lina ran to the bridge. Her hands were shaking so badly she could barely get herself strapped in, but somehow she managed it. The Sun Sphere glowed brightly, and the ship began to rise in the air.

"That was close," Ozben said, the ship rising beneath them. "Are we heading for the other side of Gazer's Gorge?"

"That's right," Lina said. "We can send the ship on its way from there, but we'll still be able to signal to Nirean to come and fly us back to Ortana."

"Good plan," Ozben said.

Lina grinned at her friend as a wave of relief swept over her. The *Merlin* was free. "I do my best," she said.

EPILOGUE

Lina set the ship down on a wide, snowy ridge on the east side of Gazer's Gorge. In the distance, the lights of Ortana glimmered faintly. Lina wrapped her scarf around her face and pulled on her mittens, but as she walked down the gangplank, Ozben trailing behind her, she realized that the snow had almost stopped. The wind still howled and burned in her lungs, but the storm was finally past.

For a moment, Lina looked not to the west, where the ship would make its journey home, but to the east, in the direction of Kalmora.

"I hope Elinore's all right," she said.

Ozben nodded. "She'll make it in time to stop the battle." His expression clouded. "I don't know what that means for the war, though. Even if my father reaches out to King Aron about peace talks, there's no guarantee he'll agree." He smiled weakly at Lina. "I don't think this is over yet."

Lina touched the *Merlin*'s metal skin. "It is for you, though," she said. A lump rose in her throat. "We can't ever thank you enough for what you did, what you risked. . . ." Her voice cracked and gave out, so instead she opened her mind to the ship and let her thoughts convey what she couldn't say.

I will always remember you. Find your way home, but know that if you ever want to come back, we'll be here for you. We'll be waiting.

Beneath her fingers, the metal of the ship warmed, and Lina absorbed that warmth. The affection and love filled her until she was crying again, the tears spilling down her cheeks in cold little tracks.

Ozben came up beside her and put his arm around her shoulder. "You saved us," he said to the ship, and his voice was unsteady as well. "I hope you have a safe journey home."

Lina forced herself to step back, drawing Ozben with her. She knew if she didn't let go now, she wouldn't be able to. The rumble of the ship's power filled the air, and for an instant, the *Merlin* shimmered and glowed like a fallen star. Lina's breath caught in her throat at the beauty of the wondrous ship. Then it rose into the black sky, hovered above them as if in farewell, and began the long journey west.

Lina and Ozben pressed together, shielding each other from the cold, and watched the ship until it looked like just another star in the sky. They stood in the silence, listening to the whistling of the wind, staring up at the deep bowl of stars shining above them.

"It's so beautiful," Ozben murmured. "If it wasn't so cold, I think I could stay out here forever."

Lina wiped her eyes. "Best view I've ever seen," she agreed. "But we can't stay." The words stuck in her throat, but she forced herself to say them. "You have to go home and see your family. You can, now that you don't have to worry about assassins. And you were right. The war isn't over yet—your family will need you."

She waited for Ozben to say something, but he didn't answer at first. He just kept staring at the sky. "You know," he said finally, "all my life I've tried to make my grandfather proud of me—to contribute to our family's legacy. But in all that time, I never stopped to think about what I wanted."

"And now?" Lina asked.

He smiled wistfully. "I think I finally know. I do want to go home and see my family. To make sure that we at least get a chance at peace with the Dragonfly territories."

"Of course," Lina said, though the words were a knife in her heart. "You'll want—"

"I wasn't finished," he interrupted her gently, still smiling. "After that, I'm going to come back here. I want to study with the archivists. I don't know if they'll take me on as an apprentice after I helped steal an airship out from under their noses, but I can at least ask, don't you think?"

Lina couldn't speak. Her heart was too full. She returned his smile. "I think they'll get over losing the ship," she said when she found her voice. "They'll let you stay. I know they will."

"I hope so." Ozben looked thoughtful. "I know the *Merlin*'s gone, but maybe someday, if we can learn enough, we could find a way to get to the uncharted lands—you and I. I think I'd like to try, anyway. And if we succeed, we could try to find the *Merlin* and the people who live on the other side of the mountains."

Lina's breath caught in her chest as she considered the idea of going with Ozben on an expedition over the mountains to find the *Merlin*'s home. It would be a long, dangerous journey—that much was certain. Maybe an impossible one.

She couldn't imagine anything more exciting.

"Lina?" Ozben asked, his smile faltering when she didn't respond. "You think I'm crazy, don't you?"

Lina wrapped her arms around his shoulders and hugged him tightly, snow glittering around them. "Completely," she said. "But I'm in. You know, Ozben, I think you'll make an amazing apprentice." She pulled back, her eyes shining. "And the two of us together?"

"We'll be incredible," Ozben said with a grin.

ACKNOWLEDGMENTS

Whenever I visit schools to talk about writing, students always ask me where I get my ideas. I try to explain that ideas are things I collect and absorb; I let them bang around in my head, sometimes for years, biding their time, waiting for the right story. This happens a lot—with dragonflies, steam locomotives, airships, even museums.

Back in 2009, I left the United States for the first time and went to Paris. While I was there, I visited the Louvre, which is one of the biggest museums in the world, with hundreds of thousands of objects in its collection. Even better, my visit happened to fall on a day when the museum was open late at night. I descended into the underground lobby and wandered the cavernous rooms and ornate galleries with my husband, thinking it would take weeks or months to see everything the museum had to offer. Wouldn't it be amazing if you could visit this place every day?

We stepped into a room full of statues and saw *Psyche Revived by Cupid's Kiss,* then peeked in another room and stumbled upon Michelangelo's *Rebellious Slave.* All those rooms, thousands of works of art—how could anyone possibly keep track of everything? Do any of these treasures ever get lost, forgotten in some musty, abandoned corner?

I left the museum and tucked all those rooms and art treasures safely away in my mind. Years later, when I took them out and dusted them off, I saw Lina and Ozben crouched in that sculpture gallery, hiding from an assassin. Then they were running through a portrait room, only to end up on a staircase holding a jar of memories. The museum in my head wasn't the Louvre anymore. It was something else. Something *new.* That's the thing about ideas. They shift shape like a chamelin, become more than what I expected.

So I'd been carrying around a museum in my head for seven years, and let me tell you, it was a weighty beast. But its story had finally come, and it was Lina and Ozben's story, the *Merlin's* story, and the story of the archivists, those wonderful, eccentric men and women who have made it their life's mission to preserve thousands of artifacts from different worlds.

But if it weren't for the Louvre and the dozens of other museums I've visited in my lifetime, this story wouldn't exist. And if it weren't for a number of talented, dedicated, and very patient people, this book wouldn't have been possible.

To my mom and dad, and to my brother, Jeff, who all told me, "Do whatever you have to do to get the book written. This is important. We will help you however we can": you may never know how much those words meant to me.

To Elizabeth, Gary, and Kelly, my extraordinary writing group, for telling me how much they loved Aethon and for making me see the story, and Lina's character, in a whole other light. I'm so lucky to have you as crit partners and friends.

To my agent, Sara Megibow, thank you for being the skilled dungeon master guiding me through publishing adventures. Yeah, she's a gamer. She'll know what I'm talking about.

To my amazing editor, Krista Marino, and to Monica Jean and everyone on the team at Delacorte Press, thank you for all your hard work and support, and thank you for loving this book as much as I do. It means the world to me.

Finally, special thanks to my husband, Tim. Yes, I put you in the dedication and you're in the acknowledgments too (hi there!), because you put up with so much while I'm writing. Thank you for Paris. I love you to pieces.

ABOUT THE AUTHOR

Jaleigh Johnson is the author of *The Mark of the Dragonfly* and *The Secrets of Solace*. She is a lifelong reader, gamer, and moviegoer and loves nothing better than to escape into fictional worlds and take part in fantastic adventures. Jaleigh lives and writes in the wilds of the Midwest, but you can visit her online at jaleighjohnson.com or on Twitter at @JaleighJohnson.